Clear Bottom Lake

Summer House &
Wellness Center

Cottage
Row

Carriage House

The Barn

The Cottage

The Inn

Hope Springs
Farm

Bek Cruddace

1

PRESLEY

Presley waits in her parked rental car across from the address she found on the torn envelope in her adoption folder. When she discovered the file in her mother's desk drawer late yesterday afternoon, she booked the next available flight to Virginia. What is she even doing here? She's not interested in medical history. A genetic testing website could determine if she possesses the dreaded breast cancer gene or whether she's at risk for Parkinson's or Alzheimer's. But Presley's test kit, purchased over a year ago from 23andMe, remains unopened in her bedside table drawer back in Nashville.

Kids on bikes and young mothers pushing baby strollers pass by, seemingly oblivious to the stranger in their midst. The neighborhood is Norman Rockwell picturesque, like one might expect in a small town called Hope Springs. Maple trees with brilliant orange leaves line the street. Pansies in yellows and purples border sidewalks leading to small front porches bearing displays of pumpkins and gourds and mums. Most of the houses are two-story brick colonials with well-tended lawns. But the whitewashed brick and Wedgewood-blue front door make number 237 stand out from the rest on Hillside Drive.

Presley drums her fingers against the steering wheel. She's been here two hours. Should she leave and come back later? She checks the time on the dash. Five forty-three. She'll stay until six.

What does she want from the people she's waiting for? Another family? Because her mother . . . her adoptive mother, Renee, died two months ago and left her all alone in the world. That's not it. Presley isn't afraid of being alone. She has no siblings. She lost her beloved father to cancer when she was a young child. This inner sense of disconnect has nothing to do with Renee's death. Presley feels a calling, like there's someone else in the universe searching for her. She's not looking to disrupt anyone's life. She simply wants to know who her people are. To look into the faces of others and see something of herself.

All her life, Presley has been a square peg trying to fit into Renee's round hole. Renee was an overachiever, a producer with one of Nashville's top country music record labels. Renee prided herself on being a hard-ass and faulted Presley for being soft. Presley prefers to think of herself as easygoing and good-natured. Renee's death was permission granted for her to find her round hole.

When a burgundy minivan rounds the corner at the far end of the street, Presley sits up straight in her seat. She glimpses the attractive middle-aged blonde behind the wheel when the van pulls into the driveway at 237. A pair of teenage girls, dressed in athletic shorts and tank tops with field hockey sticks tucked under their arms and backpacks over their shoulders, emerge from the van. Tall and lean with blonde ponytails, they look enough alike to be twins. Could these girls be her half sisters? Their mother, an older version of her daughters, is slower to get out of the car. She holds a phone to her ear and wears a scowl on her face, either angry or upset with the person on the other end.

From a distance, Presley sees no physical resemblance between the three blondes across the street and her own auburn hair and gray eyes. There's always a chance the torn envelope got stuffed in her adoption folder by accident. But not likely, since her mother's other files were in meticulous order. According to Zillow, number 237 was last sold seventy years ago. Presley assumes to this woman's parents. The official website for the town of Hope Springs identifies the owners of said property as Samuel M. and Carolyn H. Townsend. For what it's worth, the free online background check Presley conducted lists additional occupants of the home as Anna and Rita Townsend, presumably Sam and Carolyn's daughters. But this woman must be Rita because, according to Facebook, Anna Townsend—originally from Hope Springs and a graduate of Hope Springs High School—currently lives in Washington state.

This woman appears in her upper forties. No older than fifty. Presley is thirty years old. Which makes the timing right for that woman to have had an unwanted pregnancy in her late teens or early twenties.

Where are Sam and Carolyn? Do they still reside in the house? And what about this woman's husband? Is he late coming home from work? Or is she divorced?

The woman ends her call and drops her phone into her purse. Removing the mail from the black box to the right of the blue door, she sits down on the front steps and sorts through a stack of envelopes. She's smiling now, her phone conversation apparently forgotten. Presley is tempted to introduce herself. But what would she say? "Hey. You don't know me, but I think I may be your daughter."

The woman looks up from the mail and across the street at Presley. They lock eyes for a fraction of a second. A shiver runs down Presley's spine, and she averts her eyes. Did the woman see her? Is she making note of the license plate number and make and model of the rental car? Presley's not ready for this. Breathing deeply so as not to hyperventilate, she starts the engine and drives off.

She heads north to Main Street and west for another six blocks to the Inn at Hope Springs Farm. When researching hotels for the long weekend stay, she was intrigued to see the prominent luxury property had recently reopened after extensive renovations. She's booked herself a suite. After what she's been through the past eighteen months, a little pampering is justified.

Surrounded by a crop of yellow and purple pansies, the American and Commonwealth of Virginia flags flap in the breeze in the center of the circular driveway as she travels up the hill to the main building. Under the portico, a uniformed bellman awaits her arrival.

Opening her car door, he says, "Welcome to Hope Springs Farm. Are you checking in this evening?"

"Yes, sir. Presley Ingram is my name." She hands him the car keys and a ten-dollar tip. "Please make certain my suitcase gets to my room."

He tips his hat to her. "Will do, madam. Enjoy your stay."

The inn's interior is a stylish mixture of old world and new. Hardwood floors swathed in pale Oriental rugs. Antique chests and end tables combined with contemporary seating. Presley feels as though she's back home in her mother's house in Nashville as she makes her way through the wide front hall to the reception desk. A striking black woman greets her, introducing herself as Naomi Quinn, the guest services manager. Presley provides her name, and Naomi locates her reservation.

Looking up from her computer, Naomi says, "I have you booked for a one-bedroom mountain-view suite on the third floor."

"That sounds lovely," Presley says, handing her a credit card.

Naomi clicks a button and paperwork spits out of her printer. "If you'd like a cocktail or a glass of wine before dinner, off the lounge to your left is Billy's Bar. Next to the bar, our restaurant, Jameson's, serves three meals a day, including a complimentary buffet breakfast from seven until eleven in the morning." Her arm shoots out with finger pointing in the hallway opposite the lounge. "The elevators are down that way on your right."

"Thank you," Presley says, taking the key folder from her. "I'd like to have a look around down here before heading up. Will you please advise the bellman of my room number?"

She lifts a walkie-talkie. "I'll do that now."

Naomi's smile doesn't meet her eyes, and Presley senses something disturbing about her. She's friendly enough, but she seems sad. More than sad. Troubled. Perhaps Presley is seeing her own somber mood reflected in the woman's big brown eyes.

Renee had always viewed Presley's uncanny ability to read other people's feelings as a curse. But she finds her people reader helpful in gauging how to respond to them. And she's getting powerful signals to proceed with caution where this woman is concerned. *Let it go, Presley. You're only here through the weekend.*

She wanders down the hallway to the right. A couple is drinking tea by the fire in a cozy wood paneled library. A group of men dressed in khaki fly-fishing attire occupy the adjacent game room. Two of them shoot pool while the others watch a golf tournament on a large-screened television. Moving along, she discovers the octagonal-shaped solarium at the end of the hallway unoccupied. Groupings of rattan furniture, painted a forest green color with cushions covered in a tropical leaf fabric, take up much of the space. She circles the glass bubble of a room. Stone buildings dot the landscape leading to a shimmering lake, while beyond, a mountain range blazes orange with fall foliage. Tomorrow, weather permitting, she plans to explore the grounds.

Leaving the solarium, she works her way back through reception to the lounge on the other side. Richly textured fabrics in hues of gray make up the upholstered furniture and drapes adorning the floor-to-ceiling windows. Accents in various shades of blue add pops of color. The overall effect makes for a warm and inviting space to visit with friends.

She passes through the lounge and enters Billy's Bar where the patriotic décor features carpet splashed red, white, and blue, and paneled walls painted a high-gloss indigo blue. A marble-topped bar stretches the length of one wall, behind which stands an attractive male bartender approximately her age.

Presley roams about the room, studying the rock and roll memorabilia adorning the walls. Electric guitars displayed in acrylic cases. Framed collections of guitar picks, ticket stubs from famous concert tours, signed album covers of all the greats —Mick Jagger, Lynyrd Skynyrd, Van Morrison.

Presley smiles at the bartender as she takes a seat on one of the white leather stools.

"Welcome to Billy's Bar. What can I get for you?"

She opens her mouth to ask for a club soda with a lime twist and out spills, "Casamigos on the rocks, please." She rarely drinks alcohol, but after an unsettling day, she needs something to take the edge off.

"Excellent choice." He pours tequila over a block of ice in a lowball glass and sets it down on a cocktail napkin in front of her.

She lifts the glass, shakes the ice cube, and sets the glass back down without taking a sip.

She checks out the bartender, who has turned his back on her and is stacking glasses on the shelves lining the walls. While none of his features are striking, she finds the combination of reddish-brown hair, strong jaw, and electric blue eyes appealing. Black pants hug his tight butt and his starched white shirt fits snug to his torso, hinting at six-pack of abs.

What're you thinking, Presley? You didn't come here for love. A man is the last thing you need right now.

He finishes stacking glasses and returns his attention to her. When he sees her untouched tequila, he asks, "Is something wrong with your drink?"

Leaning her head down, she sniffs the tequila. The strong fruity aroma is tempting. "I'm still deciding whether to drink it. I'll pay for it either way."

"No way! I can't charge you if you're unsatisfied." When he tries to take the glass, she tightens her grip.

"The drink is fine." Presley gestures at the memorabilia on the wall behind her. "So . . . who's Billy? I assume those are his guitars."

"Billy Jameson. He's a legend around here. You've probably never heard of the Wild Hollers, an alternative rock band popular in the late eighties and nineties. He was their lead singer."

She slaps the bar. "You're kidding me? I know exactly who Billy Jameson is . . . was. Didn't he die recently?"

"About nine months ago. Billy's great-grandfather built this inn. His daughter's running it now. Have you met Stella?"

"Not yet. I just arrived an hour ago."

"You'll meet her soon. She's supercool." He leans back against the opposite counter, crossing his legs and folding his arms over his chest. "So, you're a rock and roll fan."

"I love every genre of music. But I'm from Nashville. Country is in my soul. Outlaw country is my favorite."

He nods his approval. "We have that in common. Are you in the music business?"

Shaking her head, Presley looks away. "My mother was. She passed away recently."

Genuine concern crosses his face. "I'm sorry to hear that. How'd she die?" he says and holds up his hand. "Sorry. None of my business."

She smiles at him. "No worries. Mom died of liver cirrhosis. She was a terrible alcoholic. Highly functioning until a few years ago."

When his blue eyes travel to the tequila, she pushes the glass away. "I don't know what made me order it. I'm not much of a partier. You learn a lot about what not to do when you live with an alcoholic." She decides not to tell him about the period in college when her drinking bordered on abusive, and one particularly ugly blackout drunk that scared her into sobriety.

"I don't drink much myself," he says, dumping her tequila in his bar sink.

"Oh really? Why not?" She holds up her hand. "Sorry. Now *I'm* being nosy."

He shrugs. "It's fine. I don't like the person I am when I drink."

She cocks her head to the side. "Don't you find it tempting being around alcohol all the time?"

"On the contrary. Being around drunks all the time reminds me of what I'm not missing. Besides, I enjoy meeting new people. Give someone a drink, and they'll speak more freely about themselves. I like hearing their stories." He slides a bar menu toward her. "Let me fix you something else. I have a keen knack for mixology. I can make any of the menu items sans alcohol."

She scans the menu. "I'm impressed with your use of fresh ingredients and herbs. Some of these sound yummy." She gives him back the menu. "But I'll just have club soda with a lime twist for now."

"Coming right up." He fills a glass with ice and soda, adds a chunk of lime, and hands it to her.

She glances around the empty barroom. "This place is a ghost town. Do you ever get any customers?"

"Business picks up on the weekends, when all the Jefferson College parents come into town for football games." He chuckles. "And I'm here to tell you, parents of college kids are a rowdy bunch. They're definitely living their lives vicariously through their children."

Presley thinks back to when she was in college at the University of Alabama. Her mother never missed a home football game. Renee was the life of the party, embarrassingly so at times. "I'll take that as a warning, since I'm staying through the weekend."

He fidgets with a remote control, turning on soft jazz music. "So, what brings you to Hope Springs? You're way too young to have a child in college."

Presley laughs out loud. "No children." She debates how much to tell him. He'll think she's lost her mind if she confesses she flew here on a whim to track down a lead regarding her birth mother. Running a finger around the rim of her glass, she says, "I just needed to get away. These past few months have been a challenge with Mom's death and settling her estate. Now, with the leaves changing, seemed like a pleasant time to come to the mountains."

"What do you do for a living?"

"Good question." She drains the rest of her soda. "I have a bachelor's degree from the University of Alabama, but I've been handling my mother's affairs for the last three years. Now that she's gone, I'll have to figure out a new direction for my life." Removing her wallet from her purse, she slaps her credit card on the bar. "I should freshen up before dinner. What's the food like here?"

"Jameson's offers American contemporary dishes with the freshest local ingredients. Cecily, our head chef, is amazing. I can vouch for every item on the menu. I've tried them all."

He picks up her card and studies it. "Presley Ingram? As in daughter of Renee Ingram?"

"The one and only," Presley says. "Are you a musician?"

His expression becomes guarded. "No, but everyone knows Renee Ingram. She's handled some of country music's greatest."

"Right." Everyone knows the *artists,* but only musicians hoping to break into the business know the producers.

He runs his finger over her name on the credit card. "Did your mom name you after—"

"The King? Yes, unfortunately." Presley rolls her eyes. "Mom was quite the fan. I'm thankful she didn't name me Elvis."

Laughing, he hands her the credit card without processing the charge. "Drinks are on the house."

She stares at the credit card without taking it. "I can't let you do that."

"Please. It's my way of expressing sympathy for your loss. I didn't realize Renee had passed away. That's what I get for avoiding the news. It's a sad day for country music."

"That's sweet of you to say." Rising from the barstool, she slings her bag over her shoulder. "I guess I'll see you around."

"I'll be right here all weekend. I'm Everett, by the way."

She smiles at him in parting. While he seems like a decent guy, Presley's people reader is screaming at her that he's hiding something. He's a bartender with what sounds like a troubled past with alcohol. She just buried her mother. She doesn't need that kind of headache.

2

EVERETT

As the evening wears on, Everett tries unsuccessfully to get Presley off his mind. She's smoking hot with luscious auburn hair and flawless skin. When she stares at him with those gray eyes, it's as though she's seeing his soul. But there's more to her than her looks. Good upbringing. College education. Nice family. She's the kind of girl guys fall for. Everett reminds himself that he doesn't need another woman complicating his life.

He welcomes the distraction when a disorderly group of fishermen enters the bar. They've already been in the sauce, down the hall in the game room based on their conversation. He guesses them to be in their late thirties to early forties, settling into middle age with receding hairlines and thickening waistlines. They sit at the bar instead of at one of the many vacant tables. Once seated, they shout their drink orders at him, as though he's hearing impaired.

The bald guy at the end of the bar says, "Hey, bartender, change the music. Seriously, dude, who wants to listen to jazz? Turn on some classic rock or R and B."

The man next to baldie elbows him in the gut. "Forget R and B. We want country music."

Everett tunes into his favorite country station and begins filling their drink requests. The more distinguished of the gentlemen order red wine while the drunkest ask for brown liquor on the rocks.

A man with a ruddy complexion and turkey neck asks for a Jack on the rocks. "Hey!" The man wags his finger at Everett. "I know you. Aren't you from Atlanta?"

"No, sir. North Dakota." Everett keeps his head lowered as he opens another bottle of pinot noir. The man looks familiar to Everett as well. But he can't place him.

When Everett looks up from pouring two glasses of wine, Turkey Neck is studying him closely. "Are you sure we've never met? I swear I know you from somewhere."

Despite his pounding heart, Everett lifts a shoulder in an indifferent shrug. "I'm sure you're mistaking me for someone else. I have an average face."

Everett turns his back on them, busying himself with wiping down counters. He tries to ignore them, but the fishermen are obnoxious as they try to outbrag one another about their day's catch.

Ten minutes pass and Everett assumes Turkey Neck has forgotten him. When he finally faces them again, Turkey Neck is still staring at him. "That's it!" he says, snapping his fingers. "You're a musician of some sort. What's the name of your band?"

Everett lets out a laugh that sounds more like a snort. "I'm not in a band."

Turkey Neck scowls at him. "Are you sure?"

"Positive." He fakes a chuckle. "Don't you think I'd know if I was in a band?"

Turkey Neck rests an arm on his ample gut. "Then where are you from in North Dakota?"

Is this guy for real? Everett says a silent *thank you* to his elementary teacher when he pulls the state's capital out of thin air. "Bismarck."

Everett is relieved when another fisherman summons him to the end of the bar for a refill. By the time Everett circles back, Turkey Neck has finally forgotten about him and is engrossed in a conversation about college football with the man to his right.

After several more rounds of drinks, the fishermen pay their tabs and stumble out of the bar into the lounge. It's nearly ten o'clock by the time Everett finishes cleaning up and closing out the register. When he pokes his head into Jameson's, much to his disappointment, Presley is nowhere in sight. The fishermen are the only occupants of the restaurant. Seated at the community table, they are all extremely drunk now, shoveling food and sloshing drinks. Everett sneaks through the restaurant to the kitchen without them noticing him.

Cecily is the only real friend Everett has made since coming to Hope Springs six weeks ago. His attraction to her isn't sexual. She's smart and funny and beautiful with blue eyes that light up when she laughs. But she's crazy in love with a lacrosse coach over at the college. Everett's friendship with Cecily is based on a mutual appreciation for food and drink.

She looks up from her clipboard with pinched brow. "Your dinner is in the refrigerator. Lobster-stuffed ravioli for you tonight." He loves how Cecily takes pity on his limited culinary skills, and saves leftovers for him every night.

"That sounds delicious." He peers over her shoulder at the menu on her clipboard. "What's up? Why so serious?"

"Stella booked a last-minute cocktail reception for a group of football parents on Friday night. I've told her time and again to hire an event planner. I don't mind coordinating the food, but it would be nice to have someone on the front end plan the menu and organize the extra staff."

"And the alcohol," Everett adds. "No one told me about the party, and I'm the one who has to provide the booze."

"Right." She pokes his chest with her pencil eraser. "Apparently this group has requested a signature, football-themed cocktail for their party."

Ideas flood his brain. "That could be fun. How many people are we talking about?"

She shoves the clipboard at him. "A hundred."

He flips through the menus from past parties. "That's a large party for such short notice. I have a great recipe for trash can punch."

She tilts her head to the side. "You mean fraternity party trash can punch? As in Everclear and Hawaiian Punch?"

"Yep. The Jefferson College parents love to party. They'll be all over it."

Cecily snatches the clipboard away from him. "You'd better come up with something more original with less alcohol than trash can punch."

He retrieves his to-go container from the refrigerator. "I thought Stella was actively looking for an event planner."

"She is." Cecily sighs. "I don't mean to rag on her. She's trying, but she can't find anyone suitable in this town. She needs to recruit from a big city like Richmond or DC."

He gives the messy honey-colored bun on top of her head a tug. "Why don't I come in late morning tomorrow, and we can work up a menu for food and beverage."

She smiles up at him. "Really, Everett? That'd be awesome."

"I'll see you around ten," he says and leaves the kitchen via the veranda to avoid the fishermen.

Walking the length of the porch, he reenters the building through the main back door. The night clerk is on the phone and Naomi's face is glued to a computer when he sneaks past the check-in desk. He's almost to the front door, and he thinks he's made it when she calls out to him.

"Hey, Everett! Have you gotten yourself a cell phone yet?"

He stops in his tracks. She asks him this at least once a week. She knows it irritates him. Whether he owns a cell phone is none of her business. He doesn't work for Naomi. Stella is his boss. If he doesn't owe her an explanation, why does he keep giving her one?

Taking a deep breath, he turns around to face her, but he doesn't move toward the reception desk. "I told you, Naomi. I'm not getting a cell phone. I'm trying to save money."

"But what if we need to reach you?"

"If you need to reach me, call the extension in Billy's Bar. That's where I spend 90 percent of my time. Most days, I arrive early and leave late."

"How do you stay connected with your friends and family?" She leans across the counter, as though he's about to reveal his darkest secret.

"Through email." She doesn't need to know that Everett doesn't own a computer, that he goes to the library once a week to check his email. "I moved to the mountains for fresh air and clean living. Kicking the social media habit is the first step toward a simpler life. If it's so important for me to own a phone, the inn can buy me one. But I'm not paying for something I don't need."

When she starts to argue, he cuts her off. "Why are you here so late, Naomi? And where's Jazz?"

Naomi glares at him. "She's asleep in the office, not that it's any of your business."

"It's a school night. Most six-year-olds are in bed."

"Go home, Everett." She pivots on her heels and disappears into the reservation office.

He chuckles to himself as he exits the building. What a

bully! She can dish it out, but she can't take it. Why is she working so late when they have a night desk agent and hardly any business?

There's a nip in the night air, hinting at the winter ahead. With no reason to hurry, he strolls down the long driveway toward town. He rents a studio apartment in a renovated warehouse two blocks from the farm at the intersection of Marshall and Main. Two of the three remaining apartments in the building are occupied. His landlord, a kindly old man who's a partner in the law firm downstairs, tried to convince him to rent the corner unit with the stunning view of the mountains. But Everett has no use for three thousand square feet when his list of possessions is short—an air mattress, a stack of plastic drawers that house his clothes, and his guitar.

His apartment is directly across from Town Tavern, a rowdy hangout for college kids. There's always a wait for the outdoor sidewalk seating area. On chilly nights like tonight, they put out space heaters to keep their customers warm.

He throws open the top sash of his only window and straddles the sill with one foot on the iron balcony. He's accumulated a fan club. They can't see him with his apartment light off, but they can hear him. Cheers erupt from below when he strums a few chords of his guitar and belts out the first lyrics. Continuing his music career in secret isn't cutting it for him. Something's gotta give, sooner rather than later. He came to Hope Springs out of desperation. He was running away, not running toward. Eventually his past will catch up with him.

3

PRESLEY

At seven thirty on Thursday morning, dressed in exercise clothes with her ponytail pulled through the back of a Crimson Tide baseball cap, Presley ventures over to Hillside Drive for her second reconnaissance mission. She parks her Buick sedan rental car in the middle of the block, close enough to see any activity at number 237 without raising the blonde woman's suspicion. At ten minutes before eight, when the burgundy minivan leaves the driveway, she follows at a safe distance. She assumes the mother will drop her girls at school before continuing on to her workplace. But she's surprised when the van parks in the side lot of a towering two-story red brick building that appears old enough to be the town's original high school.

Presley pulls into a nearby parking space, takes the car out of gear, and tugs the lid of her baseball cap low over her face. Mother and daughters pile out of the minivan and walk together across the parking lot toward the building. Is the mother on staff here? Or is she here to conference with one of the girl's teachers? Maybe she volunteers in the office a few days a week. The daughters sport matching green uniforms—skirts with jackets over tank tops—with their blonde hair in single braids down their backs. Game day. Will they play at home or away? Presley notices a turf field behind the school with a scoreboard that reads Home of the Hawks.

She waits forty-five minutes, but the mother never emerges from the building. Returning to the inn, she leaves her car with the valet attendant and stops by the coffee bar in the lobby for a to-go cup of hot brew before continuing out back. A wide veranda extends the width of the building. Breakfast is being served on the side of the porch to her left, while to her right, guests read newspapers and fiddle with their phones in a long line of rocking chairs. A semicircular stone terrace extends from the veranda. Moving to the waist-high wall at the edge of the terrace, Presley stares out across the grounds. While the view of the mountains from her third-floor suite is spectacular, from the terrace, she can better see the other buildings that make up Hope Springs Farm. Closest to her is a large barn constructed out of the same stone as the main building. There's a tiny cottage with black shutters and an inviting front porch. Farther down the hill from the cottage is a structure that Presley assumes once served as a carriage house. A brick sidewalk stretches between the barn and carriage house from the terrace to a large lake at the base of the mountains. On the shore of the lake, partitioned off by orange fencing, a building of considerable magnitude is under construction.

Curious, she takes off on foot down the sidewalk. As she draws closer, she can see this new structure is a modern version of the same stone architecture as the main building. She stops at the orange fence and watches a crew of workmen pour concrete to form the base of an outdoor pool.

There's a chill in the air, and as she tilts her head back, the sun warms her face. Without a cloud in the cobalt sky, the weather is autumn perfect.

A female voice startles her out of her reverie. "What do you think of our future spa?"

Presley didn't hear her approach, and she's surprised to see a woman about her age standing next to her. "Impressive. So, I was right? I guessed a spa, slash, fitness center, slash, pool."

The woman adds, "Slash, casual restaurant offering healthy brunches, lunches, and snacks. The pool facility will encompass our natural hot spring."

The thought of soaking in a hot spring on a bright autumn day like today brings a smile to Presley's face. "That's way cool."

"And way warm." The woman giggles at her own joke. "The wooden hut currently houses the hot spring." She points at a rickety building at the far end of the construction site. "We'll demolish the hut, and the spring will be open air to allow guests to enjoy the view. We haven't decided what to call the complex yet. I figure I'll know it when I hear it." She extends her hand to Presley. "I'm Stella Boor, general manager here. Welcome to Hope Springs Farm."

Presley takes her hand. "Everett mentioned you. You're Billy Jameson's daughter."

"I am." Stella's smile spreads across her lips, connecting high cheekbones. Brown curls spring out from her head, a hairstyle that hints at a spunky personality. "You sound as though you knew Billy. Did your family vacation here?"

Presley shakes her head. "This is my first visit to Hope Springs. I never met Billy personally, but I know his music." She places her hand on her chest. "I *love* his music, actually."

"Me too." Stella stares up at the mountains, a faraway look on her face.

Presley waits for Stella to say more. When she remains quiet, she wonders what is running through Stella's mind. Is she conflicted about her feelings for her father?

Minutes pass before Stella returns her attention to Presley. "Are you enjoying your stay so far?"

Presley nods vigorously. "Very much so. I'm no expert, but I've stayed in my share of luxury hotels. Whatever the inn was like before, the renovated product is five-star in my book. That it's been around for nearly a century makes it all the more intriguing."

Stella appears impressed. "You've done your homework."

She laughs. "I read your website."

Stella beams. "I wrote the history myself."

"If you don't mind me asking, how did the inn get so rundown?"

Stella smiles warmly. "I don't mind at all. Sadly, Billy had a chronic heart condition. About ten years ago, when his health declined, he allowed the buildings to deteriorate. The place was an absolute disaster when I first got here. We've come a long way. But we still have a long way to go."

Presley angles her body toward Stella. "How so?"

"As long as the college is here, we will have weekend guests. We were once a popular spot for small firms who hosted their conventions here during the week. We're facing some challenges in recovering that corporate business."

Presley's gaze shifts back to the construction. "When will the spa open?"

"By early spring at the latest. The Summer House, as they called it back in the day, was nothing more than a glorified porch used for bingo nights and dances. I'm hoping the spa and fitness center will help to attract those small conferences."

Lifting her chin, Presley stares up at the sky. "Summer House. I like it. Makes me think of the movie *Dirty Dancing*. Why not call the complex the Summer House Wellness Center?"

Stella's blue eyes grow wide. "That's perfect! The Summer

House part will remind our older repeat customers of days gone by, and the Wellness Center will appeal to the younger generation keen on being fit and healthy. You're a genius, Presley."

Presley smiles at her. "Hope Springs Farm is ideal for destination weddings. Are you marketing to brides?"

"Hmm . . . good question. Whether we're officially marketing to them, we're doing all right in the wedding department. We have one booked nearly every weekend next summer. If only I could find an event planner to work with the brides and their mothers. I've been recruiting, but no one in this town meets the criteria. I need to broaden my search to the larger Southern cities."

"How hard will it be to entice someone to move from a cosmopolitan metro area to a small town? Hope Springs is quaint, but . . ." When her voice trails off, Presley's implication hangs in the air between them.

"Quaint or not, Hope Springs is still a small town. He or she will face a culture shock to be sure. I did when I moved here from New York." Stella chuckles. "It's funny. I considered myself the quintessential New Yorker, but I love living in the mountains with all this wide-open space to breathe in the fresh air. *Quaint*, in my mind, means old-fashioned. Once you get to know the town better, you'll realize it has a certain laid-back sophistication about it."

"So, tell me more about the job. I'm from Nashville. I may be able to help you find someone. You mentioned convention and wedding planning. What other types of events do you anticipate?" she asks, more curious about the job than anything.

"Well, let's see. Besides graduation and parents' weekends, we have many events associated with Jefferson College, like alumni and prospective students' weekends. We're scrounging around today to host a last-minute booking for a group of football parents tomorrow night."

"What about your locals? I imagine your beautiful new facility would be a hotspot for the citizens of Hope Springs."

"I'm not sure why the local business has been so slow to come back," Stella says, her expression pinched. "I have confidence in our menus. Our food is spectacular and reasonably priced. We went down to the wire on the renovations. We almost didn't reopen on schedule. I'd hoped to have a party, a large open house, to celebrate with the community, but I've been too busy to plan it."

"You should make your party a priority. Bringing locals in for a free event would give them the opportunity to see the renovated building and sample your cuisine. And do it while the weather is still nice, so your guests can tour the grounds." Presley places a hand on Stella's arm. "I'm sorry. I don't mean to sound so bossy."

"No apology necessary," Stella says.

A white pickup truck appears on the narrow road leading from the main building. The driver, wearing jeans and a hard hat and holding a travel coffee mug, waves over at them as he gets out of the truck. Stella blows him a kiss in return.

Presley's gaze travels to the silicone band on Stella's left ring finger. "Your husband?"

"Fiancé. He's also our contractor." She gestures at the building. "Jack is very good at his job."

"I can see that. When are you getting married?"

"Probably not until next summer. We haven't even picked out an engagement ring yet." She turns away from the construction site. "If you're headed back up, we can walk together."

"I'd like that." As they're making their way back to the sidewalk, Presley notices another area of construction partially hidden by the forest off to her left. "What's going on over there?"

"That's Cottage Row. We've demolished the original cottages

and are rebuilding them exactly as they were. They'll be ready by next summer. Our plan is to offer them for weekly rentals."

"How much land do you have here?"

"Seventy acres total, but much of that is wooded." As they stroll back to the main building, Stella tells her about the hiking trails and the local bike shop owner who offers guided trips on mountain trails.

Most of the tables on the veranda are occupied. Stella grabs a menu from the hostess stand and shows Presley to a table for two on the edge of the porch. "I need to take care of some business, but I've enjoyed chatting with you. If you're in the mood for decadence, try the french toast with maple sausage links."

"I might just do that. Thank you." Presley rarely strays from her strict nondairy, gluten-free diet. But today, when the server comes to take her order, she asks for the french toast. Why not? She's on vacation.

The fishermen she noticed in the game room last night eat in silence at the two tables nearest her. Their bloodshot eyes tell of their hangovers, and as they pay their bills, she overhears them groaning to their waitress about their long drive back to Atlanta.

As Stella said, the french toast is total decadence, and Presley eats every morsel on her plate. She sits on the veranda for a long time, staring out at the mountains and replaying in her mind the past three years. The time is a blur with her mother's debilitating disease followed by the funeral and preparations for putting Renee's house on the market. The realtor has assured Presley that, in the current seller's market, they'll have multiple offers the first day. While she has no use for a five-thousand-square foot house, once it's sold, Presley will be a homeless orphan.

4

STELLA

As I pass through the lounge, I glimpse my reflection in an antique mirror. Pausing in front of it, I run my fingers through my unruly mop of brown curls. I noticed Presley eyeing my hair. From shaved head to my current labradoodle look, I should be used to people gawking by now. The truth is, I'd do it all again. My grandmother, Opal, has told me many times how much my support means to her. And that means all the world to me.

I straighten my shoulders, and with head held a little higher, I continue on my way.

I'm alarmed to find my uncle, Brian, waiting for me in my office. I'm always on the alert these days, waiting for the other shoe to drop.

"Brian." I kiss his cheek when he stands to greet me. "I wasn't expecting you. I hope nothing's wrong."

"Not at all. I was in the neighborhood and thought I'd check in with you."

"You're lying," I say with a laugh, even though I'm being serious. "Your visits always have a purpose."

He snickers. "True. But you need to relax a little."

"How can I relax when I'm on an emotional roller-coaster ride? My life has been out of control since this past April, when you suddenly appeared in my life and announced that my supposed sperm donor of a biological father was none other than rock legend Billy Jameson."

"That's fair. You have been through a lot. Your hair is growing out."

I smooth my curls. "This particular punishment was self-inflicted. How was Opal's doctor's appointment yesterday? She hasn't called, and I've been so worried."

"She wanted to tell you in person, so be surprised when she comes by later today. The leukemia is in remission."

"That's fabulous news." I throw my arms around him, and he lifts me off the floor. When he releases me, I plop down in the chair behind my desk.

He takes a seat opposite me and asks, "How're things here?"

"Slow. The weekends are busy, but on Sundays, the inn becomes deserted. Are you sure we can afford to keep our doors open?"

"I'm positive. By the way, I'm glad you pushed me to hire an accountant. Diana is excellent. I've just come from a meeting with her, and we are rock solid. At least for the time being."

I furrow my brow. "What're you keeping from me, Brian?"

"The spa facility is running a little over budget, which I fully anticipated. But there is plenty of money in the estate to fall back on if we get in a jam. I've told you before, Stella, you have to spend money to make money. We're in a transition period. Things will turn around soon. Once we get the spa building and Cottage Row open, guests will swarm the place like bees on honey." His confident tone contradicts the worry lines around his eyes.

"I hope you're right."

"I am. You'll see." Brian crosses his long legs. "Now, tell me about Jazz. How's she doing?"

"Fine. I guess. I see little of her these days. I know we agreed to give Naomi a chance, but I can't get rid of this sick feeling in my gut that something is wrong in Jazz's world."

"That's because you're more than a sister to Jazz. You've been her stand-in mother these past few months. It's normal for you to experience separation anxiety."

I hold his gaze. "And what if something happens to Jazz?"

"We'll be here to rescue her. Naomi is Jazz's mother, Stella. She's earned the right to prove herself."

"If you say so. But as you well know, I am extremely wary of the alcoholic mother of my six-year-old half sister."

"How's Naomi performing at work?"

"She hasn't burnt the place down yet. I suspect my father kept her on staff for the same reason I do—to have her close to keep tabs on her. I'm sorry to be so negative about Naomi. She just gets under my skin."

Brian gives a curt nod. "I understand. She's given you plenty of reasons to feel that way." He rises from his chair. "I should get to the office. Call me if you need anything."

I walk him to the door. "I will. Thanks for stopping by."

He chucks my chin. "Try not to worry so much, Stella. Business will turn around soon, and we'll be building an annex to accommodate the overflow."

I smile at him. "That would be a good problem to have."

I lean against the doorjamb watching Brian walk down the hall. When he disappears around the corner, my gaze shifts to the photographs of generations of Jameson family members lining the walls of my office. Sitting at the same mammoth desk where my ancestors sat for nearly a hundred years gives me a sense of belonging like I've never known before. But also, a sense of dread for fear I'll disappoint them.

I'm so lost in thought, I don't hear Jack sneak up from behind.

"Come with me." Taking me by the arm, he walks me down the hall in the direction from which he came, through the library, and out the french doors on the front of the building to his truck.

"Where are we going, Jack? I have work to do."

"You can spare a few minutes for your fiancé." He blindfolds me with a red bandana and helps me into the passenger seat.

I can't see anything, but I hear his boots on the pavement and his car door slam. The engine starts and we speed off. We make a quick left turn, followed by a sharp right before coming to a stop. Jack turns off the engine, and his door closes again. He's at my side, holding on to my arm while I climb out.

"You'd better not let me fall, Jack."

"Hush your complaining." Hands on shoulders, he marches me a short distance. When he removes the bandana, the manor house—a mini replica of the inn with a stone facade and dormer windows—stands tall and proud in front of us.

I shake my head in confusion. "I don't understand. What're we doing here?"

"We're going to live here. I bought you your dream house."

His hand is on the small of my back. When he nudges me forward, my feet remain cemented to the sidewalk.

"Wait a minute, Jack." I swat his hand away. "How did you know this is my dream house? True, I've secretly fantasized about living here, but I've never told a soul, not even you."

"I've seen the way you look at it when we drive by. Your grandfather built this house. Why wouldn't you want to reclaim your family's ancestral home? You're a Jameson, Stella. It's only fitting for you to live here."

"But you've poured your heart and soul into *your* dream house. I can't ask you to leave it."

27

"Too late. The current owners already accepted my offer. Yes, I love where I live now. But this house is special, Stella. Wait until you see the inside." Taking me by the hand, he drags me up the sidewalk to the covered front stoop. "The owner, Luke Connor, is a friend of a friend. He called me a while back, asking for the name of a roofer to replace some missing snow guards. When he told me he was putting his house on the market, we got to talking and I made him an offer he couldn't refuse. He never even contacted a realtor."

"That explains why I never noticed a For Sale sign out front. The owners aren't home now, are they?"

"Nope. They moved to Charlotte last week."

Humph! I never noticed a moving truck either. Guess I need to be more aware of my surroundings. "So, you've known about this for a while?"

Jack grins at me. "About six weeks."

My mouth falls open. "Six weeks? Are you kidding me?" I backhand him playfully in the stomach. "Never let anyone accuse you of not being able to keep a secret, Jack Snyder."

Jack twists the key in the lock, and when he swings the heavy wooden door open, I gasp at the sight of the sweeping staircase. He scoops me up and carries me over the threshold. "Welcome home, Stella."

"Can we afford this?" I ask, still in his arms.

"I promise you, sweetheart, I will never let us live beyond our means."

"But what if the inn fails? I won't be able to contribute to the mortgage."

He sets me down on my feet. "Your salary is not a factor. If things don't work out at the inn, you can be a stay-at-home mom for our brood of children." Bracing my shoulders, he gives me a gentle shake. "But things will work out. You need to think positively."

I give him a peck on the lips. "I wish I had as much faith as you." Turning my back on him, I wander through the downstairs. A wide central hallway leads to a room at the rear of the house with windows overlooking the sprawling backyard. The kitchen is circa early eighties and could stand an update, but the rest of the first floor—living room, dining room, library, and great room—appear in excellent shape with random-width oak floors, handsome woodworking, and twelve-foot ceilings. I feel like Julie Andrews in *The Sound of Music* as I ascend the stairs to the second floor.

Through the window at the top of the stairs, I spot a detached building at the rear of the leaf-covered lawn. "Oh, look at that charming building! Is that a guest house or a garage?" I ask Jack, who's behind me on the stairs.

"A garage with a second-floor apartment for when your mothers come to visit."

I bark out a laugh. "*If* they ever come for a visit, Hannah and Marnie will stay at the inn."

"Then you can use it as your yoga studio," Jack says.

"Or a home office for you."

We tour four nice-size bedrooms and two full baths before ending up in the master suite, an enormous room with a gas fireplace and sumptuous white marble bathroom.

Jack and I stand together at one of two windows in the bedroom. "How bizarre to think my great-grandfather stood in this very spot, watching over his inn when he was away from his office. I wonder if he felt the same obligation I feel to stay near the guests in case of an emergency."

"That explains why you never stay over at my house." Jack wraps his arms around me from behind, hugging me tight. "Is this house close enough for you?"

I lean back against him. "This house is perfect, Jack."

He plants a trail of kisses on my neck. "We'll be happy here, raising our children and growing old together."

More than anything, I want to have Jack's children. But there's another little girl I can see myself raising in this house. My half sister. Jazz should have a happy home with lots of younger siblings to dote on.

"Are you ready for surprise number two?"

I turn to face him. "You can't be serious."

He removes a ring box from his coat pocket. "Marry me, Stella." He opens the box to reveal a large diamond surrounded by a halo of smaller ones.

I flash back weeks ago to the young couple who got engaged at the inn. He gave his fiancé a ring nearly identical to this one. My brain is a jumble of thoughts, and I struggle to form a coherent sentence. "But . . . It's . . . Where'd you get . . . How did you know?"

His hazel eyes sparkle with mischief. "I heard you compliment the woman. When you stepped away, I asked if I could take a picture of her ring."

I palm his cheek. "You're too much, Jack Snyder."

"I'm desperate is what I am. Since I couldn't get you to go ring shopping with me, I had to resort to drastic measures." He slips the ring on my left hand.

I stare at the diamond, glimmering pinks and blues from the sunlight streaming in through the window. "I absolutely adore it." Pinning him against the wall, I kiss him with all the love and passion I feel for him.

When the kiss ends, in a breathy voice, he says, "Does this mean we can get married before next summer?"

"How about next spring, after we open the spa building?" When disappointment crosses his face, I add, "Spring is sooner than summer."

"And winter is sooner than spring," he says with a shy smile.

"No way! I can't swing a wedding so soon. Not with all the uncertainty with the inn and Jazz."

Jack appears wounded. "If I didn't know better, I'd think you were having doubts."

I lay my head on his chest. "No doubts. We agreed to wait, Jack. We've only known each other a few months."

Those months now seem like years, and I'm ready to be with him. Or am I? *Am I having second thoughts about marrying him? Is that what's causing this uneasy feeling in my gut?*

After locking up the house, Jack and I go to the lunch counter at the Hope Springs Pharmacy on Main Street for a bowl of homemade chili. While we eat, he shows me drawings for remodeling the kitchen in the new house. "This is over the top, Jack. Shouldn't we wait?"

"Take my word for it, we do not want to live through a kitchen renovation." He rolls up the plans and secures them with a rubber band. "Stop worrying about money, Stella. I stand to double what I've invested in my house. I'll get a lot of the materials at cost and do much of the work myself." He bonks me playfully on the head with the plans. "If it makes you feel better, you can pay for lunch."

I laugh out loud. "I'll have to pay you back. I don't have my purse with me."

He cuts his eyes at me. "You're a high maintenance woman, Stella Boor."

He pays the bill and we drive back to the inn. Naomi is at the check-in desk when I walk through to my office. "You look flushed," she says to me. "Did you have a little lunchtime delight with your *boyfriend*?"

Naomi claims my engagement to Jack isn't legit, because he

hasn't given me a ring. I get warped pleasure out of flashing my new diamond at her. "Fiancé, Naomi."

Her face turns to stone, and I don't even try to hide my smile. "So, are you making any progress in booking new conferences?"

She glares at me. "I'm working on it."

"That's what you said when I asked you about it a week ago. You've been the inn's guest services managers for years. You helped coordinate conferences in the past. You know the contacts at these companies. Are you dragging your feet to annoy me?"

"Get over yourself, Stella."

"We need this business, Naomi."

"Okay. I'm on it."

"What about our marketing campaign? If we're not already, we should target brides looking for a destination wedding."

She glares at me. "I'll get right on it."

Jazz emerges from the office, licking chocolate-smudged lips. Her face lights up when she sees me. "Stella!" She runs over and hugs me.

I lift her into my arms. "What're you doing here, kiddo? Why aren't you in school?"

"I have a dentist appointment."

I raise an eyebrow. "You're eating chocolate before you go to the dentist?"

She hunches her tiny shoulders. "Why not? The dentist is gonna clean them, anyway."

I laugh, kissing the tip of her nose.

When a guest approaches Naomi with a question, Jazz and I step away from the desk. "How are things at home, kiddo?"

Tears well in Jazz's amber eyes. "I miss you and Jack."

I thumb away a tear on her cheek. "Oh, honey. We miss you too. It's natural for us to miss one another. We lived together all summer."

"Can I come live with you again? Mommy ignores me. She never watches TV with me or reads me books. All she does is play with her phone."

Typical. "How's your reading coming?"

"My teacher thinks I'm getting better. Mommy says I don't need to go to my tutor anymore."

I manage a smile. "Good girl! Keep up the hard work." I feel totally frustrated by this situation. When Jazz moved back in with Naomi at the start of the school year, Naomi agreed, at my insistence, to let Jazz continue with her tutoring sessions and ballet lessons. Naomi is her biological mother and legal guardian. As much as it pains me to admit it, she doesn't owe me any explanations about reading tutors or ballet lessons.

5

EVERETT

O n Thursday morning, after a five-mile run, Everett makes his weekly trip to the town's library. Sitting down at one of the public-use computers, he signs into his Gmail account and deletes all of the expected emails from Carla and Louie without reading any. His mom has written her usual chatty email, relaying funny stories about the rich women who pay her to alter their expensive clothes. She talks about these women as though they're her friends. She has no other social life. When she's not sewing, she's taking care of his diabetic father who doesn't appreciate the sacrifices she makes for him. Everett is her only child, and he suspects not having him around has been difficult for her. But she's a good sport. She doesn't ask where he's living or when he's coming home. She understands he needs time to himself to sort through some issues.

He types out a quick response, telling his mom he loves and misses her, and clicks send.

Everett takes his time walking to work, enjoying the warm autumn weather. Despite the early hour, tourists and locals crowd the sidewalks, window shopping and dog walking. Like most college towns, boutiques and eating establishments, many of them geared to students, line Main Street. Caffeine on the Corner offers a mean Frappuccino, but he prefers to satisfy his sweet tooth with two scoops of butter pecan ice cream from Dairy Deli across the street. The locals claim Elmo's Bistro has the best food in town. He's only been there once for Sunday brunch, but in his opinion, it can't compare to Jameson's.

When he arrives at the inn, he's relieved to see the fisherman loading luggage into two cars. He feels Turkey Neck's eyes on him as he rounds the side of the building to the kitchen entrance. Turkey Neck knows Everett from somewhere. It's entirely possible he heard Everett sing at Blue By You.

He shakes off an uneasy feeling as he enters the kitchen. Cecily, who is pacing the floor and gnawing on a fingernail, appears to have her own brand of nervous energy.

He drops his backpack on the counter. "What's wrong?"

She continues to wear out the tile floor. "My shipment of seafood is late, and salmon is one of our specials tonight."

"Have you called the vendor?"

"Duh. They said it was on the way, should be here any minute."

"Okay. Stop." He grabs her by the arm. "The pacing is making me nervous. Talk to me. Why are you so stressed out?"

When she looks up at him, Everett sees genuine fear in her eyes. "This job means a lot to me, Everett. If Jameson's doesn't work out, I'll have to move away from Hope Springs. And I really like it here."

Everett pinches her cheek. "You mean, you really like a certain lacrosse coach who lives here."

A pink blush travels up her neck. "I don't *like* Lyle. I *love* Lyle. I want to make a life with him. And his job with the college is secure."

"Come with me." Taking her by the hand, Everett cracks the door to the dining room, and seeing there are no guests, he drags her over to a table by the window and pulls out a chair for her. Sitting down opposite her, he says, "You need to get a grip, Cecily. Business may not be what we hoped for, but Stella has assured us the inn is financially sound. We will weather this storm."

"I know that."

"Then what else is bothering you?"

"The same thing that was bothering me last night. The menu for the football party. You promised to help me with it." She removes a pen and notepad from the pocket of her black apron, tossing both on the table.

He picks up the notepad. "The page is blank. What happened to the menu you were working on last night?"

"I scratched it," Cecily says. "I need fresh menu ideas, and I can't come up with any." She buries her face in her hands. "We've only been open six weeks, and I've already reached my professional peak."

Everett chuckles. "All your ideas are still fresh. And your old menu items are *very* good. Incredible, even." He jots down his five top favorite menu items she serves at parties. Sweet Potato Ham Biscuits. Pecan-Crusted Chicken Skewers. Mini Crab Cakes. Tuna Tartare on Toast Points. Pimento Cheese Bites. "This is a start. I can think of more."

"Not necessary. I have a file with hundreds of recipes on my computer." Lifting the notepad, she studies his menu. "None of these relate to football."

He falls back in his chair. "We're not hosting the Super Bowl, Cecily. And we aren't throwing a tailgate party. Our guests don't want buffalo chicken dip. Have your pastry chef make football-shaped brownies or something. No one cares if the food has a theme as long as it's tasty."

She hangs her head. "I guess you're right. I'm worried I'm losing my creative edge."

"You're barely thirty years old. You're just getting your creative juices flowing." He sits up straight again. "You're putting too much pressure on yourself. I've sampled most of your specials. They're inventive and flavorful. You're offering our guests fresh ideas every single night."

"Do you think so, really?" she says in a pathetic tone.

"Now you're fishing for compliments."

She laughs. "You're right. I am fishing for compliments. My ego needs a boost." She drops her smile and looks closely at me. "Why doesn't a nice guy like you have a girlfriend?"

Everett smiles at her. "I'm recovering from a relationship gone way wrong."

"I'm afraid to ask." Her gaze shifts to something or someone behind him. "She's into you, you know?"

He turns in his chair to see his part-time bartender standing in the doorway. "Kristi's sweet, but she's just a kid."

When Kristi waves him over, he holds up a finger to let her know he'll be there in a minute. He turns his attention back to Cecily. "So . . . about the party. Do you want me to come up with a signature beverage?"

"That would be great. As long as it's not trash can punch." Cecily wears a dazed expression, as though her mind's running in a million different directions. "What if it rains?"

"Is it supposed to rain? I haven't heard the forecast."

Cecily pushes back from the table. "A hundred percent chance, remnants of that tropical storm in the Gulf of Mexico. The forecast predicts the bulk of the rain will hold off until Saturday morning. Fingers crossed." She lifts her hand to show him her fingers are just that.

"That sucks for the football game." He stands to face her. "But that's not our problem. Let's not worry about rain until we have to. Okay, Cecily?"

She smiles at him. "Okay, Everett. Thanks for the pep talk."

He gives her arm a squeeze. "Anytime."

Everett and Kristi spend the next couple of hours mixing their way to a cocktail they call the Sparkling Hail Mary—a combination of apple juice, orange liqueur, and Prosecco with slices of fresh apples and pears. He's taking inventory of their supplies, preparing to place an order for Friday deliveries with their local beer, wine, and liquor distributors, when he feels someone watching him. Turning, he sees a pair of golden eyes peeking around the corner of the entryway at him. Crouched down, he hurries toward his young friend.

"What're you doing sneaking up on me like that? Huh? Huh?" He pokes the child in her tummy several times until she giggles.

"Turn me upside down, Everett!"

"You mean like this." In one swoop, he lifts her up by the ankles." Her knit top slides down, revealing her belly button. When he tickles her tummy, she squeals. "Stop! Everett!"

He looks up to find Naomi glaring at him. "Put her down, Everett. We have guests in the house."

"Sorry, Jazzy. Your mom says I have to put you down." He lowers the little girl until her hands are on the ground before letting her feet drop.

"And why aren't you in school?" he asks Jazz, patting the top of her head.

"I got out early to go to the dentist." She sticks out her tongue. "Yuck."

"Let's see." Bending over, he opens her mouth and inspects her teeth. "I don't see any cavities. You should be fine."

She shoves him away. "You're not a dentist."

He laughs. "No doubt about that. Do you have ballet today?"

Everett has seen this kid dance. He doesn't have to be an expert to recognize talent.

Jazz bobs her head up and down.

"Will you dance for me afterward?"

"Yes!"

He offers her a high five. "I'll be waiting."

She cranes her neck to look back at him as she walks off hand in hand with her mother.

He waves at her, fingers wiggling under chin. "Bye, Jazzy."

Suddenly at his side, Kristi says, "She's a cute kid. Too bad she has such a bitch for a mother."

His neck snaps as he looks down at Kristi, who rarely says anything negative about anyone. "Something's going on with Naomi. I'm still trying to figure out what it is. For Jazz's sake, I'm hoping it's just a phase."

Everett thinks about what Cecily said earlier about Kristy being into him. No doubt she's beautiful with a tight body and pert breasts. She's always flirting with him, and he wouldn't have to try very hard to get into her pants. But, not only is he her supervisor, he's not that kind of guy anymore. At least he's trying not to be that kind of guy. He's had more than his share of hookups in his life. Groupies throw themselves at him, offering more than applause for his performances. Sometimes it's hard to say no. All the more reason to stay secluded in the mountains a while longer. There are two types of girls in this town. College kids who hang out at the bars on Main Street, and guests at the inn who are mostly older than forty. Not that some college moms aren't cougars. And plenty have made passes at him.

Since coming to Hope Springs, he's only met one woman who intrigues him. He's been on the lookout for Presley all day, but so far, much to his disappointment, he hasn't seen her.

6

PRESLEY

According to the high school's website, the varsity girl's field hockey game against Lynchburg's E.C. Glass is scheduled for four o'clock on home turf. At three thirty, Presley leaves the inn and drives over to the school. She's among the students and parents packing the bleachers when the referee blows the whistle for the face-off. Based on the conversations around her, the Hilltoppers are the Hawks's biggest rival.

The woman sitting next to her, the proud mother of the Hawks's goalie and team captain, has a stack of rosters, and she's happy to give one to Presley. There is one pair of sisters on the varsity team. Emma and Abigail Reed. Emma, number twelve, is a senior while her sister, number twenty-three, is a junior. Both are in the starting lineup, but within minutes, it's clear that Abigail is the team's star. By halftime, she has five goals to her credit.

Three minutes into the second half, Abigail scores again, prompting the woman behind Presley to say to her friend sitting next to her, "Did you hear Abigail is being recruited by UVA?"

The friend says, "I guess so. Her father's some bigwig alumni there. I'm sure he's trying to get back into his daughter's good graces after he left her mother for another woman."

Presley's ears perk up.

"He's trying to get her a scholarship is what he's doing," the first woman says. "He's bankrupt."

The friend gasps. "You don't say."

"Yep. He owned a chain of high-end restaurants in Charlotte. Ran them all into the ground."

"So that's why Rita moved back in with her parents," Friend says. "I thought she was living with them while she looked for a house."

"She's not living with them. They *gave* her the house. They moved into independent living at Shady Grove before they were even ready to be in a retirement facility."

It strikes Presley that these women are talking about her biological grandparents. Will Presley ever get to meet them?

"Can you imagine?" Friend says. "How humiliating for poor Rita."

There is no sympathy in the woman's voice, and while Presley can't see her, she imagines the malicious smile on her face.

Presley spots the woman, whose name she now knows is Rita, three rows down in the middle section. She's totally engrossed in the game, oblivious to what these catty women are saying about her. If she's not Presley's biological mother, she's her aunt, and Presley takes offense to their gossip.

Now is Presley's big chance. She could politely ask Rita, who is seated at the end of the bleacher, to slide over and make room for her. The imaginary scene plays out in her head. She joins Rita, and they strike up a conversation about the game. Presley makes up a lie as to why she's here. She tells Rita that she came to pick up her little sister from school. Her sister is a freshman and wants to stay until the end of the game. Rita tells Presley her daughters are numbers twelve and twenty-three, and Presley congratulates her on their performance. Presley asks Rita if she has any other children, and she tells her she had another child once, a daughter she gave up for adoption.

The buzzer sounds, signaling the end of the third quarter and jerking Presley back to reality. Rita has enough on her plate —dealing with the divorce, being a single mother, and moving her parents to a retirement home. And what if her ex-husband can't afford to pay her alimony? She may be struggling financially. She doesn't need the child she put up for adoption thirty years ago wreaking havoc on her life.

Standing, Presley crawls her way over the row of spectators to the aisle and hurries out of the stands to the safety of the parking lot. She drives around town for an hour trying to figure out her next move. She made a mistake in coming to Virginia. For Rita's sake and her own, she should let the matter go. But she's not sure she's ready to do that. What exactly is she afraid of? Of disrupting Rita's life? Or the possibility of rejection? Should she cut her trip short and go back to Nashville? Why do that when there's nothing and no one waiting for her there. Better to be here amongst strangers than with her mother's ghost in her cavernous house.

Presley turns back toward the inn. She'll stay a while longer. Maybe by Sunday, she'll have a better idea of how she wants to handle the Rita situation. If she wants to handle it at all.

She parks under the portico and hands her keys to the valet. Wandering aimlessly around the lounge, she admires the exquisite collection of landscapes by an artist who signs her work *Opal*. Even though she skipped lunch, she's still full from her french toast breakfast. When she hears cheers coming from a crowd gathered in Billy's Bar, Presley investigates the focus of their attraction. She nudges her way through to the front of the crowd where a precious little girl is dancing ballet to

Prokofiev's *Peter and the Wolf*. While Presley knows music, she knows very little about dance. From what she sees, this kid is exceptional, poised and graceful for someone so young. She's dressed all in white—tights, leotard, and tutu—with pink ballet shoes tied up her toothpick legs. Her hair is pulled back in a tight bun, and her eyes are the same golden brown as her skin.

When the song ends, she dances on her toes over to Everett, who lifts her onto his shoulder and parades her toward the entrance. When he puts her down, she glides through the lounge and out of sight.

Everett catches sight of Presley and waves her over to the bar. By the time she gets through the horde of people, he has a club soda with a lime twist waiting for her.

"Your little ballerina is amazing," she says, taking a sip of club soda. "Who is she?"

"Her name is Jazz, short for Jasmine." His blue eyes twinkle when he talks about the child, and the notion he's a decent guy at heart strikes Presley again.

"What's she doing at the inn? Is her family staying here?"

He shakes his head. "Her mother, Naomi, is our guest services manager."

"Oh, right. I met Naomi yesterday when I was checking in."

A customer seated at the bar summons Everett for a refill. When he returns, he asks, "Have you enjoyed your first day in Hope Springs?"

Presley thinks about the field hockey game. *Enjoy* is not the word she'd use to describe it. "For the most part. I had a nice chat with Stella this morning. I really like her."

"I knew you would," Everett says with a nod. "She's pretty special."

"I went out to explore the town. While I was gone, a few hundred guests checked in."

He chuckles. "That's the way it is around here on the weekends."

When a gentleman seated next to where she's standing vacates his barstool, she quickly claims it.

"If you're thinking of dining in-house tonight, I've sampled the specials, and I highly recommend the scallops. If you're not a fan of seafood, you can't go wrong with the rack of lamb or roasted duck. Jameson's is booked for reservations, but the community table is first come, first served."

"Good to know. And I love seafood. Thanks."

Customers suddenly inundate Everett with drink orders. With only her empty hotel room waiting for her, Presley remains at the bar, taking her time in finishing her drink. When Everett finally gets a break, she tries to give him her credit card, but once again, he refuses to take it.

"Then charge it to my room," she says and gives him her room number.

"It's club soda, Presley. It's not worth the effort."

"At least let me tip you." She places a five-dollar bill on the bar.

"Fine, but only because I don't want to argue with you," he says and pockets the five.

Presley leaves the stuffiness and noise of the bar and ventures out to the terrace for fresh air. The sun has begun its descent over the mountains and the view is breathtaking. An attractive group of women is chatting and laughing around a fire pit. One of them smiles at Presley and moves over, silently inviting her into their fold. The women bombard her with questions about herself, and she quickly learns about their lives. They are mostly from the Carolinas and Virginia, except for one from New Orleans. They left their husbands at home for this long-planned girls' weekend. Their daughters, all seniors at the college, belong to the same sorority. The girls stopped by the inn earlier to visit with their moms but have returned to campus to log a few hours in the library before going to a late-night party. When the moms invite Presley to join them for dinner at Jameson's, she eagerly accepts. She feels more at ease with these women, whom she's only known for an hour, than she ever felt with her own mother.

It's this place, Presley decides, as she's walking back to her room after dinner. Everyone is in a good mood here. They are on vacation, relaxing on the veranda, breathing mountain air, and eating delicious food. They all have problems awaiting them at home, but they've put those problems on hold for the weekend. Presley could totally get use to this fairytale way of life.

With rain in the forecast for the weekend, Presley books a bike outing for Friday morning with Allen Farmer, the town's bike shop owner. The workout is rigorous and the views are stunning. It's pushing three o'clock by the time she returns to the inn. When she enters Jameson's for a late lunch, she hears loud arguing coming from the kitchen. Recognizing one voice as Everett's, she sticks her head through the door.

Everett, who hasn't yet changed into his bartender clothes, is sporting a Widespread Panic T-shirt that shows off his biceps and the outline of very nice abs. He's squared off against a woman wearing a chef's coat and frantic expression.

"Sorry for the intrusion," Presley says. "You might want to lower your voices. I can hear you out here."

Stella appears behind Presley, pushing through the swinging doors. "I heard you all the way out in the lounge. What on earth is going on?"

"The weather forecast changed," the chef says. "The rain is moving in earlier than predicted. The restaurant is booked solid.

Where are we going to put these hundred football parents of yours? The veranda isn't big enough."

"Can you rent a tent?" Presley suggests.

"We called the local rental companies," Everett says. "There are no tents available."

"With a property this size, you should probably own your own tents." Presley's hands shoot up. "Sorry. None of my business. But something to think about for the future."

Stella's fingers graze her arm. "That's actually a wonderful idea, Presley. And come to think of it, I may have seen a tent in the attic at the barn. Let me check with my groundskeeper." Removing her cell phone from her back pocket, she steps away to place the call.

Presley holds out her hand to the chef. "I'm Presley Ingram, nosy guest."

The chef shakes her hand. "Cecily Weber, head chef. And your nosiness is greatly appreciated. Do you know Everett?"

Everett and Presley exchange a smile. "We've met," she says.

Stella rejoins them. "Katherine confirmed that there is at least one tent in the attic, but she thinks there may be more. Her crew is getting them down now."

Everett says, "Katherine's crew comprises mostly non-English-speaking Mexicans. I doubt any of them knows how to put up a tent."

"We'll get Jack to help us," Stella says.

"Good thinking," Everett says. "Jack knows how to do everything."

Cecily rubs the back of her neck. "This whole situation is stressing me out. We really need to hire an event planner, sooner rather than later. You know what a team player I am, Stella, but I don't feel like I can give the restaurant my undivided attention if I'm having to organize all these parties."

Stella falls back against the stainless-steel counter. "I know, and you're right. What do you say, Presley? Are you interested in being our event planner?"

Stella's tone sounds like she's joking, but her eyes are fixed on Presley as she waits for her reply.

"Believe it or not, I have a degree in hospitality management with a concentration in event planning."

Stella's mouth falls open. "Then it's fate. Will you consider taking the job?"

Presley laughs. "I'm not sure I'm ready to move to Hope Springs, but I'd be happy to help out tonight."

Relief crosses Stella's face. "That would be wonderful. Let's get through this party, and tomorrow morning, we'll have a serious chat."

7

EVERETT

Kristi holds down the fort in Billy's Bar while Everett helps set up for the party. Presley is a miracle worker. Not only does he enjoy watching her hot little body run around in form-fitting exercise attire, she has a solution for every problem they encounter.

Cecily freaks out when a server calls in sick. "This is a disaster. We were short-staffed to begin with. I can't pull anyone from the restaurant."

"Why don't you recruit some servers from the college?" Presley suggests. "I'll bet plenty of them have restaurant or catering experience. It's not like passing a tray of food is rocket science. Besides, college kids are always eager to earn beer money."

Cecily's face lights up. "That's a brilliant idea. My boyfriend is a lacrosse coach. I'll have him spread the word."

Cecily texts Lyle, and within the hour, four students contact her for the details.

When Presley goes to her room to change for the party, Everett walks with her to the elevators. "I'm impressed with your ability to think fast on your feet. What kind of job experience do you have?"

"I worked in event management for a country club in Nashville for a few years out of college. Until Mom's condition worsened and I began managing the social aspects of her career. Which, as you might imagine for a music producer, was a full-time job."

"The other night you mentioned you're looking for a new direction for your life. Might event planning for the Inn at Hope Springs Farm be that?" Everett flashes her his most brilliant smile.

They reach the elevators, and Presley jabs at the up button. "I will eventually look for a job. Right now, I'm taking some time for myself. I'm not sure I can see myself living in a small town like Hope Springs."

"To be sure, it's an adjustment. But small town living definitely has its perks. The cost of living is way less. I can walk almost everywhere I need to go. And there's a ton to do if you enjoy outdoor activities."

"I experienced that today on my bike tour." Presley punches the up button again. "Do you live nearby?"

"Yep. In a studio apartment two blocks down on Main Street. Our building has a vacancy if you're interested, the best unit with lots of windows overlooking the mountains. I'm happy to show you the building after I get off work tonight." When Presley hesitates, he quickly adds, "I promise not to make a move on you."

She laughs, a delightful giggle that's both childlike and sexy as hell. "In that case, I accept your offer. Seeing the building will help when I talk to Stella tomorrow morning."

"So you *are* considering the job."

The elevator doors open, and a handful of guests emerge.

"Let's just say I'm exploring my options." She steps inside the cart and the doors close.

Everett experiences the strangest feeling of loss. In the brief span of a few hours, this girl has gotten under his skin.

Despite being crazy busy, the minutes drag until he sees her again at almost midnight. He finds her waiting for him in the lounge outside Billy's Bar.

"We've been slammed all night," Everett says. "I never had time to get over to the party. How did it go?"

Presley stands to face him. "Aside from a small leak in the tent's corner, everything went off without a hitch. Stella seemed pleased. I'm meeting with her at nine in the morning." She glances at her Apple Watch. "It's late, and it's been a long day. I understand if you'd rather show me your building another time."

"Not at all. I'm still wired from work. I'm game if you are." He holds his arm out to her and she takes it.

The hallways are empty as they walk toward the front of the building. Most of the guests have retired for the night in anticipation of the big game tomorrow. The rain has momentarily stopped, and they stroll leisurely down the front driveway. They make it to Main Street before the skies open up again. Everett takes Presley by the hand, and they run two blocks to his building. They're dripping wet by the time they arrive. Under her cashmere wrap, Presley's maxi dress is soaked through and clinging to her curves. He can barely take his eyes off her as he leads her up the back stairs to the second floor. By the time he unlocks his door, she's shivering. He grabs two clean towels from the bathroom, and while she's drying off, he slips his guitar into the closet. They've only just met. He's not ready to share his music with her.

"Thanks." Presley hands him the wet towel and looks around

his apartment. "Your decor gives new meaning to spartan. Where's all your furniture?"

He laughs. "I'm a man of few needs."

"Apparently," she says, with her infectious giggle.

"So, there are four apartments. Mine is the smallest. The available apartment is next door." He throws his thumb over his shoulder at the wall behind him. "If you're interested, I'll put you in touch with the landlord tomorrow. Basically, the unit is a one-bedroom, thousand square foot version of mine with heart pine floors, oversized windows, and exposed brick walls. Girls go nuts over exposed brick walls."

She cocks an eyebrow. "And men don't? Brick walls add character."

He gestures at his air mattress. "Obviously, I know nothing about interior design."

She wanders over to his galley kitchen. "What do you remember about the kitchen in the available unit?"

"It's larger than mine."

She turns to face him. "Yours isn't technically a kitchen. It's a stove built into a counter in the corner of your apartment. What about the appliances next door?"

"All new. The landlord has owned the building for decades, but he only recently converted this floor into apartments."

Moving to the window, she looks out at the rainy night. "Have you tried any of the restaurants on Main Street?"

He goes to stand behind her. "A few of them. I spend most of my time at the inn. If you don't mind the college crowd, Town Tavern"—he nods at the restaurant across the street—"has excellent bar food."

Everett breathes in her scent. She smells like lemons and summer rain showers. She turns around and they're face-to-face, their bodies inches apart. Leaning down, he brushes his lips against hers. She tastes delicious, like dark chocolate and strawberries, and he's hungry for her. He teases her lips open with his tongue, and she presses her body against his. When she wraps her arms around his neck, he's all over her, hands on breasts and sliding down to her thin hips. He wants her more than he's ever wanted any girl. His bed, such as it is, is merely feet away. He could strip off her clothes and have his way with her. He hasn't had sex in six weeks. The last time was with Carla. The thought of his old girlfriend, his friend with benefits, brings his desire to an abrupt end.

He's about to push Presley away when she beats him to it.

"I'm sorry, Everett. I don't know what got into me. I'm not in a good place right now. My life is . . . um . . . complicated."

Hands in the air, he takes a giant step backward. "No problem."

"I've offended you. I'm sorry, Everett. It's not you. Really. It's me."

Is he offended? A little, maybe. Mostly he's relieved. He has his own complicated life to sort out. Besides, he might only get one chance with Presley, and he doesn't want to screw it up. "No worries. I totally understand."

She holds her hand out to shake. "Friends? I could really use one right now."

Everett takes her hand in his. "Friends." As the words leave his lips, he realizes that a friend is what he needs right now too. He's tired of going it alone. His gut tells him he can trust Presley. Maybe she can help him figure a way out of the mess he's made of his life.

A gust of wind drives heavy rain against the window. "Ugh!" Presley says. "I hope this town has Uber."

"If you want to call it that. We have only a handful of drivers, and the service is spotty. Don't worry. I'll take you back in my truck."

She appears relieved. "Are you sure you don't mind?"

"Positive." He flashes her a grin. "What're *friends* for?"

Helping her into his only raincoat, he pulls a baseball cap over his head and shows her down the backstairs to the parking lot. They make a run for his truck. Fortunately, it's raining too hard for Presley to notice his Georgia license plate. They're soaking wet again, and it takes a minute for the heat in his clunker to come on.

Once they're on the way, he asks, "Did seeing the building help you decide about the job?"

"Yes and no. Based on yours, I'm sure the available apartment is lovely. The location is ideal. But I don't think now is the right time for me to be making such a drastic move. Mom has only been dead two months."

"Speaking from personal experience, getting away helps put your life into perspective. There's something magical about this place, the history of the inn and being in the mountains. And Stella has done a commendable job of recruiting her management team. We work well together. Most of us are young and hungry for success."

Presley nods. "I'll keep that in mind when I talk to Stella tomorrow." She removes her phone from her purse. "What's your number? I'll text you mine, so you can share your landlord's contact information."

Here we go, Everett thinks. *Why does every conversation circle back to the phone?* "I don't have one."

"You don't have what? A phone?" she asks, distracted as she thumbs through texts. "Did you leave yours back at the apartment? You can text me the information later."

"No, Presley. I don't *own* a phone. I'm taking a break from social media. I highly recommend it. There's a withdrawal period of about a week. But now, I'm way more productive and much less *distracted.*" He clears his throat to emphasize his point.

Presley looks up from her phone. "Oh. Sorry." She drops her

phone in her bag. "You're crazy, Everett. Not having a phone is social suicide."

He laughs. "You should try it sometime. You might be surprised."

He feels her eyes on him, studying him. She's suspicious of him because he doesn't own a phone.

The portico is empty of valet attendants and guests when Everett pulls up in front of the inn. "I plan to be here early tomorrow," he says. "I imagine a fair number of guests will spend the day drinking in the bar instead of standing in the rain at the football game. I have the landlord's contact information at my apartment. If you decide you want to get in touch with him, stop by after your meeting with Stella, and I'll give it to you."

"Sounds good." She opens the passenger door, but she doesn't get out. "And Everett, I didn't mean to judge you about the phone thing. Maybe I need to try life without mine. Maybe a drastic change of lifestyle will show me the path to the future. Because, after these last few years with my mother, I seem to be treading water, not sure in which direction to swim."

"If you truly feel that way, Presley, I recommend you think seriously about taking this job, if only for a year or two."

"I will. I promise."

"One more thing, Presley. I think ditching your phone would mean career suicide for an event planner."

Presley laughs. "I think you're probably right. Goodnight, Everett." She slides out of the truck and hurries inside, his red rain jacket flapping in the breeze behind her.

8

PRESLEY

P resley spends a sleepless night contemplating every aspect of accepting the job. Planning events and weddings at a resort like the Inn at Hope Springs Farm is her dream job. She'd prefer to live in a Southern city like Savannah or Charleston or Richmond. To be considered for a job of this magnitude in any of those places would require experience she doesn't have. At Hope Springs Farm, she'd be the primary event planner. She'd be in charge, answering only to Stella and the guests whose parties and weddings she's organizing. After two or three years, when she's more qualified, she can apply for jobs in a more glamorous city.

Logistically, the move wouldn't be difficult. She'd fly back to Nashville on Sunday as planned, load up her Volvo with clothes and other essentials, and return to Hope Springs on Monday. Her realtor can handle the sale of her mother's house. Most of her high school friends are living elsewhere. There's absolutely nothing else keeping her in Nashville.

Rita ends up being the deciding factor. While Presley's not yet ready to reveal her true identity to Rita, the thought of living in the same town with her biological mother appeals to her. It buys her time, allowing her to warm up to the situation. Maybe Presley will become friends with Rita, before she confesses that she may be Rita's daughter.

By the time Presley enters the general manager's office at nine o'clock sharp on Saturday morning, she has talked herself into accepting the job. Stella—looking stylish in black leggings, booties, and a gray knit top—comes from behind her mahogany desk to greet her.

The office is handsomely decorated with a small conference table, comfortable seating area, and two large windows over-looking the front lawn. Presley circles the room, studying the framed photographs of famous people who've visited the inn over the years. She recognizes musicians and actors and politicians. There's even one of John and Jackie Kennedy.

"I had no idea the inn was such a hot spot for the rich and famous," she says.

"In its heyday, the Inn at Hope Springs Farm was one of the South's best-kept secrets. If you're interested, check out some of the old photo albums in the library."

Presley gives her an eager nod. "I'll be sure to check them out."

"Shall we?" Stella motions her to the seating area. "I had breakfast sent over from the kitchen."

Presley sits down in one of four leather chairs. On the coffee table is a tray that bears an insulated coffee carafe and a platter of pastries.

Sitting down in the chair nearest her, Stella pours coffee into two china mugs. She hands a mug to Presley and then peels back the plastic wrap on the pastries. "Help yourself."

"They look delicious." Presley chooses a cinnamon roll and one with cream cheese and blueberries.

Stella says, "I'd like to congratulate you on a job well done last night. I'm comping your room, unless you'd rather I pay you outright."

Presley smiles at her generosity. "Neither is necessary."

"Oh yes, it is. You worked hard, and you earned your keep. Your stay this weekend is on the house." Coffee mug in hand, Stella sits back in her chair and crosses her legs. "Now, what's it gonna take to get you to accept the job permanently?"

Presley lets out a little laugh. "Not much, actually. I'm thrilled about the opportunity. But I have a few reservations I'd like to discuss with you before I commit."

"You can talk to me about anything, Presley. Now and in the future."

Stella's warmth and kindness set her at ease. "My mother recently passed away, and I'm in the process of settling her estate."

Stella touches her fingers to her lips. "I'm so sorry. I didn't know."

"Thank you." Before Stella can question her further about Renee's death, Presley continues, "Mom's house goes on the market on Monday, but my realtor can handle the showings. At some point, I'll need to make a trip to Nashville to clean out the house. But, until I have a contract, I won't know when that'll be."

"Understood," Stella says." We'll figure it out when the time comes."

Presley takes a bite of the cream cheese pastry, closing her eyes while she savors it. "I have to stop eating like this if I'm going to be working here. I'll gain ten pounds the first month."

Stella laughs. "Isn't that the truth? I stay away from the kitchen as much as possible."

Presley adds cream to her coffee and takes a sip. "You, being from New York, should understand my hesitation in moving to a small town. I'm not convinced I'll love Hope Springs as much as you do. But I'm willing to give it six months. If I'm not happy, I'll turn in my notice. But I won't leave you in a bind. I'll stay as long as it takes to find a replacement and train him or her. I hope this is something you can live with."

Stella doesn't bat an eye. "I totally understand. It's my job to make you happy, so you'll stay. I appreciate your honesty, Presley. You'll be a welcomed addition to the team. Now, about salary," she says and tells Presley the amount she's willing to pay her.

"Wow! That's extremely generous."

"Believe me, you'll earn every penny," Stella says. "When can you start?"

Presley tells her about the apartment in Everett's building, and her plan to fly to Nashville tomorrow and drive back early in the week with her belongings. "I should be able to start on Tuesday, Wednesday at the latest."

"That would be outstanding." Stella is visibly relieved, as though hiring an event planner had been weighing heavily on her. "We have plenty of rooms available next week if you need a place to stay while you make this transition."

"Thanks. I'll keep that in mind. But I should be fine." Presley pops the rest of the cinnamon roll into her mouth. "You mentioned hosting a party for the townspeople. If you're serious about it, we should plan something for the last weekend of October or the first weekend in November. Any later and we'll be getting close to Thanksgiving. How do you feel about a Sunday afternoon event? After the weekend guests check out."

Presley can see the wheels spinning in Stella's head as she thinks about it. "I love the way you dive right in. But are you sure it's not too much for you, with moving and starting a new job?"

"I'm positive. In my opinion, we should make this party a priority."

"I agree wholeheartedly." Stella leans forward in her chair. "I say we go for it. I'll talk to Cecily and Naomi about which date works best. When you get back from Nashville, we'll set up a meeting. In addition to this party, we need to start planning for the holidays and working with the brides on their wedding plans for next summer." She uncrosses her legs and gets to her feet. "In the meantime, go enjoy what's left of your weekend. This might be the most relaxation you have for a while."

Presley stands to face her. "No relaxation for me. I'm on my way to see a man about an apartment." They cross the room together. When they reach the door, Presley turns to her. "Thank you for this opportunity, Stella. I promise to give this job a hundred percent."

Stella smiles warmly at her. "I have faith that you will."

Presley nearly skips down the hall to Billy's Bar. Her new job is a solid gig. The work excites her, and the salary is way more than she expected. Although she's not ready to give up her cell phone, she'll borrow from Everett's playbook and use her time in Hope Springs as a hiatus from the real world. Who knows? She might enjoy small-town living. If nothing else, she'll figure out what she wants to do with the rest of her life.

When she enters the bar, Everett looks up from tallying credit card receipts. "You took the job!"

She slides onto a barstool. "How can you tell?"

"It's written all over your face." He stuffs cash and credit card receipts into a bank bag and zips it up.

Presley notices Everett's damp hair and shirt clinging to his broad shoulders. "Oh shoot! I forgot to give you back your raincoat last night. I left it in my room. I'll bring it down later. You didn't walk to work this morning, did you?"

He combs fingers through wet hair. "I always walk, rain or shine."

She offers a guilty smile. "I'm sorry."

He shrugs. "What are friends for?"

Presley thinks back to their kiss last night. She must forget about his sexy lips on hers if they're going to just be friends.

She looks through the lounge to the windows. "I'm glad I don't have to go to a football game in this weather."

"Right! We're gearing up for a busy afternoon. I imagine a lot of parents will bail on their tailgate plans." He hands Presley a slip of notepaper with a phone number and the name Ruben Sanders scrawled in messy handwriting. "In case you're still interested in the apartment."

"I'm definitely interested." She unlocks her phone screen. "It's almost ten o'clock. Is it too early to call him now?"

"Go for it. I've seen no one coming in or out of the apartment. I assume it's still available."

She narrows her eyes at him. "It better be, now that you got my hopes up."

Ruben Sanders answers on the second ring. She introduces herself and explains her situation. "Is the apartment still available?"

"Yes, ma'am." He sounds like a Southern gentleman. "When would you like to see it?"

"I can be there in twenty minutes?"

He chuckles. "You're an eager one. Let's make it thirty."

She ends the call and sets her phone on the bar. "How old is that guy?"

"Old. He's super nice, though, and cool in an old-fashioned kinda way. He's the most senior partner at his law firm, which takes up the whole first floor of the building."

Presley gets to her feet. "I need to run up to my room before I meet Mr. Sanders. Do you mind if I borrow your raincoat again? I promise to bring it back this afternoon."

"Take it," he says, flicking his wrist at her. "You'll need it. Park on Marshall Street if you can find a spot. You'll be closer to the entrance to the stairs."

She takes note of his suggestion, but when she arrives at the building, all the parking spaces on the street are taken. She parks in the back lot beside Everett's Ford pickup. In the dim light of a rainy day, she sees how old and worn out it is. Noticing his Georgia tag, she makes a mental reminder to ask if he's from Atlanta. And if he is, whether he knows any of her many college friends from there.

Ruben Sanders, wearing a Barbour coat and an Orvis fedora, is waiting for her in the hall outside the corner unit. He reminds her of her late grandfather with a slight build and jolly looking face.

As he's unlocking the door, he talks about his grandson, Jackson, who is on the football team at Jefferson College. "My daughter insists my wife and I go to the game in this nasty weather, even though Jackson probably won't see any playing time. Between you and me, I'd rather be at home in front of the fire watching Alabama beat the tar outta Mississippi State on the television." He chuckles, nudging Presley with his elbow.

Presley's face lights up. "I went to Bama. Roll tide!"

He punches the air. "Roll tide, roll! I didn't go to Alabama, but I'm originally from Mobile."

"The apartment is over a thousand square feet. I haven't been able to find a tenant. Most people want two bedrooms in an apartment this size." He opens the door and motions her inside ahead of him. "Make yourself at home."

Presley wanders through the empty rooms. The apartment is scrumptious, like Everett's but on a larger scale. The enormous bedroom includes a walk-in closet and the spotless bathroom shines with white subway tile and a shower stall. Shelves line the walls in the kitchen, and the base cabinets are black with fake marble tops. There's a gas stove, dishwasher, and stainless side-by-side refrigerator. In the living room, the windows are floor-to-ceiling, two on Main Street and another pair looking out in the direction of the inn. She can't see much through the fog, but on a clear day, she'll have a marvelous view of the mountains.

Ruben joins her at the window. "I've owned this building for decades. As Everett probably told you, my law practice occupies the first floor. But I only recently converted the upstairs into apartments. If you lease it, you'll be the first to live here."

"How much is the rent?" she asks, even though it doesn't matter. She'll take the apartment at any cost. She's never had her own place. Something about the space feels right. Like home.

When Ruben tells her the amount, she asks him if she can move in right away. The rent is a fraction of what an apartment of this caliber would cost in Nashville. He presents a lease, she signs it, and writes him a check to cover the security deposit and first month's rent. He gives her the keys and they walk to the door together.

"Thank you, Mr. Sanders. I promise I'll be an ideal tenant."

"I believe you will, Miss Ingram. If you need anything, do not hesitate to call."

After he leaves, she roams from room to room, imagining a bed here and a sofa over there. Presley has some furniture in storage from previous apartments, most of which is junk and not worth the effort to move. She tries to envision the apartment outfitted with the somber furnishings from her mother's house. Once she sells the house, she'll bring back a few of the more valuable accent pieces, but she's going for a more youthful and contemporary vibe for her new home. At least she'll have no trouble outfitting the kitchen. Her mother fancied herself a gourmet chef, but she rarely cooked.

On her way back to the inn, Presley makes a detour past 237 Hillside Drive. The minivan is parked in the driveway and dim lights burn from within. How does a single mother and her teenage daughters spend a rainy day together? Are they playing board games or in the kitchen baking cupcakes? Is Rita reading a book in front of a fire while the girls listen to music and Face-Time with their friends in their respective rooms?

As she drives away, Presley has a gut feeling she's making the right decision in moving here, that given time she will come to know her biological mother and half sisters.

Back at the inn, after retrieving her laptop from her room, she stops by Billy's Bar to return Everett's raincoat. But Everett is too busy to talk, and she leaves the raincoat folded at the end of the bar.

The lunch crowd swarms Jameson's. She adds her name to the list, and she's rewarded for her thirty-minute wait with a table by the window. She orders a crab cake sandwich, and while she eats, she explores websites of popular furniture stores. Reid and Tarten, a nationwide chain with a store in nearby Roanoke, best suits her taste. When she calls the number, she's connected to a helpful salesclerk. Room by room, she orders a few primary pieces of furniture including a blue velvet sofa, coffee table, bed, and dresser. With a stroke of luck, the store has a delivery time available for this coming Tuesday morning.

She thanks the salesclerk and ends the call. She orders a coffee and stares out at the rain, thinking how drastically her life has changed in three short days.

9

EVERETT

Everett arrives at work early on Sunday morning. While he takes an inventory of his liquor supply, he keeps one eye on the doorway, hoping Presley will stop by. He missed her when she dropped off his raincoat yesterday afternoon, and he's curious what she thinks of the apartment. When lunchtime rolls around with no sign of her, Everett assumes she's already checked out and headed back to Nashville. Their kiss remains at the forefront of his mind. He can taste Presley's sweet lips and feel her slim hips beneath his hands. While he wants more from her, friendship will have to be enough for now.

A few guests linger after checkout time, brunching in Jameson's and then stopping in afterward for one last Bloody Mary or mimosa before heading home. Two local men spend the afternoon drinking craft draft beer and watching the Redskins lose to the Eagles.

Everett drags his heavy body from one task to the next. He hasn't felt this down since he quit drinking years ago. Do his Sunday blues have anything to do with Presley? Or is it because he's currently holding himself hostage while he figures a way out of the mess he's made of his life?

By six o'clock, the football fans have gone home, the Redskins game is over, and the Giants are now playing the Cowboys. Everett is reconciling his register in preparation of closing early when Jazz comes flying around the corner into the bar. He holds open his arms, and she leaps into them, burying her face in his chest.

"What's wrong, Jazzy?"

Raising a tiny arm, she points a finger at Naomi and Stella, who are standing just outside the bar in the lounge. He can't make out what they're saying, but their voices are raised and their expressions pinched.

"Would a Dizzy Fizzy Ballerina make you feel better?"

She nods into his chest. He deposits her onto a stool and goes behind the bar. When he changes the TV channel to Nickelodeon, Jazz's face lights up at the sight of SpongeBob.

"How was your weekend?" he asks, and she answers, "Fine."

He mixes Blood Orange SanPellegrino with papaya nectar and a splash of cranberry—Jazz's very own signature mocktail he designed especially for her. He adds a sprig of rosemary and slides the glass across the bar to her. He leaves Jazz and goes out to the lounge, standing awkwardly nearby while Naomi and Stella continue to argue.

Naomi's nostrils flare as she glares at Stella. "If you're accusing me of something, come right out and say it."

"I'm not accusing you of anything, Naomi. I'm asking why you haven't reached out to organizers of past conferences when you promised me weeks ago you'd make it a priority."

Naomi's posture is stiff, her shoulders squared. "I never promised you anything. I said I'd get to it when I had a chance. And I've been busy."

"Busy doing what? There are no guests in the house tonight. Not a single room is booked." Stella sweeps an arm at the empty lounge. "Every week is like this, Sundays through Wednesdays, sometimes even Thursdays. We can't survive if we don't start hosting conferences."

The hatred in Naomi's brown eyes makes Everett's flesh crawl. "If it's so important, do it yourself."

Stella's body tenses. When she balls her fists at her sides, Everett worries she might hit Naomi. "I will. Send me the list of contacts."

"It'll take me some time to pull the information together. God, I hate working for you."

When Naomi storms into the bar, Stella mumbles to her retreating back, "Then why don't you quit?"

Alone in the lounge, Stella looks over at Everett. "Sorry you had to witness that."

"It's none of my business, but why do you put up with her behavior?"

Stella shakes her head. "I ask myself that question nearly every single day."

From where they stand, they watch Naomi snatch the drink out of her daughter's hands and slam it down on the bar. "Come on. Time to go." She lifts Jazz off the barstool into her arms.

Jazz squirms. "Stop, Mommy! I want to finish my Dizzy Fizzy Ballerina."

Naomi tightens her grip. "It's time to go, Jasmine."

"Put me down. I want Stella." Jazz kicks and claws her way out of Naomi's arms. She runs out of the bar to Stella, hugging her waist. "I want to spend the night with you, Stella."

Stella smooths the child's unruly hair. "It's fine with me."

"Well, it's not fine with me," Naomi snaps.

"Naomi," Stella says in a warning tone.

Shooting Stella a death glare, Naomi bends over, with hands on knees, to speak to her child. "I was going to take you to Lucky's for dinner."

"I thought you said we couldn't go to Lucky's," Jazz says, her face planted in Stella's abdomen.

"Well, I changed my mind." Naomi tugs on Jazz's shirtsleeve. "If we go now, we might beat the dinner crowd."

Jazz tilts her head back and looks up at Stella. "Do I have to?"

Stella pries Jazz's arms free from her waist. "Of course, you do, sweetheart. You always have to listen to what your mommy says. Besides, Lucky's is your favorite. Will you eat some french fries for me?"

"No! Get your own french fries." Jazz stomps off with Naomi on her heels.

Stella's shoulders cave as she exhales a breath of air. "I need a drink after that."

"Me too," Everett says. "And I don't even drink."

Stella manages a weak smile. "I'm sorry you got caught in the middle of that."

Everett shrugs as if to say no big deal. "I have an open bottle of that Oregon pinot noir you like. Can I pour you a glass?"

"Please!" she says, and they enter the bar together.

Everett aims the remote at the television, which is still tuned to Nickelodeon. "Do you want to watch the game? The Giants are playing."

"I'm not a football fan. But thank you."

He clicks off the television and turns on Pandora, tuning into the Wild Holler's station. The sound of her father's voice brings a smile to Stella's face.

Everett pours a healthy serving of red wine and hands the glass to her.

"I shouldn't let Naomi get under my skin. She infuriates me. I seriously want to strangle her." Stella holds her hands out, fingers forming a circle as though wrapped around Naomi's neck.

He busies himself with tidying up the mess he made in

fixing Jazz's drink. In his experience as a bartender, Everett has discovered that people are more willing to open up if they think he's preoccupied with other tasks. Sure enough, a faraway expression settles on Stella's face, and she talks out loud, more to herself than to him.

"I'm to blame for giving Naomi additional responsibilities when I know she won't deliver." Stella sips her wine. "If not for Jazz, I'd fire her in a heartbeat."

Everett wipes an imaginary spot off the marble. "Jazz seems afraid of her mother."

"There's no doubt about it," Stella says. "You saw the way Naomi jerks the poor kid around. Truth be told, I'm a little afraid of Naomi myself."

"Me too," Everett says with a chuckle. "I feel sorry for Jazz the way Naomi keeps her here so late at night."

Stella frowns. "What're you talking about? Naomi works nine to five."

Oops. Everett didn't mean to get Naomi in trouble. Or did he? "Several times in the past few weeks, when I'm leaving to go home around nine or ten o'clock at night, Naomi's been at the reservation desk and Jazz asleep in the office."

"Naomi has some serious emotional problems. And she's a recovering alcoholic." Stella blushes, as though she'd like to eat her words. "That isn't public knowledge, Everett. I shouldn't have told you."

"Bartenders are required to take oaths to keep their customers' secrets. Or in your case, their boss lady's secrets." He drags his fingers across his lips. "What's said in Billy's Bar stays in Billy's Bar. Is Naomi still drinking?"

"She'd better not be. She's supposed to be attending weekly AA meetings. It's one of my conditions for employment." Stella plants her elbows on the bar and stares down at her wine. "Jazz's life has not been easy. She was a sad little kid when she came to stay with me last summer. Telling no one where she was going, Naomi flew off to rehab in Arizona and left Jazz in my care for six weeks. I'd only been in Hope Springs a month, and I had no clue about Jazz being my half sister. During Naomi's absence, Jazz contracted bacterial meningitis and was hospitalized for a week. Poor kid had a tough go of it. We both did. But we grew close because of it. I'm more like Jazz's parent than her sister, and that confuses her sometimes."

Everett has stopped the busywork and is now listening intently. "That explains the exchange I just witnessed."

"Jazz runs to me every time she disagrees with her mother. Because she's Jazz's mother, I have to support Naomi's decisions as much as it kills me. But I pick my battles. I don't always let Naomi have her way."

He pours a little more wine in Stella's glass. "Were Naomi and Billy married?"

"Nope. My father's relationship with Naomi was complicated."

He stuffs the cork back in the bottle. "How so?"

She pauses, as though considering how to answer. "Naomi cared more for Billy than he cared for her. She got pregnant to trap him into marriage, and when he refused, she married the first guy who came along."

Sweat trickles down his back at the familiarity of the situation. "Is she still married to him?"

"No. She's separated from Derrick. Good thing, too. I don't think Derrick was much of a stepfather. But Billy adored Jazz. He provided well for her in his will. Part of the reason Billy gave me the farm is so I'll be close to Jazz in the event Naomi goes off the deep end. That kid means everything to me. I'll protect her at all costs, even if it means petitioning the court for custody."

"I don't understand how things like that work. Is it a possibility?"

"It would be a last resort. Jazz deserves happiness. Her father is dead, her mother is unstable, and her stepfather wants nothing to do with her. I may be the only one who can give her that happiness. If I petition for custody, I want the situation to be permanent for Jazz's sake."

"How does Jack feel about all this?"

Stella takes a gulp of wine. "Jack adores Jazz. He would have no reservations about raising her as his own child."

Everett leans across the bar. "When are the two of you getting married?"

"That's the million-dollar question. Jack promised not to pressure me, but his patience is waning." Stella drains the rest of her wine. "The last thing I need is to complicate our lives with planning a fancy wedding."

He holds up the bottle. "More?"

Stella waves off the offer. "I've had enough. I can sleep now." She pushes her stool back. "You're an excellent listener, Everett. I rarely open up about my problems so easily. What's said in Billy's Bar—"

"Stays in Billy's Bar," he finishes. "You have my word."

As he watches Stella disappear into the lounge, his hand that's holding the bottle of wine shakes. He could so easily pour himself a glass. He quickly stores the bottle out of sight. Will the temptation ever fully go away?

10

PRESLEY

A wave of profound sadness washes over Presley as she backs out of her mother's driveway. She's closing a chapter on the life she's known for thirty years. This house, her home, holds good and bad memories of holidays and birthdays, sleepovers with friends, the succession of springer spaniels who once ruled their yard. She has no remorse. But, while she's excited for her new apartment and career awaiting her in the mountains of Virginia, the fear of an uncertain future is unsettling.

Before rounding the corner at the end of their block, she takes one look back at the house. Patricia, her listing agent, is at the front door greeting their first potential buyers. Patricia is confident they'll have multiple offers, perhaps even a contract, by this evening.

She squeezes her eyes tight, the tears streaming down her cheeks. Her mother's voice rings in her head. "You've got this, Presley. You can accomplish anything you set your mind to." Renee wasn't such a bad mom, for a high-strung control freak whose only form of recreation was partying. She gave sound advice, was an excellent provider, and supported Presley in her many ventures. So what if Renee never exhibited her love. Maybe Presley expectations were too high.

Rummaging in her bag for a tissue, she wipes her eyes and leaves the neighborhood one last time. Through the rearview mirror, she can barely see over the clothes and kitchenware, lamps and bedding packed in the back of her SUV as she makes her way through town. Once she's on the interstate, she adjusts her seat and settles in for the seven-hour drive to Virginia.

She places a hands-free call to her mother's primary antiques dealer. When she explains the situation to Hubert Brock, he expresses interest in buying back many of Renee's pieces. Presley promises to get in touch when she's ready to clear out the house. After hanging up with Hubert, she makes a mental list of her friends who work for small to midsize companies that might be interested in hosting conferences at Hope Springs Farm. Her mind drifts to the party. She has several ideas for themes, but one keeps coming back to her. She calls Stella to run the idea past her.

"What do you think of *Homecoming* as a theme for the town party? After all, the inn is like home for many of the townsfolk, those who have lived in Hope Springs all their lives and have fond memories of time spent on the farm growing up."

When silence fills the line, Presley worries that Stella hates the idea. "We can brainstorm something else."

"Not at all. I absolutely love it, Presley! I've spoken with Cecily and Naomi. We agree the weekend following Halloween is best."

"Perfect! That'll give me an additional week for planning." Presley pauses while she passes another car. "By the way, is it okay if I start work tomorrow afternoon? I need to be here in the morning when the truck arrives with my furniture."

"Presley, please! Take a couple of days to unpack and rest up after your drive. I'm afraid you won't have much free time going forward."

"But I'm eager to get started. I'll come in on Wednesday morning. What time should I be there?"

"On Wednesday? Let me see." Presley hears Stella clicking on her calendar. "I have an early meeting with my architect at the spa building at seven. Why don't you come in around nine? We have limited office space in the main building. For now, you'll have to share with Karen, the concierge. Did you meet Karen during your stay?"

"Yes! She booked my bike tour."

"Since this job will demand a lot of your weekend time, I'm fine with you setting your own hours. Because the office space is tight, feel free to work remotely from your apartment if you need to spread out."

Presley eyes Renee's large screen iMac strapped into the passenger seat beside her. "I may do that. Thanks for allowing me the flexibility."

Presley and Stella talk for a few more minutes about ways to raise awareness of the resort. She admires Stella's keen business sense and the way she stays on top of every department without being overbearing.

After stopping for lunch and gas in Knoxville, she gets on Highway 81 and cranks the volume on her road-trip playlist, a mixture of her favorite classic rock artists. Heavy tractor-trailer traffic adds ninety minutes to her trip, but excitement overpowers her exhaustion when she finally arrives at almost six o'clock. She's making her first trip up the stairs to her apartment, her arms loaded with hanging clothes, when Everett appears from work.

"Presley! You're back. Let me run this stuff up to my apartment"—he holds up his backpack in one hand and a take-out food container in the other—"and I'll help you unload your car."

"I've got it, Everett. Don't let your dinner get cold."

"I'm not really that hungry. Besides, it'll take you until midnight if you do it alone."

She flashes him a grateful smile. "In that case, I accept your offer."

An hour later, they carry the last load up the stairs, adding it to the pile of cardboard boxes and plastic bins in the center of the living room. Everett collapses onto a mountain of bedding and throw pillows. "You were gone for thirty-six hours, and a portion of that was spent traveling. How did you pack all this stuff up in such a short amount of time?"

She drops to the floor beside him. "I stayed up most of the night."

Staring up at the ceiling, he says, "Where're you planning to sleep tonight?"

"I'll make a bed out of the pillows and comforter you're lying on. Truthfully, I'm so tired, I could sleep standing up."

He rolls over on his side to face her. "I'll bet you are. I'm sure you're hungry too. I've got a hankering for a pie from Ruby's pizzeria. They're located just up the street. Should I run get us one while you locate your toothbrush?"

"Pizza sounds awesome. But only if you let me treat you for helping me unload." Crawling around on her knees, she locates her purse and removes thirty dollars from her wallet. When she tries to give it to him, he stares at it.

"Are you sure? I'm fine with going dutch."

She folds the money in his hand. "I'm positive. I'd still be unloading my car if not for you." With one hand on his back, she walks him to the door. "Now go. I'm starving."

He starts down the hall toward the stairs and turns back around. "By the way, what do you want on your pizza?"

"Anything but anchovies." She closes the door behind him and returns to the mess in the living room. Her toothbrush can wait. Right now, she's craving a cup of tea. She attacks the kitchen boxes until she locates her Keurig machine, two coffee mugs, and a box of chai tea. She fills the Keurig with water, steeps the tea, and takes her mug over to the window. The sun is a glowing ball of orange as it dips below a mountain ablaze with red and yellow tree foliage. The setting moves her to tears. Her first night in her new home.

Her phone vibrates in her back pocket with a call from her listing agent. "We've got ourselves a bidding war," Patricia blurts when Presley answers. "I've received three contracts, all for full asking price."

Presley continues to stare out at the mountains. Is she doing the right thing in selling the house? Even if she ends up back in Nashville, she has no use for a five-thousand-square-foot house. She can hear her mother now, dry martini in hand. "Dump the house, Presley. Invest the money. When the time is right, buy something more suitable for you."

Let go, Presley. Time to move on with your life.

"That's exciting, Patricia. How do we decide?"

For the next few minutes, they talk about Patricia's strategy to get the interested parties to increase their bids. Presley has no sooner hung up with Patricia when Everett returns with the pizza. She brews him a cup of tea, and using washcloths for napkins, they eat the entire pizza straight out of the box. Afterward, they stretch out on the hardwood floor with their heads propped on pillows.

"So, Presley, I'm curious why you picked little old Hope Springs for your weekend getaway? The inn isn't *that* special. There are equally desirable resorts closer to Nashville. Like Blackberry Farm, for example. I'd understand if you were meeting a friend or family member. You had to purchase a plane ticket to get here, for crying out loud."

"If you must know, I came here on a mission." She tells him about the adoption file she found in her mother's desk and the woman who lives at 237 Hillside Drive whom she believes to be her birth mother.

Everett brings himself to a sitting position. "Whoa. That's some story." With knees bent, he rests his head on folded arms. "Did you know you were adopted before you found the file?"

"Yes," she says. "My father died from cancer when I was six, but my mother has always talked openly with me about my adoption. She and my dad couldn't have children. They were blessed to have gotten me."

"That must have been hard for you growing up without a father."

Presley hangs her head. "Dad and I were close, and even though I was so young when he died, I still miss him a ton."

"Do you have any idea who your birth father is?"

She cuts her eyes at him. That's a strange question. Then again, maybe not so strange coming from a male perspective. "No clue."

"Did you ever consider trying to find out about your biological parents on one of those websites like 23andMe?"

"I thought about it a lot, actually. I have the test kit to prove it. But I never pursued it out of respect for my mother—my adoptive mother, that is. It's funny. Before I found that envelope, I never thought of Renee as my *adoptive* mother. She was just my mom. I'm grateful to her for giving me a wonderful life. At the same time, I'm grateful to my biological mother for giving me life."

"You mean instead of aborting you?"

At first, Presley thinks Everett is kidding, but his face is serious. And troubled.

She gives him a shove. "Jeez, Everett. Way to be blunt about it!"

He shrugs. "Why sugarcoat it? What would you do if you found yourself burdened with an unwanted pregnancy?"

"That's a loaded question." Presley gets to her feet and goes to the window. "Because I *was* adopted, I've thought about it a lot over the years. Putting a baby up for adoption is the ultimate sacrifice. Suffering through nine months of pregnancy, only to give your baby away. I couldn't do that. I'm thankful I haven't had to make that decision. If I got pregnant now, at age thirty, I would raise the baby on my own."

"What if the baby's father wanted you to have an abortion?"

Presley is glad her back is to Everett. She doesn't want to see his expression, to know what he's thinking. "I would never do that. It would help if the father wanted to be a part of the baby's life. A child should have two parents. But it wouldn't be a deal breaker. I have enough love in my heart to be both mother and a father."

"So, you don't think the father has a right to insist the woman have an abortion?"

Presley twirls around to face him. "How did this turn into an ethical discussion?"

"Right. Sorry." Everett's eyes are glassy, as though he's returning from a faraway place. "Aside from the address on the torn envelope, do you have any other documentation to prove this woman is your biological mother?"

Turning back to the darkened window, she mumbles, "No." She thinks of Rita and her daughters in their house on Hillside Drive. They've finished dinner by now, and the girls are probably doing their homework. She wonders if Rita is folding laundry. Or planning a trip on her computer. Or grading papers if she's a teacher at the high school. "The last thing I want to do is cause trouble for her. I'll understand if she wants nothing to do with me."

"She'll be thrilled, once she gets to know you." Everett comes to stand beside her at the window. "Thank you for trusting me enough to tell me. I apologize for what I said about the abortion. It was inappropriate."

She smiles over at him. "No worries. If you don't mind, though, I'd like to keep this between us. It's not a secret, exactly, but it's personal."

"You have my word. I won't tell a soul." He kisses her cheek. "Sleep tight in your new apartment."

Presley remains at the window for a long time after he lets himself out. She doesn't know what prompted her to confide in him. She's not a very open person. Even when she had a whole sorority of girlfriends at Bama, she kept things to herself. But Everett is different. Although she doesn't know him well, she feels like she can trust him. With so many changes taking place in her life, she's glad to have a friend.

11

EVERETT

E verett sleeps fitfully, dreaming of fatherless babies crying for attention. When he wakes with a start at daybreak, he sits bolt upright, bathed in a cold sweat and unable to breathe. Rolling off the mattress to his feet, he takes big gulps of air as he moves about the room. Once his breathing steadies and his heart rate slows, he throws on workout clothes and hits the pavement. By doubling the distance he normally runs, he succeeds in chasing away the demons plaguing his conscience.

After showering and dressing and eating a bowl of Cheerios, he walks over to the library and waits for it to open at ten. Today, instead of deleting emails from Carla and Louie, he reads the most recent from both. Nothing in their messages surprise him. More pleas for Everett to get in touch as soon as possible. His mom, on the other hand, delivers disturbing news in her weekly communication. His father suffered a minor stroke over the weekend. He's out of the hospital now, and while there's no major damage, the doctors warn that another, more severe stroke, is possible. His diabetes complicates his condition, putting him at an even higher risk. While his mom assures him that everything is fine, Everett reads the worry between the lines. Even though his father is eligible for Medicare and Medicaid, his mom, on her limited income, won't be able to afford the hospital bills.

With a heavy heart, Everett leaves the library and heads in to work. When he enters the building, his mind elsewhere, he forgets to check for Naomi at the front desk. Spotting him, she chases him down as he hurries through the lounge.

"Everett, I need a word with you." He slows his pace, and she catches up with him. "In private."

He glances around the empty lounge. "But there's no one here." She glares at him, and he adds, "Whatever."

They walk together to Billy's Bar. Everett goes behind the bar, dumps his backpack on the counter, and flicks a series of switches that bathes the room in light. "Okay, Naomi. What's this about?" he asks with an exasperated sigh.

"I received a disturbing phone call this morning from one of last week's guests." Standing near the end of the bar, Naomi consults the notecard in her hand. "A Mr. Mack Lambert. He was part of the group of fly fishermen here last week."

Turkey Neck, he thinks. "And what did Mr. Mack Lambert have to say, Naomi?"

"He was asking a lot of questions about you, Everett. Do you remember him?"

Everett examines his fingernails, pretending to be bored despite his heart hammering against his rib cage. "I remember the group, not the man specifically. What kind of questions was he asking?"

"He claims he knows you from somewhere, but he can't place you, and it's driving him crazy. You know how that is."

Everett knows exactly how that is. He's still trying to figure out how he knows the ruddy-faced fisherman as well.

He feels Naomi's eyes on him, watching closely for his response. "When I can't remember someone, it bugs me for a few minutes, an hour max. But those men checked out nearly a week ago. If this Mack person is still trying to place me, he seriously needs to get a life."

Naomi waves the notecard at him. "That's the thing, though. He's certain he knows you from Atlanta, yet you told him you're from North Dakota. Mack wants to know why you lied. He thinks maybe you're wanted by the police." She sets her intense gaze on Everett. "Are you, Everett? Wanted by the police?"

Fear creeps down Everett's spine. "That's ridiculous. Mack is mistaken. You know the old saying that everyone has a twin."

Naomi holds out her hand. "Let me see your driver's license."

Everett digs through his wallet and hands her the fake license. If she investigates him, she won't have to dig hard to find out he's originally from Georgia.

Naomi studies the license and returns it to him. "I've got my eye on you, Everett. You're hiding something, and I aim to find out what it is."

"You're wasting your time, Naomi. From what I hear, that's what you do best."

Naomi opens her mouth *to* speak, but then closes it again. Spinning on her heels, she flees the bar.

Everett pours a shot of Patron. With a shaking hand, he lifts it to his lips. His mom's voice echoes in his head. *Don't do it, Rhett. You're better than this.*

Am I, Mom? I'm not so sure. He pours the tequila down the drain and slumps against the bar. Will the end ever justify the means? Why not go home to Atlanta and face the firing squad? In the grand scheme of things, his crimes aren't serious. He's done nothing illegal. He's not wanted for murder. He's not even wanted by the police. Sure, what he did was morally wrong, and his conscience is eating away at him. But throwing in the towel would mean giving up on his dreams. And he's not ready to do that just yet.

And what about Presley? Whatever is going on between them is more than friendship. If he wants a chance at a meaningful relationship with her, he must take things slowly. But his time is in short supply.

Only two customers enter the bar during the afternoon. A businessman who sits at a table, guzzling a beer while speaking animatedly to someone on his AirPods. And an older woman in town visiting her daughter who just had a baby. The woman's been up all night at the hospital and has returned to the hotel for a nap. She sits at the bar, sipping a glass of champagne while telling Everett more than he ever wanted to know about the process of childbirth.

Everett can't seem to get away from pregnancy and childbirth and adoption.

Stella sticks her head in the bar around four o'clock. "I wanted to remind you about parents' weekend this weekend. We're booked solid beginning tomorrow night." Her smile is forced, the worry apparent in the lines around her eyes.

Everett makes a sweeping gesture at the gleaming shelves of liquor bottles. "I'm on it! All stocked up and waiting."

If business doesn't improve, the decision whether to stay in Hope Springs may be out of Everett's control. His salary, alone, won't pay his rent. For a bartender, tips are necessary for survival. No way he can afford to help his mom with his dad's hospital bills.

Everett closes the bar around six and walks home. When he reaches the top of the stairs, the sight of Presley's door ajar makes his heart skip a beat. A dose of her spunky personality is exactly what he needs.

As he draws closer to her apartment, he hears the pounding of a hammer coming from within. He nudges the door open. "Knock knock," he says but doesn't wait for a response before entering.

Presley is teetering on the back of a blue sofa, driving a picture hook into the drywall. "Careful, Presley. You might fall."

She turns to look at him and tumbles to the sofa. "Too late," she says, laughing. "Don't sneak up on me like that."

"I didn't. You left the door cracked. I called out before I came in."

She rolls off the sofa. "I'm glad you're here. You can help me hang this beast." She crosses the room to a large abstract painting of a flower leaning against the far wall. "It's not heavy. Just awkward."

He takes the painting from her, and they wrestle the canvas onto the hook, standing back to admire it. The petals of the flower are white and pink, highlighted with streaks of yellow. Peeking through the outer petals are slivers of blue-gray sky, the same color as her new velvet sofa.

"Nice couch, Pres." He performs a flying leap onto the sofa and breaks into a Tony Bennett rendition of *Blue Velvet*. He sings the entire song with Presley staring at him slack-jawed.

"You have some serious vocals, Everett. You've been holding out on me. I know a lot about music and you've got talent. I'm not the first person to tell you that, am I?"

A lie is on the tip of his tongue, but when he looks up at Presley, so honest and good, the words remain unspoken. He makes a joke out of the situation instead by bursting into Nickelback's "Rockstar."

Presley smacks him in the head with a throw pillow. "Stop! I hate that song." In a fit of laughter, she falls onto the sofa beside him.

Loud and intentionally off-key, he sings the song in its entirety. With hands covering ears, she laughs until tears stream down her face.

When he's finished, he rests his head against the back of the sofa and takes in her apartment. There's a fake antelope rug on the floor and a large square coffee table with gold base and glass top. He imagines Presley watching the sun set over the mountains while working at the white lacquer writing desk positioned between the two windows facing the inn.

Recovering from her laughing fit, Presley tosses her head back against the cushions beside his.

"The place really looks great, Pres." He runs his hand against the soft velvet. "I particularly like the blue velvet . . ." His tone becomes melodic.

She shoves a pillow in his face. "No. More. Singing."

"Okay! I promise," he says, his voice smothered by the pillow.

She removes the pillow from his face and places it behind her head. "I need to go to the grocery. Wanna come?"

"Nah. You go." He closes his eyes. "I'll wait for you here on Big Blue."

"Big Blue? So, my sofa has a name now?"

"Yep. Your apartment's badass, even if it is a bit girlie for my taste."

Presley smacks his abdomen with the back of her hand. "You have furniture envy, because all you own is an air mattress."

"That might have something to do with it." He cracks an eyelid to look at her. "I'm not kidding. I could stay here forever. I don't even need food or water. Lock the doors and keep the world out."

She rolls on her side to face him. "You're in a strange mood. Did something happen today?"

"Nothing you want to hear about." Sitting up, he smooths out his wiry hair. "Let's make a deal. I'll go with you to the grocery store if you'll have dinner with me at Town Tavern. Tonight is two-for-one burger night. My treat."

She laughs. "How is that a treat? You're only paying for one burger, regardless."

"Can't blame a guy for trying."

"Fine. But after tonight, we go dutch. We're just friends, remember?"

He rolls his eyes. "As if I could forget."

The chemistry between them is undeniable, even if Presley isn't ready to accept it. But she will, once she settles into her new life. In the meantime, if financial circumstances dictate it, he'll look for another job in Hope Springs to stay near her. Carla and Louie be damned.

12

PRESLEY

The first day of my new life, Presley thinks as she watches the sunrise from her second-floor window. She wraps her arms around her midsection, embracing the warmth radiating through her body. Everything about this town feels right. *Please let it be real.*

After a thirty-minute Peloton yoga workout, she pulls on a fleece, stuffs AirPods in her ears, and leaves the building. She's incognito, a local out for her morning walk. No one has reason to suspect she's spying on the family who lives at 237 Hillside Drive.

Her timing is impeccable. As she rounds the corner onto the street, Rita and the girls emerge from their house. Seeing Abigail's and Emma's bare legs in short flouncy dresses makes Presley shiver. Does that mean no field hockey game for them today? Rita wears a Barbour coat over her khaki pants. What is it with the Barbour coats in this town? Everyone appears to own one.

As Presley strolls by on the sidewalk, one of the girls, Abigail, she thinks, the younger of the two, lifts a hand at her in a shy wave. Presley wishes her a good morning in return. She smiles to herself as she continues down the street. Her first contact with her half sister.

As she roams the neighboring streets, Presley, enamored by so many charming homes, loses track of time and is nearly late for her first day of work. She chooses a simple long-sleeved black sheath and tall boots, but she feels overdressed when she sees Stella waiting for her at the front door in jeans and a black turtleneck. She reminds herself that Stella has been meeting with the architect at the construction site.

Stella holds the door open for her. "Good morning. Welcome to the team."

"You have no idea how much this means to me." It's been a long time since Presley has been a part of anything.

She gives Stella a quick hug, and they enter the building together. "We'll stop by your office first. Then, we can discuss plans for the homecoming party while I give you a tour of the facilities."

Presley smiles at Naomi as they pass through reception. Naomi nods at her, but she doesn't smile back. *What is up with her attitude?*

Karen, the concierge, is on the phone at one of two desks cramming the small office. She flaps her hand at Presley. Karen's warm welcome sets Presley at ease after Naomi's chilly reception.

In a low voice, so as not to disturb Karen, Stella says, "I'm hoping to relocate security to a different building, which will open up the office next door for you."

Presley's fingers graze Stella's arm. "This is fine. Really. I'll work remotely from home whenever necessary."

"Please let me know if it gets to be a problem." Stella turns back toward the door. "Are you ready for the tour?"

"Let's do it." She removes her iPad from her bag and drops the bag on the chair at the empty desk.

Starting at the solarium, they work their way through the first floor of the inn before moving on to the outbuildings. Presley falls in love with the barn at first sight. "No matter what season, this will make for a fabulous wedding reception venue."

"I think so too," Stella says.

"For the party, why don't we book a bluegrass band and have an oyster roast out here?"

Stella's face lights up. "Brilliant suggestion. Cecily has an excellent source for oysters. Coincidentally, I've purchased three tents in varying sizes, and I'm having a Sperry Tent custom designed to cover the terrace at the main building."

"Wow! Our brides will love it." A sailcloth tent of that quality must cost a fortune.

They continue down toward the lake, stopping in at the carriage house. The building houses two two-bedroom suites on the second floor with a kitchen and lounge area on the first.

Stella explains, "In 1923, when my great-grandfather built the inn, even though the use of automobiles had become more widespread by then, they still needed a place to store their guests' horse-drawn carriages."

"I love the way you kept the integrity of the building when you renovated," Presley says. "How do you plan to use the carriage house?"

"To accommodate brides' families during wedding weekends and corporate executives who need a quiet place away from their employees during conferences."

"Are we using the carriage house for the party?"

Stella shakes her head. "I don't think we need it. But I envisioned us having an inflatable or two for kids on the lawn out front."

"Fun! We can come up with some other activities to keep the kids occupied while their parents enjoy themselves."

Stella gestures at the construction site. "You've seen the spa, which is now officially the Summer House Wellness Center thanks to you." They walk back up the hill to the main building. "I have a surprise that I hope will take some responsibility off of your shoulders."

Presley palms her chest. "Ooh. I love surprises. What is it?"

"As of Monday, our wine shop and cellar are officially open for business." Stella motions Presley through the door. "Come on. I'm dying to show it to you."

On the way down in the elevator, Presley asks, "Who is running the wine shop?"

"Our sommelier, Lucy Jordan. Lucy has worked at the inn on and off for much of her life. In her younger days, she was a server in the dining room. After college, she attended sommelier school and trained at French Laundry, a Michelin three-star restaurant in Napa."

Presley nods. "I know it well. The food is amazing. My mother and I visited the wine country several times. She always insisted we eat at French Laundry."

"I've heard it's over the top. I feel blessed to have Lucy on our team."

The doors part at the basement level, and the women enter another world. In one direction, a tunnel of a room, cool and damp with an arched stone ceiling, stretches as far as the eye can see. Lining the walls are oak shelves housing hundreds, if not thousands, of bottles of wine. A long wooden tasting table with matching backless stools occupies the center of the room. In the other direction, partitioned off by glass, is the wine shop with a checkout counter in the center surrounded by shelves of upright wine bottles.

An attractive woman in her fifties with shoulder-length mahogany hair comes from behind the counter, extending her hand to Presley. "I'm Lucy Jordan. Welcome to the team!"

There it is again. *The team.* Presley loves the way everyone refers to the staff as one working unit. "Thank you. Your cellar is impressive."

"Lucy designed it herself," Stella says proudly.

"With a lot of help from Stella." Behind black frame glasses, laugh lines crinkle at the corners of Lucy's brown eyes. Presley's people reader kicks into action. There's something special about this woman. Yet she's sending off a mysterious vibe as well. Is she struggling with inner demons? If so, she's doing a stellar job of not letting it show.

Stella glances at her watch. "Oops. I'm due at another meeting. I'll leave you two to get acquainted. Presley, full steam ahead with the plans for homecoming. I'll email the list of brides to you by the end of the day. And check with Cecily as soon as you can. We have a few small parties booked for parents' weekend on Friday and Saturday nights."

"I'm on it." Presley gives Stella a thumbs-up, and waits for her to leave before asking Lucy, "When are you hosting your first tasting?"

"On Friday night, for college parents on a first-come, first-served basis."

Presley asks, "Would you like for me to arrange a charcuterie board with cheeses and meats that pair well with your wines?"

"I've already spoken to Cecily about it," Lucy says. "You're knowledgeable about wine. I guess that's a given in your industry."

"My mother was a connoisseur. We went to a lot of tastings together." Presley learned what *not* to do from her mother. One *tastes* wine to savor the aromas and flavors. One doesn't drink wine to get drunk.

"Was? Is your mother . . ."

"Dead? Yes, she passed away two months ago." Presley changes the subject. She's not in the mood to talk about her mother's death. "Stella mentioned you worked at French Laundry. How did you end up back in Hope Springs? I hope I'm not being too personal."

"Not at all. Mine is the age-old story. I married my high school sweetheart. Grant, my now ex-husband, loves Hope Springs. He refused to live anywhere else. To be with him, I had to move back to Virginia. Around that same time, the sommelier here, at the inn, passed away, and I took his job. After my son was born five years later, I was a stay-at-home mom. Billy Jameson was managing the inn back then. His health had begun to decline, and he was letting things slip. He chose not to hire anyone to replace me."

"So, you and the inn are starting over together."

Lucy nods. "In terms of networking. But I never stopped studying wine. I've traveled a lot and received several important certifications. I feel as though I've been given a golden opportunity."

Presley smiles at her. "We have that in common." She removes a bottle of bordeaux from a shelf. She recognizes the label from her mother's cellar, a vintage worth over a thousand dollars. "Where did all these wines come from?"

"Believe it or not, a lot of them were already here. They were well-preserved, and we have some exquisite vintages in stock like the one you're holding."

"Does the wine shop have a name?"

"Hope Springs Cellars," Lucy says. "Our program isn't just about our restaurant's wine list, although Jameson's plays an important role in our overall success. I want our guests to enjoy a delicious bottle of wine at dinner and purchase a case to take home with them. The opportunities for tastings and wine education with our in-house guests will be limitless, and on slow nights, I'd like to host wine dinners for the locals."

The women talk for nearly an hour, discussing ways to grow the cellar's reputation. Presley finds Lucy's passion for wine infectious, and has faith that she will put Hope Springs Cellars on the map as one of the best in the state if not the country. As she talks, her face comes alive and her eyes twinkle. She is vibrant and intelligent, yet she also has a gentle way about her. Their guests will enjoy working with her to plan the wines for their events.

13

STELLA

In a leap of faith, Jack insists on putting both our names on the manor house title. His gesture, meant with the best intentions, makes me nervous when we haven't even set a date for our wedding. I'd feel better if he'd let me invest in the property, but when I offer my meager savings, he refuses to take it. I'm overjoyed at the prospect of one day living in my ancestral home. After he receives the official documents on Wednesday morning, Jack and I spend that afternoon picking out paint colors and going over the kitchen designs one last time before committing to the contractor.

When Jack returns to work, I stay behind to explore the yard. I'm delighted to discover my father's name etched in the trunk of an old maple tree at the back of the property. I sit on the ground at the base of that tree, imagining the time he spent here as a child. While I never knew Billy, never got to call him Daddy, oddly enough, I feel my connection to him getting stronger every day. Now that I'll be spending more time in the house where he grew up, he'll never be far from my mind.

The familiar fear of an uncertain future comes rushing back. What if the inn doesn't make it? What will happen to my career? There are no other hotels of that caliber in Hope Springs. Returning to New York is out of the question. I could never leave Brian and Opal, Jack and Jazz. Maybe I could get a job Charlottesville. I could suffer through the hour commute twice a day for a while, but it wouldn't be practical once we start our family. I've grown professionally these past few months. Managing the inn fulfills me in a way I never thought possible. Would I be happy as a stay-at-home mom? I have my doubts.

In order for my dreams to come true, I have to make certain the inn succeeds.

Getting to my feet, I walk through the house one more time before dragging myself back across the street. The inn has become a hostile environment with Naomi lurking around every corner. The look of dismay on Everett's face during our conversation on Sunday afternoon still haunts me. I'm losing his respect by allowing Naomi to walk all over me. Yet, I can't get rid of her unless I have absolute proof of wrongdoing. Even then, I risk losing Jazz. And that's a risk I'm not willing to take. If only I could figure out why Naomi has been keeping late hours at the inn. I would classify her work ethic as average. She's certainly not trying to impress me. I made a point of stopping by the reservations desk after dinner last night and the night before. Inez, our night agent, reported that Naomi had long since gone home. It's possible Everett's mistaken. But something tells me he's not.

I work in my office later than my usual six o'clock until I can no longer ignore my rumbling stomach. When I pass through reception, Inez's face is glued to the computer and her ear to the phone. The office behind her is empty. Naomi is nowhere in sight. I continue through the lounge to Jameson's. A foursome of elderly women are the only occupants of the restaurant.

As I enter the kitchen, I paste on a cheerful face for Cecily who is putting the finishing touches on four plates of food at the prep counter.

I wait until a server swoops the tray of entrees away before asking Cecily, "What's for dinner?"

"A salad with leftover grilled shrimp. Want one?" Cecily busies herself with cleaning up. Why can't she look me in the eye? Has she, too, lost respect for me?

I pull a stool up to the counter. "Sure. If you don't mind."

Cecily has been down in the dumps these past few weeks. Like me, she's concerned about the success of the inn. Jameson's is her big chance to make a name for herself. I try to make conversation with her while she throws together the salad— fresh mixed greens, grilled shrimp, and her homemade ginger dressing—but she has little to say. The bubbly Cecily I first met in May when she was a barista at Caffeine on the Corner is in hiding.

"Try not to worry so much, Cecily. We're in a transition period. Things will get better. Our homecoming party is the key to bringing in the townspeople," I say, wishing I felt as confident as I sound.

"I hope you're right," Cecily mumbles, setting my salad on the counter in front of me.

"Is something else wrong? You know you can talk to me about anything."

Cecily's lips curl up in a smile. "I'm fine. You have enough on your plate without worrying about me."

I tell her about the manor house while we eat, but I'm unsuccessful in drawing her out of her funk. It dawns on me that I'm being insensitive in talking about my fiancé and our new home when Cecily wants nothing more than to put down roots in Hope Springs with Lyle.

After cleaning my plate, I say goodnight to Cecily and leave the kitchen. At the reception desk, Inez is smiling at her cell phone, probably texting with her boyfriend. Behind her, the office door is closed.

Inez looks up at me, and her smile disappears. "Stella, what're you doing here so late?"

"Finishing up some work." I nod toward the closed door. "Who's in the office?"

Her gaze shifts from me to the door and back to me. "Oh . . . um . . ."

"What's going on, Inez?" I move behind the counter toward the office door.

"Don't go in there," Inez says, stepping in my path. "Jazz is asleep."

"Jazz? What's she doing here?"

Inez stares down at her feet. "I'm babysitting her."

"Where's Naomi?"

"Um . . ." She chews on her lip.

"Your loyalty to Naomi is admirable, Inez. But I'm the one paying your salary."

"She's with one of our guests."

Through gritted teeth, I say, "What guest, Inez? Tell me everything you know."

"Some businessman, in from out of town. This is his third or fourth time staying here. I don't know where they go or what they do together."

I know exactly where they are and what they're doing together. "When do you expect Naomi back?"

"She said by midnight."

My heart pounds in my ears, and I want to give Inez a proper lashing, but I hold my tongue. None of this is her fault. She's covering for her boss and earning extra money babysitting. I step around her and enter the office, closing the door behind me. Jazz is sound asleep on the floor in the corner, curled in a ball with her head resting on one arm. I take her coat from the back of Naomi's chair and drape it over her, tucking it in around her small body.

Sitting down at Naomi's computer, I plant my face in my hands. This is so wrong. This woman does not deserve to be anyone's mother. I have to get my sister away from her, but I have to be smart about it.

I click on the mouse, engaging Naomi's computer. I sort through files for more than an hour before I comprehend the method to Naomi's madness. She's saved files in folders with names that have nothing to do with information held within. I find the document I've been hounding Naomi about labeled Cleaning Supplies and attached to a folder marked Housekeeping. I click on the Excel spreadsheet and the contact information for every conference booked at the inn for the past ten years appears. The file was created in December 1999 and last updated six months ago. Naomi has had this information at her fingertips all along.

I access my Gmail account and email the document to myself. I keep searching. Buried in a folder marked Linens are five files from advertising agencies bidding for our business. Last summer, when Naomi returned from rehab and I was looking for something to occupy her time while the inn was under renovations, I put her in charge of researching marketing agencies. She's had plenty of experience with advertising in the past, and she assured me she could handle this monumental task. The fees on all five agencies are comparable, but creatively, any of four would have been a better choice than the one Naomi chose for us. She deliberately picked the worst firm. This one's on me. I made the drastic mistake of giving her too much authority.

Outside the door, I hear loud talking, and Naomi bursts into the office. Jazz bolts upright and, disoriented, begins to cry. When Naomi yells at me for using her computer, Jazz cries harder.

I jump to my feet. "Admit it, Naomi! You're deliberately trying to sabotage me. You want to see the inn fail."

She glares pure hatred at me. "I want what's rightfully mine. You stole this farm from me."

I go around the desk to face her. "How do you figure? You and Billy were never married."

"And *you* never even knew Billy, yet here you are running the inn." Naomi jabs a finger in Jazz's direction. "Jazz loved Billy and he loved her. This property belongs to her. And since she's my daughter, it's my responsibility to manage her investment."

"I couldn't agree with you more. My dream is for Jazz and me to run this business together, one day, when she's old enough and you're no longer in the picture."

Naomi's face turns a deep shade of purple. "You won't last that long, Stella. Not if I have my way about it."

I step closer to Naomi. She smells rank, like day-old underwear, but she doesn't reek of booze. "You're fired, Naomi. Pack your things and get out of my inn." So much for being smart about how I handle her.

"If you fire me, I'll take my daughter and leave this town. You'll never see your beloved baby sister again."

Jazz darts across the room to Inez. Seeing my sister turn to someone else for comfort sobers me. I'm her safe haven, but I've scared her. I'm no better than her mother.

"Come on, sweetheart. It's time to go home." Naomi yanks Jazz free of Inez and lifts her into her arms. She grabs the child's pink backpack and coat and turns back to me. "We'll talk more about this in the morning. Once you've had a chance to calm down." She swaggers out of the office as though she's won the battle.

Naomi may have won the battle, but I intend to win the war.

I wag my finger at Inez. "Not one word of this to anyone. Understood?"

With quivering chin, she nods her head. "Yes, ma'am."

I brush past her on my way out of the office. With tears blurring my vision, I leave the main building for my cottage. I belly dive onto my couch and have a good long, much-needed cry.

I've really blown it this time. I can add Inez to the growing list of employees who no longer respect me thanks to Naomi. Her threat comes back to me. *You'll never see your beloved baby sister again.* She has me right where she wants me—in the palm of her hand. Naomi will eventually slip. And when she does, I'll be there to watch her fall.

14

PRESLEY

Presley dives headfirst into her new job. Collaborating with others passionate about their work inspires her. They're not merely her teammates. They're quickly becoming her new friends. The team meets nearly every day, occasionally in Stella's office but more often in the kitchen. Everett is a genius at mixing herbs, fresh juices, and blends of alcohol into tasty cocktails, and Lucy knows exactly which wines to pair with Cecily's sumptuous farm-to-table cuisine. But the mood is not festive. Their intense focus on details is riddled with anxiety because of all that rides on the successful outcome of this party—the future of the inn as well as their jobs. And some of them handle the stress better than others.

Presley catches glimpses of Cecily's bubbly personality, but mostly, the head chef is wired as tight as a guitar string. Cecily confides in her what Presley already knows. "Jameson's is make or break for my career."

Stella is a great faker, except for when it comes to Naomi, who fails to show up for their meetings more often than not. While Naomi's lack of interest in the homecoming party appears to irritate Stella, Presley is secretly relieved. Naomi sucks the air out of the room with her hostile attitude.

Presley is grateful for Everett, who tries to lighten the mood with upbeat playlists and terrible jokes, and Lucy for always being optimistic and cheerful.

Presley has the least interaction with the head groundskeeper. Katherine is friendly enough, but quiet with an aura of sadness about her. On Friday afternoon at the end of Presley's first full week at work, after an exceptionally long meeting in Stella's office, Katherine invites Presley to go for a walk. "I want you to see what I've been working on."

They take the winding narrow road that runs along the perimeter of the property down to the maintenance shed, which isn't a shed at all but a sizeable steel building someone had the excellent sense to hide behind a row of Leyland cypress trees.

Katherine shows Presley around the side of the building facing the lake. There's a rectangular greenhouse filled with potted orchids, mums, and lilies in fall colors. Stretching down both sides of the greenhouse are raised flower beds planted with rose bushes and hydrangeas and a host of perennials Presley doesn't know the names of.

Katherine plucks a drooping pink rose from one of the bushes. "I got a late start last summer, but next spring I hope to plant early. Flower arranging is a hobby of mine. I did the flowers for a few weddings when I lived in Savannah. When I moved here, I decided to grow my own flowers." Katherine tugs her phone from her back pocket and shows Presley photographs of her most recent arrangements. "I created these with my first crops."

"These are impressive, Katherine. And I know a bit about flowers. My mother entertained a lot, and I organized the arrangements for many of her functions. Would you consider doing the flowers for some of our events?"

Katherine's lips part in a rare smile. "Yes! That's what I wanted to talk to you about. Stella has already given me her blessing. I'm considering partnering with the owner of a small flower shop on the outskirts of town. Claire is talented. She purchases her stems from a wholesale florist. My goal is to become her primary supplier." She sweeps her hand at the flower beds. "What you see here is just the beginning. I've signed the lease on a field close to here."

"That's exciting, Katherine. I'm happy to support you in any way. The woman at Mountain Flowers on Main Street is working up a price for the homecoming party, but I wasn't that impressed with her work. If you'd be willing to do the flowers, I'd rather give you the business."

"I would love that. Just tell me what you need. The inn has a spectacular collection of containers."

As they walk back to the main building together, they talk not only about the flowers for the party but also about decking the inn with trees, wreaths, and poinsettias for the upcoming holidays. When they part on the terrace, Presley feels like she's made a new friend.

Entering through the back door, she's on her way to her office to talk to Karen about renting a hayride for the party, when Naomi pulls her aside.

"I had a call from one of your brides yesterday afternoon. She claims you quoted her the wrong discount rate on blocks of rooms."

Presley is thrown off guard at first, alarmed she could have made such an error when she's well aware of the block room rate. But then, she realizes Naomi's trying to cause trouble. She's notorious for it. She fails to deliver important phone messages and neglects to forward inquiry emails received through the general inbox to the appropriate department. And she blows complaints from guests out of proportion, making a big deal out of nothing when a simple apology to the guest would suffice.

"I don't know how that's possible, Naomi. Every bride receives the same packet of information with the 10 percent discount rate clearly stated."

Naomi raises her hands. "Don't shoot me. I'm just the messenger, repeating what your bride told me. She says you offered her a 30 percent discount."

Presley's jaw goes slack. "That's absurd. Who's the bride? I will reach out to her."

"That's not necessary," Naomi says. "I calmed her down. I told her you were new here and unfamiliar with our policies."

Presley glances around the reception area, making certain they're alone, before leaning across the check-in counter. "Why would you tell a bride her event planner is new to the job? We want our guests to have confidence in us. Now, tell me the name of the bride."

"Jody Butler, if you must know. But you'll only make matters worse if you call her."

"I know how to handle it, Naomi. And, in the future, I would appreciate it if you'd direct any calls relating to weddings directly to me." Presley whirls around and storms off.

She knows Naomi is lying. Out of all her brides, Jody Butler is the least worried about costs. But Presley calls her anyway.

"I just wanted to make certain you received the wine list I emailed you yesterday," Presley says when Jody answers the phone in her bubbly Southern girl voice.

"I got it!" With a giggle, Jody says, "My daddy is a wine snob. He wants to be the one to choose which wines we serve. He hasn't had a chance to look at the list, though."

"No rush," Presley says. "If he has questions, he can contact our sommelier. I included Lucy's contact information in the email. She's quite knowledgeable. Your dad, being a wine enthusiast, might enjoy talking to her."

"Cool! I'll be sure to tell him that."

"Is there anything else I can help you with?"

Jody pauses a fraction of a second. "Nope. FYI, I booked my block of rooms earlier today. Y'all are so nice to offer a 10 percent discount. A lot of hotels don't do that."

Presley grips her phone. So, Naomi was lying. "We appreciate your business, and we are excited about your wedding next summer." They talk for a few minutes about food and bands before hanging up.

Presley contemplates her options. While she's tempted to tell Stella about the situation, she decides to talk it over with Everett first. But, with the inn booked to capacity for the college's alumni weekend, she doesn't get a chance to do that until Sunday night.

They are camped out on Big Blue with a leftover pizza from Jameson's between them. Since her return from Nashville, Presley has spent what little free time she has in the evenings with Everett. They watch movies and eat tubs of popcorn. Sometimes they sit in the dark, with the lights from Main Street streaming through the windows, and talk for hours. She shares much about her life while he shares little about his. Presley was raised by an alcoholic. She knows when someone's hiding something. And Everett is totally hiding something. But, despite having met only a little over two weeks ago, she feels as though she's known him all her life. Whatever he's keeping from her, she believes he'll tell her when he's ready.

"I'm telling you, Ev. I wanted to strangle Naomi."

Everett rolls his eyes. "Everyone has issues with Naomi. Too bad we can't get rid of her."

"Why would Stella keep someone like that around?"

Everett takes a bite of pizza and stares up at the ceiling as he chews. How much do you know about the Jameson family?"

"Not much. Except what you've told me about Billy and Stella."

He points his pizza at her. "You can't tell anyone I told you this. Cecily is my primary source of information, although some of it I've heard directly from Stella."

"You have my word." She holds up three fingers for Scout's honor.

Everett sets down his pizza and wipes his mouth. "So, Billy had an older brother, Ethan, who was killed in a plane crash in the early nineties. He was living in DC at the time. He'd chartered a private plane to fly home for his wedding."

Presley's eyes get enormous. "His wedding? That's so tragic."

"Everything about this family is tragic." Everett stuffs the last bite of crust in his mouth and wipes his lips with a napkin. "Both Billy's parents died within a few years of Ethan, allegedly from natural causes but many believe from broken hearts. Billy and Stella's mother spent their summers together here, on the farm, when they were growing up. At some point they became romantically involved. At least long enough for Stella to be conceived. Stella's mother is now living with another woman as an openly gay couple in New York. Her lesbian mothers led Stella to believe that her father was a sperm donor."

Presley blinks. "Are you kidding me? That's insane."

"Billy wasn't thrilled when Stella's mother took off to New York with his unborn child. Sometime later, he struck up a relationship with Naomi, and the two of them produced another child, born out of wedlock. That child is Jazz."

Presley's lips form an O. "I get it now. Stella is stuck with Naomi because she's the mother of Stella's half sister."

"Exactly." Everett closes the lid on the pizza box and tosses it like a Frisbee across the room.

Presley cuts her eyes at him. "What was that for? Are you angry about something?"

"Never mind." Leaving the sofa, he picks up the pizza box, sets it on the coffee table, and walks over to the window.

Presley goes to stand beside him. "Seriously, Everett. I can tell something is bothering you." She nudges him with her elbow. "You can trust me. Is it something at home? Are your parents okay?"

He doesn't speak for a long time, but when he does, his voice is calmer. "My dad just got out of the hospital. He had a stroke. Fortunately, there was no permanent damage. He's doing better now, but I feel bad, not being there for my mom."

"I'm sure you do. Should you go home for a visit?"

"I should, but I'm not. I can't leave work right now. I wish I could send them some money to help with the bills. But, with business so slow, I can't spare a dime."

Presley places a hand on his arm. "Hang in there, Ev. We're working as hard as we can to change that."

They stand together in silence for a long time, staring out at a quiet Main Street. The businesses are shut down, and everyone has gone home to prepare for the start of another work week. Presley feels sorry for Everett. She knows all too well the worry associated with having a sick parent. She appreciates him opening up to her, but she senses there's something more he's not telling her.

15

EVERETT

Everett goes to the library early on Monday morning to check his email. There are no new emails from Carla or Louie. He hopes this means they are finally giving up on tracking him down. He suddenly remembers his dream from last night of Carla and Louie chasing him. When Everett comes to a cliff, he jumps off, tumbles through the air, and lands in Clear Bottom Lake. When he sinks to the bottom of the lake, Naomi, wearing a mask and snorkel, comes after him wielding a long spear like a lobster diver.

The news from home is grim. His mom, who is usually so upbeat, appears to be reaching the end of her rope. Physically, his dad is fine. Emotionally, he hasn't fully recovered from his stroke. According to his mom, his dad is argumentative and verbally abusive. He's reverted to the man of five years ago before the diabetes got the best of him. His mom doesn't outright admit it, but Everett suspects he's physically abusing her. Everett's mom is too proud to ask for money, but he senses their financial situation is becoming desperate. He signs into his bank's website and transfers every dime he can spare, which doesn't amount to much.

On the way to work, Everett considers looking into part-time positions at some of the businesses on Main Street, but with his erratic hours at the inn, he doubts he'll find anything that will mesh with his job at the inn. Besides, the majority of the guests at the inn have money, and most of them are big tippers. Perhaps he should wait it out at Billy's Bar a little longer. If business hasn't improved by Thanksgiving, he'll move on.

Everett arrives as his coworkers are congregating in Stella's office for a staff meeting. Sitting across from Naomi at the small conference table, he feels Naomi's suspicious eyes on him, watching his every move. He can't go on like this much longer. The stress is getting to him. He's been distracted at work, breaking things easily, messing up drink orders, and misinterpreting things his coworkers say to him. He doesn't mean to lash out at them, but controlling his temper is becoming increasingly difficult. He worries he's turning into his father.

Music has been the one constant in his life that has brought him any semblance of happiness. With Presley living next door, he can't risk playing for his audience at Town Tavern. He was forced to ignore them last week when he heard them chanting, "Music Man. Music Man. Music Man."

After the meeting, he overhears Presley making plans with Lucy to drive to Richmond for a wine tasting this afternoon. Lucy and Presley have been hanging out a lot lately, which Everett admits makes him jealous. After work, with a bag of leftovers from the kitchen in hand, he rushes home to his apartment, grabs his guitar, and throws open the window. Usually, when he has an audience, he plays popular tunes, encouraging them to sing along. But tonight, with the sidewalk tables at Town Tavern empty, he sings his original songs.

He works on a new composition for a while before slipping into some of his favorite old ones. For the first time in weeks, he's able to relax. He strums the first chords of "Show Me the

Way." The lyrics, country music heartbreak at its finest, are told from the perspective of a young man struggling with alcoholism who turns to his mama for help when he reaches rock bottom. The song takes Everett back to the night his life crashed and burned.

It's late August, Saturday a week before Labor Day weekend, a typical sultry summer night in Georgia. Inside the Blue By You, the air is stifling, despite the commercial air-conditioning units blowing at full steam. But the crowd, their sweaty bodies pressed together on the dance floor, doesn't seem to mind the heat. They're as rowdy as Everett has ever seen them. Do they sense there's a VIP in the house?

The guys in the band are Everett's homies. Louie on drums. Danny on keyboard. Malcolm on bass, and Duane on electric guitar. And they rock the house that night. Everything that can go right does just that. Everett saves "Show Me the Way" for last, and his fans go crazy. He'd produced the solo earlier in the summer, and it had gone viral with the Atlanta crowd, bringing him a minute of fame and attracting the attention of said VIP.

Wade Newman pulls him aside after the show, heaping praises on his performance. "You're the next Johnny Cash." He motions Everett to the door. "I've gotta be somewhere. Come outside with me while I wait for my Uber."

When Everett opens the door, a wave of humid air steals his breath. "I hope this heat wave ends soon."

On his heels, Wade says, "Tell me about it. I'm headed to the beach in South Carolina tomorrow. My wife's the only fool who wants to be on the beach in this kinda heat." Wade leans against the building, lights a cigarette, and offers Everett the pack. "Want one?"

"No thanks." Everett doesn't want a cigarette. He wants Wade to give his pitch before his Uber arrives.

"So . . . here's the thing, Rhett. You've got real talent, as a

ASHLEY FARLEY

singer, a songwriter, and a guitar player. Unfortunately, the rest
of your group is only mediocre."

"But we've been together since high school."

"All the more reason to make the break now. You've gone as
far as you can with them. If you want to grow as a musician, you
need to spread your wings." Wade grinds his cigarette butt into
the pavement with his loafer. "Listen, man. You have a distinct
tone to your voice. Like I said, Johnny Cash. People will hear you
on the radio and know it's you. That immediate recognition will
make you a star. If you're willing to work hard, and I believe you
are, you can go all the way to the top."

At what price, Everett wonders. He can't leave his homies
behind. Or can he? Hasn't he always known this might happen?
The other guys are good, but they aren't great. And they're definitely not driven. While Louie is technically the manager,
Everett is the one hustling for gigs.

Everett is at a loss for words. He can't tell a guy like Wade
Newman that he needs to think about it. Fortunately, Wade
beats him to it. "Take a few days to think it over. You know how
to reach me if you have questions." He chuckles. "I'll welcome
the phone call. I'm facing a boring week of sitting inside the air-
conditioned beach house while my wife bakes in the sun."

Everett shakes his hand. "Thanks for coming, Wade. I'll be in
touch."

A black Toyota 4Runner pulls to the curb, Wade climbs in,
and they speed off.

Everett feels as though he just got run over by the 4Runner.
He doesn't need a few days to think it over. He doesn't need a few
minutes. He'll be taking Wade up on his offer. After he figures a
way to tell the other guys in the band.

As he turns to go back inside, Waylon, the owner of the bar,
bursts through the door. "Dude, where's Louie? I've been
looking all over for him."

Everett shrugs. "Last I saw him, he was inside."

"Here." Waylon shoves a thick envelope at Everett. "Give him this. Tell him I had to split. My wife's keeping my kid awake until I get home."

Everett takes the envelope from him. "What is it?"

"Money I owe him. He'll know what it's for. See ya, man." Waylon tosses a wave over his shoulder as he disappears around the corner of the building to the parking lot.

Everett pinches the envelope between two fingers. Feels like cash. A lot of cash. He'd expressed his concern to Louie many times. Why, when they're playing gigs five nights a week, are they always broke? Is Waylon paying him a portion of their fee on the side?

Stuffing the envelope in his pocket, he reenters the building. When Carla sees him, she's all over him. "Rhett! You were fabulous tonight. Let's go celebrate in private." She walks her hands up his chest and nibbles at his chin.

Carla is only average-looking with shoulder-length brown hair and hazel eyes. But she has a body that won't quit. Older than him by two years, she works as a pediatric nurse at one of Atlanta's best hospitals. She'll make someone a wonderful wife. But that someone won't be him. He likes her fine. He just doesn't have the forever feelings for her. But he's a man, and she's smoking hot in bed, so he says, "Sure! Your place or mine?"

She smacks his chest. "Aren't you the funny one!"

It's a joke between them, since he lives with his parents. Everett moved back in with them two years ago when his dad's diabetes forced him to retire early from his plumbing job and when . . . Everett can't bring himself to think about the when. Living at home isn't all bad. Being able to help out with the bills gives Everett satisfaction and his mom peace of mind. While he'd rather not have to see his father's angry mug every day, his mom's cool. But she would freak out if he brought someone home. Even Carla. His mom adores Carla.

Jumping into his truck, he tosses Louie's envelope in his glove box and follows Carla to her apartment. During the twenty-minute drive, he listens to outlaw country radio on Pandora as he reflects on his conversation with Wade. *You're the next Johnny Cash . . . All the more reason to make the break now . . . If you're willing to work hard, you can go all the way to the top.*

Johnny Cash, wow! Everett wants success so bad he can taste it. Is he ready to leave Louie and the band behind? Heck yes! What about Carla? How will she take the news? She knows their relationship isn't permanent. He can't break the news to her tonight, not until he tells Louie first.

Inside the door of her apartment, Carla tears off her clothes first and then his. Everett picks her up, and she wraps her legs around his waist. Her fingernails dig into his back as she smothers him with kisses. Walking her to the sofa, he trips over a small table and knocks it over. When Carla bursts out laughing, he silences her with his mouth.

Two hours later, having moved from sofa to floor to her bed, they lay spent in each other's arms. He's drifting off to sleep when Carla, says, "We're good together, aren't we, Rhett?"

Uh-oh. That dreamy quality in her voice has nothing to do with the stream of orgasms she just experienced. "Sure." His eyes remain closed, and she pinches his nipple to get his attention. "Ouch! Jeez, Carla. That hurt."

She sits up in bed, not bothering to cover her milky plump breasts. "I'm trying to tell you something, Rhett. Neither of us is getting any younger, and . . . well, I'm pregnant. And don't insult me by asking if the baby is yours, because I haven't slept with anyone else in over a year."

Everett takes the sheet with him when he scrambles out of

bed. "Pregnant? How did this happen, Carla? You told me you were on the pill."

She gnaws on her lower lip. "I *was* on the pill. But then I stopped taking it."

"Why'd you do that?"

"Because I'm ready to have a baby. If you won't marry me, I'll raise it on my own. You're a good guy. You'll be a part of his or her life, won't you, Rhett? You'll make such a wonderful daddy."

Daddy. Seriously? "I don't even know what to say to you Carla. You're trying to trap me into something I'm not ready for."

Finding it difficult to breathe, he hurries from her bedroom. He gathers his clothes and is tugging on his jeans at the front door when she comes at him, pressing her naked body against his. He pushes her away, and she snatches his shirt off the floor, hiding it behind her back.

"Please, Rhett! Don't leave angry. We can work this out."

Grabbing his boots, he flees her apartment barefoot and bare-chested, slamming the door behind him. He makes a pit stop at home, the one-story brick rancher in a neighborhood of cookie-cutter houses out near the Atlanta airport. He stuffs as many clothes as will fit in a duffel bag, powers off his phone, and slides it under the mattress.

His father is passed out in his lounger while his mother sleeps with her head resting on the back of the sofa and her latest sewing project abandoned in her lap. Placing the sewing on the coffee table, Everett lifts her legs onto the sofa and covers her with a blanket. He's kissing her forehead when he notices his father watching him.

"Where you going?" his father grumbles, eyeing the duffel slung over his shoulder.

"Away," Everett says. "Can I count on you to be good to Mom?"

His father grunts and closes his eyes again.

Everett bolts out of the house, despite the feeling of dread gnawing at his stomach. He gets on the interstate intending to land in DC or New York. But as he's driving through Charlotte, on a whim, he veers off toward the mountains. Hours later, he stops at a roadside motel on the outskirts of Hope Springs. The following morning at Caffeine on the Corner, when he overhears a customer say the Inn at Hope Springs Farm was hiring, he applies for the job as bartender and begins his self-imposed exile.

In hindsight, Everett doesn't know what prompted him to run away that night. He just freaked out. Two monumental events happened to him in a few brief hours. Wade offered the fame he coveted, and Carla broke the news that she was pregnant with his baby. But once he started running, he kept on going.

He forgot all about Louie's envelope until a week later when he lost his sunglasses and was searching his glove compartment for his extra pair. Everett is not a thief. But the more he thought about it, the more convinced he became that he was owed money. Louie is the sketchy sort. He could see Louie working deals on the side that would enable him to keep some of the proceeds from their gigs. Regardless, Everett hasn't touched the money. The envelope is hidden in a zippered pocket in his backpack in his closet. But desperate times call for desperate measures.

Reluctantly, he puts his guitar away and stretches out on the air mattress, pulling his fleece blanket over him. His journey into the past, reliving the night that forever changed his life, has served as a reminder of how important music is to him. As he watches shadows from headlights on Main Street dance across his ceiling, he makes two monumental decisions that he prays will set his life back on track.

For the first time in a week, he doesn't dream about Carla and Louie and Naomi, and he wakes feeling rested. On Tuesday morning, when the local branch of his nationwide bank opens at nine, he deposits Louie's cash into his account. Tomorrow or the next day, once the deposit posts, he'll transfer the entire amount to his mom. When he leaves the bank, he continues to the library where he sends an email to Wade Newman. Blaming his father's illness, he apologizes for the delay in getting back to him. When he clicks send, his flesh crawls with chill bumps. No matter what happens with Carla and Louie and Presley, if Wade will still have him, he's going to Nashville.

16

PRESLEY

Homecoming has come to mean more to Presley than a theme for the party. Now that she's settled into her new job and apartment, she never wants to leave Hope Springs. Work feels like play. Her coworkers are her family. The picturesque town is her home.

She's so wrapped up in finalizing plans for the party, she doesn't leave work until nearly eleven o'clock on Tuesday night. Despite the late hour, she moseys home in the unseasonably warm night, stopping to admire a fake fur coat on the mannequin in the window of her new favorite boutique. A block away from her building, she hears cheering and applause coming from outside Town Tavern. She draws closer to get a better look at the crowd. Some of the patrons are seated while others are standing. The majority are women, their gazes lifted upward. The subject of their attraction is a man playing a guitar from the second-floor window of the apartment building across the street. *Her* building. The apartment next to hers. The man with the guitar is Everett.

To avoid being seen, she darts into the side door and dashes up the stairs. Inside her apartment, without turning on any lights, she drops her work tote on the sofa and listens at her window for a brief moment before easing it open. Straddling the sill, she cranes her neck, so she can see down the side of the building. Everett is also seated astride his window with one bare foot planted on the balcony. With head bowed, he's hunched over his guitar, seemingly oblivious to his audience.

Presley rests her head against the wooden window frame. His music stirs something deep inside of her, particularly a song with lyrics that sound vaguely familiar about a young man who's lost his way. She's been around musicians all her life, but she's never had one move her so profoundly. Her mother would describe his music as soulful. His tone is unique, deep and smooth as honey, and his lyrics tell heartfelt stories of love, tragedy, and loss.

He plays until well past midnight. If he's aware of her presence, he doesn't acknowledge her. His gaze never strays from his guitar. After the last of his audience has left the restaurant, he remains at his window, the silence hanging in the air between them.

"Why didn't you tell me about your talent?" she says finally.

Standing, he makes his way down the narrow balcony to her. "Can I come inside? I'm afraid of heights."

She bites down on her lower lip to keep from laughing. "Only if you play me a song."

"Haven't you been listening? I just played at least twenty."

"I want my own song."

"Fine. Move over." Nudging her with his knee, he sits down beside her.

He sings a beautiful ballad about a woman desperate to escape her loveless marriage. The woman, Mary, pines for the days of her youth with her parents on their homestead out in Texas. When the song ends, Everett swipes at his wet eyes with the back of his hand.

Presley leans into him. "You sound like Johnny Cash. Has anyone ever told you that?"

He smiles. "I've heard it before."

"Is Mary your mama?"

"Yes," he says in a soft voice, but he doesn't elaborate. "Can we go inside now?"

She barks out a laugh. "We can go inside now."

They climb in the window and race each other to the sofa. She beats him, and he falls on top of her. With his face close to hers, he stares into her eyes and she thinks he's going to kiss her. She *wants* him to kiss her, and she's disappointed when he rolls off of her.

With heads back against the cushions, they stare into the dimly lit room. "You never answered my question. Why did you hide your music from me?" Presley runs a hand over the soft fabric of her sofa. "You sang "Blue Velvet" the night my furniture came. When I commented on your talent, you intentionally sang off key. Why did you do that?"

He rakes his hands through his brown hair, leaving several strands sticking up. She reaches over, as though to smooth the wayward hair back into place, and then snatches her hand back.

Everett doesn't appear to notice. He's deep in thought, the lines in his brow pinched. "I'm at a crossroads with my music, which is one of the reasons I'm hiding out in Hope Springs. I came here to clear my head."

"And have you? Has the clean mountain air helped clear your head?"

"I'm getting there." He shifts on the sofa to face her. "I'm still trying to figure out how you fit in."

"How I fit in where?" She knows what he means. She just wants to hear him say it.

"How you fit in my life."

Her stomach does a one-and-a-half somersault dive. She

has no clue how they fit together. She doesn't care about forever. She only cares about the here and the now. The man sings like an angel. The sound of his voice sends jolts of electricity to parts of her body that haven't been loved in way too long.

He fingers a strand of hair out of her face. "I realize we agreed to be just friends, but I can't ignore the attraction anymore. Give me a reason to stay in Hope Springs, Presley."

Leaning toward him, she cups the back of his neck and brings his lips to hers, kissing him ever so tenderly. He crushes his mouth to hers, prying open her lips with his tongue, in a kiss that lasts forever and sets her on fire with a passion she's never known. He stretches out on the sofa, pulling her on top of him. Straddling his waist, she presses her hands to his chest and slides them down his tight abs. When she goes for his belt buckle, it becomes a free-for-all of tugging and unzipping until they're both naked with her now lying beneath him.

Presley loses count of the number of times they make love. At some point, he carries her from the living room to her bed. It's almost three o'clock in the morning by the time they're satiated, their bodies aching all over. They've taken a shower together and are lying side by side, limbs intertwined, on the bathroom floor.

"I've gotta be at work earlier than you," she says.

He belts out a slower, more somber version of "Should I Stay or Should I Go."

Pressing her ear against his chest, she listens to his voice reverberate through his body until the song is over. "I'll tell you what you should do. You should promise never to deprive me of your talent again."

"I promise." He kisses her hair. "Now, answer the question. Do you want me to leave or can I stay?"

"Hmm." She doesn't want to be without him ever again, not

even for a minute. "I would love to wake up in your arms. Is your front door locked?"

"Yes." He pushes himself off the floor, so he can see her. "What does my doorknob have to do with anything?"

"Do you have your keys with you?"

"No. They're in my coat pocket in my apartment. Why?"

With a smirk on her lips, she says, "Because the only way for you to get into your apartment is through the window. Do you really want to make the crawl of shame across the balcony in the morning? All the God-fearing citizens of Hope Springs driving to work on Main Street will see you."

He palms his forehead. "You're right. I guess that answers my question. As much as I hate it, I must leave your beautiful body." He reaches over and yanks a towel off the rack.

She grabs the towel from him, covering her body. "There is one other option."

He sinks back to the floor beside her. "Talk to me."

"You can set your alarm for sunrise."

He touches her nose. "We can set *your* alarm since I don't own a phone."

"Tell me again why you don't have a phone."

"Another time. I'm too tired to talk anymore." Getting to his feet, he picks her up, tosses her over his shoulder, and carries her to bed.

Having Everett in her bed feels right. Everything about her new life feels right. She came to Hope Springs for one reason, but she's staying for so many others.

When her alarm wakes her at six thirty, Everett has already gone. How did he sneak out without her hearing him? She resets her alarm for forty-five minutes later, but despite being exhausted, she can't fall back asleep. She stares at the ceiling as she replays their night together over in her mind. Even though she's alone in her bed, she blushes at the thought of the things they did together. With Everett, none of it felt kinky. He's her person. Her guy. They are meant to be together. She feels it in her soul.

She lounges in bed until seven fifteen. Skipping her yoga workout, she dresses in exercise pants and a fleece and heads out for a walk.

The sidewalks in the neighborhoods of Hope Springs are in a state of disrepair from tree roots buckling bricks. By now, she knows the worst areas, one being in front of 237 Hillside Drive. She's stepped over and around the buckled bricks many times, but today, in her state of post-lovemaking bliss, she trips and falls hard to her hands and knees. As luck would have it, Rita and the girls are in the yard in front of their house, and they rush to her aid.

She's discerned much about the girls over the past weeks. Emma, the eldest and prissy one, takes time to put on makeup and style her hair every morning. Abigail is a tomboy, dressed most days in jeans and T-shirts with her face free of makeup and hair in a ponytail. She's the one who helps Presley to her feet.

"Are you okay?"

"I'm fine." Presley is more embarrassed than anything. She's imagined this moment happening dozens of different ways, but never like this.

Mother and daughters are even prettier up close. Presley studies their faces, looking for something of herself but finding nothing. They are blue-eyed blondes with remnants of golden summer tans. She's a redhead with gray eyes and skin that burns on cloudy days.

Rita gives Presley the once over, her eyes landing on her

hands. "Oh, goodness. You're bleeding. Let me go inside for my first aid kit."

Presley's palms and knees sting, and when she looks down, she sees that her nylon pants are torn at the knees.

When Rita starts toward the house, Presley says, "Please, don't bother. I live close by, up on Main Street."

"That explains why you walk past our house every day. Are you stalking us?" asks Emma in a tone that is anything but friendly.

Abigail covers her mouth to hide her smile.

Tears prick Presley's eyelids, and she's grateful to be wearing sunglasses. "I'm a creature of habit, I guess. Have a nice day," she says and hurries off before she makes a fool of herself.

17

PRESLEY

By the time she showers and dresses for work, Presley has recovered from her humiliation. She drives to the inn instead of walking, making a detour by 237 Hillside Drive to slip a flyer for the homecoming party in the mail slot. She's been holding off inviting Rita and the girls to the party. Before, she was a stranger to them. Now, she's the girl who fell on her face in front of their house. Now that she's broken the ice with them, she's ready to make their acquaintance.

Presley's curiosity about the occupants of 237 has grown. Abigail and Emma seem so different. What makes them tick? What other sports does Abigail enjoy? What makes Emma so guarded? Do they have boyfriends? Where do they want to go to college?

Presley's mind drifts as she imagines the inside of the house. What if she'd taken Rita up on her offer of first aid? Would Rita have invited Presley inside to the sunny yellow kitchen of Presley's imagination? Would Rita have told Presley more about herself while she nursed her wounds with Neosporin and Band-Aids? Would Presley have blurted, "I think you might be my biological mother?"

A car horn jerks Presley out of her reverie. The red light in front of her has turned green. Waving at the person in the car behind her, she turns left onto Main Street and continues toward the inn.

There's only a slim chance Rita and the girls will come to the party. But Presley will be on the lookout for them, and if, by some stroke of luck, they show up, she'll use the opportunity to give them a tour of the inn.

She arrives before anyone else for the meeting in Stella's office. Even Stella is nowhere to be seen. Making herself comfortable at the conference table, she opens her laptop and accesses her inbox. She's humming one of Everett's tunes while scrolling through emails when Lucy enters the office.

"Someone's in a good mood." Lucy eases into the seat next to Presley. "What gives? You're practically radiating. Who's the lucky guy? A certain bartender I know?"

"How'd you—"

"I recognized the attraction the first time I saw you two together." Lucy smiles.

Presley sees no point in lying to her. Aside from Everett, Lucy's her closest friend in town. "Okay, fine. You're right. Everett and I hooked up last night. Only it was more than a hookup. It was incredible. I think he might be the one, Lucy."

"Lesson number one," Lucy says, holding up her pointer finger. "Never mistake lust for love."

Presley snaps her laptop shut. "Give me some credit, Lucy. I'm thirty years old. I've been in love before."

"Mm-hmm. With whom?" she asks in a skeptical tone. Lucy either doesn't believe what Presley experienced before was love or thinks she's too young to have ever been in love.

Chin out, Presley says, "My college boyfriend."

"And what happened to that relationship?"

"He moved to New York after graduation and found someone new."

Lucy targets that same pointer finger at Presley. "See! Men are not to be trusted. Which is lesson number two. Take it from someone who knows. I'm the ex-wife of an untrustworthy man. My son, Chris, is still innocent, but it's only a matter of time before he becomes one too."

Lucy rarely mentions her ex, and Presley has been waiting for the right opportunity to ask about her divorce. "I never realized you were so cynical about love. What happened to your marriage?"

"That's a long story," Lucy says with a sigh. "I'll tell you about it sometime over a glass of wine. Well, I'll have wine and you can have tea."

"Better yet, why don't you tell me over lunch?"

Lucy considers the idea. "Let's do it. And we can expense it if we go to the new sandwich shop that just opened on the other end of Main. One of Cecily's friends has been raving about their sesame-ginger chicken salad. Cecily is dying for one of us to try it out."

Presley claps her hands. "Undercover! I love it. Can you go today?"

Lucy shakes her head. "Sorry. I have to go to my son's school for an awards ceremony."

"That's exciting. What kind of award is Chris getting?"

"An English one. It appears as though my son is on his way to becoming the next Ernest Hemingway." Lucy pulls her phone out, accessing her calendar. "Tomorrow we have the meeting with the tent company at noon. What about Friday for lunch?"

"It's a date! Twelve o'clock on Friday," Presley says and creates an event in her electronic calendar.

Everett walks in just at that moment. "Where are the two of you going on Friday?"

"To lunch," Lucy says. "But don't worry. I won't steal her away from you."

Presley glares at Lucy. Why would she say that to him? Now he thinks Presley was blabbing to Lucy about their sexual encounter last night.

She casts a tentative glance at Everett and is relieved when he kisses the top of her head. "I'm glad you told her about us. Do you think Stella will approve of our workplace relationship?"

When Naomi saunters in, Presley mumbles, "Stella's not the one we have to worry about."

"So, Everett, I just got off the phone with your friend from Atlanta. He booked two rooms for this weekend. I convinced him to stay through Sunday to attend the party."

Presley observes the color draining from Everett's face. Why is Everett afraid of the friend from Atlanta?

"Great!" Everett says in a deadpan tone. "I look forward to pouring him some drinks."

Stella arrives within seconds of Naomi, bringing with her a gush of chilly air and the scent of pine. "I'm sorry I'm late. I've been down at the spa. The building is taking shape. I can't wait for you guys to see it. And wonderful news! Jack thinks he might finish early, in March instead of April."

Naomi grunts. "When have you ever known a contractor to finish a project early?"

Stella presses her lips thin. "If anyone can do it, Jack can."

"That's significant in terms of conferences and weddings," Presley says. She's met Jack several times. He doesn't seem the type to make such a promise without being certain he can deliver.

Stella joins them with her laptop. Her eyes travel the table. "Where's Cecily? Has anyone seen her today?"

"Here I am." Cecily appears in the doorway with a dining cart loaded with coffee carafes, china mugs, and a plastic-wrapped platter. "I hope you brought your appetites. I've been experimenting again. I made some sausage and cheddar biscuits. And I brought coffee."

Cecily is transferring the platter from the cart to the table when Presley spies a diamond engagement ring on her left hand."

"Cecily—" Presley starts, but Stella beats her to it. "What's that on your finger?"

Cecily's grin spreads from ear to ear. "Lyle proposed last night." Snatching a napkin from the tray, she dabs at her eyes. "I haven't stopped crying since. I'm just so happy. If it's okay with you, Stella, we'd like to get married here." Sniff. "At the inn." Another sniff. "At Christmas."

"Yes! Of course! But why so soon?" Stella furrows her brow. "Are you pregnant, Cecily?"

Cecily laughs as she shakes her head. "I wanna marry him before he changes his mind."

Stella rolls her eyes. "As if that would ever happen. Lyle adores you."

Cecily holds her ring out in front of her. "He does, doesn't he?" Stuffing the napkin in her apron pocket, she goes about pouring coffee for everyone. "Anyway, I haven't seen my family in over a year. They're all coming for the wedding. Will you plan my wedding, Presley? Mom and I have already discussed budgets. We can afford nice but not fancy."

"It would be my pleasure. You can do a super nice Christmas wedding on a budget with all the poinsettias and trees and wreaths. You should book your rooms now, though." Presley looks across the table at Naomi. "And remember, your guests get a 10 percent discount."

"Ten percent?" Stella says in a tone of outrage. "We can do better than that for Cecily. We'll double the discount for your family and throw in a suite in the carriage house for your parents for free."

Presley can almost see the steam puffing out of Naomi's ears, and she's ever so tempted to stick her tongue out at her.

Leaning over, Cecily wraps her arm around Stella's neck from behind. "You're the best," she says, kissing her cheek. "Thank you so much."

"You're quite welcome. I'm happy for you." Presley detects something hidden beneath Stella's smile. Is she envious that Cecily is getting married at Christmas? She spots a diamond ring on Stella's hand. Where did that come from? What happened to her silicone band? Presley won't say anything now, for fear of spoiling Cecily's big moment, but the ring is gorgeous.

The meeting goes on longer than expected. When Lucy excuses herself a few minutes before twelve, Stella realizes the time and announces the meeting adjourned. Presley is on the way to her office, when Everett catches up with her.

Placing a hand at the small of her back, he leans down and whispers in her ear. "Last night was fun. Can we do it again tonight?"

She laughs. "On three conditions." She ticks them off on her fingers. "One, you sing to me. Two, you come in through the door and not the window. And three, we start earlier so we can get some sleep."

"Deal. I'll even buy dinner."

"From Jameson's? You big spender, you."

"Not from Jameson's. I was thinking pizza," he says with a twinkle in his electric blue eyes. Given the opportunity, Everett would eat pizza three meals a day.

"Why don't I cook for us? Do you like chicken parmesan?"

"It's one of my favorites." When they stop outside her office door, Everett glances down the hall in both directions as though making sure the coast is clear. "I'm dying to kiss you right now. But if I know Naomi, she's watching."

Whatever secret he's keeping, Naomi knows something about it. And how does the friend from Atlanta fit in? While she's tempted to question him about it, now is not the time or the place. And she'd rather wait for him to tell her when he's ready.

She puckers her lips, kissing the air. "We'll save the real kissing for later."

18

STELLA

After the others leave, as we clear the conference table of dirty dishes, I press Cecily for the details about Lyle's proposal.

A dreamy expression settles on her face when she says, "He was so romantic about it. He was waiting for me after work last night. We drove to an overlook in the mountains. I've never been up there at night. It was so peaceful and beautiful. I wish you could've seen it, Stella. The stars were bright and the lights from town twinkled. The air was balmy; we didn't even need our coats. Lyle spread out a blanket on the ground, and we drank champagne, and he popped the question."

I'm hanging on her every word. "And then what?"

Cecily giggles. "We hurried back to my apartment to call our parents. Of course, my parents already knew. Lyle had spoken to my dad on the phone earlier in the day to ask his permission."

My arms break out in goose bumps. "I'm so happy for you, Cecily. I know this is what you wanted."

"You have no idea. Can you believe it, Stella? We're both getting married." Her gaze shifts to my left hand, and her blue eyes grow wide at the sight of my engagement ring. "When did you get that?"

Self-consciously, I cover the sparkling diamond with my right hand. "Jack gave it to me last week."

Cecily appears wounded. "Why didn't you tell me?"

I let out a sigh. I don't like keeping secrets from my best friend. But she's been so out of sorts lately, and I've been . . . I don't know what I've been. "The same reason I didn't tell you Jack bought the manor house."

"Get out of town! He bought you an estate and a diamond the size of a boulder. Let me see that." She grabs my hand and studies the ring. "I can't believe I haven't noticed it before now."

I jerk my hand away. "You haven't noticed it, because I've only been wearing it around Jack. And Jack and I haven't seen each other much these past few days. Truth be told, Cess, I'm confused about a lot of things right now."

"That's unlike you." Cecily drapes a linen cloth over the cart and pushes it against the wall, out of the way. "Come with me." She takes me by the hand and drags me out of my office.

"Where're we going?" I ask, tripping along beside her.

"To get some air. I have a headache. I drank too much champagne last night." We burst through the back door onto the veranda. "Sit." She motions me to a rocker, turns on a propane space heater, and plops down in the chair beside me. Our few guests from last night have checked out, and we have the porch to ourselves.

"Talk to me, Stella. You're not having doubts about marrying Jack, are you? You love him, right?"

"Of course, I love him." I spread my arms wide at the grounds and the mountains in front of me. "But I love all this every bit as much. I don't know what I'll do if I lose it."

Cecily pumps her legs, rocking her chair back and forth.

"We all want the farm to succeed. But it won't be the end of the world if it doesn't. You'll find something else to do."

I stare at her, mouth agape. "This from the woman who's been so stressed out about her career she's been biting everyone's heads off for weeks."

Cecily sinks into her shoulders. "Sorry."

"You're forgiven," I say. "Anyway, what else would I do? I'm not sure I'd be happy scooping ice cream at the Dairy Deli."

"But you'll still have Jack. Isn't that enough? I'd be happy scooping ice cream as long as I have Lyle."

"Ha. I know you, Cecily. You might be happy for a while. But you would grow bored quickly, and then what would you do?"

Cecily palm-slaps the arms of her chair. "I'll have babies. Duh. Don't you want a family, Stella?"

"Yes, I want children. I just don't know if being a stay-at-home mom is enough for me."

"Have you considered that maybe you don't love Jack?"

My throat swells, tears fill my eyes, and I turn away from her. When the wave of emotion passes, I say, "Is it so wrong of me to want a family and a career?"

Cecily lets out a sigh. "Not at all. Like you, I want both. I'm mentally preparing myself in case things don't work out at Jameson's."

I rest my head against the back of the rocker. "Listen to us. We're being so negative. Brian has assured me we're a long way from closing our doors. Even if the party bombs, we have the opening of the wellness center next spring to look forward to. With a spa and state-of-the-art fitness center, we'll be able to market ourselves as a resort."

"That's true," Cecily says. "I hate to say it, but with everyone being so health conscious these days, not having a fitness center hurts us."

Katherine's grounds crew draws near with leaf blowers, and

we have to wait for them to move on before continuing our conversation.

"You know, Stella, you should tell Jack how you're feeling. When Lyle asked me why I've been so irritable lately, I shared my concerns about the possibility of losing my job and having to move away from Hope Springs. He asked me to marry him the next night." She flashes her ring at me. "He'd already bought this and was planning to propose at Christmas. But he gave it to me now, so I won't be stressed anymore."

I smile at her. "He's a great guy, Cecily. I'm so happy for you."

"That means a lot." Cecily shifts in her chair toward me. "I hope you'll be my maid of honor."

Gasping, I bring my hand to my chest. "I would love that. I'm flattered you asked me, Cecily." I reach over the arm of the chair and hug her. "Christmas is less than two months away. That's not a lot of time to plan a wedding. Are you sure you don't want to wait?"

Cecily shakes her head. "Christmas works for both our families. Thank goodness we have Presley to work her magic." She stands and stretches. "I need to find some Advil for this headache. Are you coming in?"

"You go ahead. I'm going to sit here a minute." As soon as she leaves, the tears I've been holding back spill from my eyelids. *I do love Jack. But do I love him enough to suffer through thick and thin?*

As though I've summoned him through mental telepathy, the door opens and Jack emerges from the building onto the porch. "There you are. I've been looking for you. We have an issue with the women's locker room in—" He stops in midsentence when he sees my face. "What's wrong?"

"Nothing. Everything." I run my thumb along the band of my engagement ring. "I'm not sure I can marry you, Jack."

"What're you talking about? What happened?" He drops to

Cecily's vacated chair, and I repeat everything I told Cecily about my concerns for my career if the inn goes bust.

He listens without speaking until I'm finished. "Are you having doubts about your feelings for me?"

I care about him too much to lie to him, and he can't help me unless I'm honest with him. "I don't think so, but I'm not sure."

The muscles in Jack's face tighten, but he doesn't appear angry. "Think about how drastically your life has changed since April, Stella? You found out about the father you never knew you had. You moved from New York City to a tiny town in the mountains of Virginia. You nursed your baby sister through meningitis. You managed the multi-million-dollar renovations on the inn. The reopening wasn't as successful as you'd hoped, and now you're worried you'll have to close. Not to mention your constant concerns for Jazz's well-being. And those are only the highlights of the past six months. Anyone else in your shoes would've long since had a nervous breakdown. I think it's only natural for you to be having doubts about your future."

"When you put it like that . . . I guess I have been through a lot. I adore this town and living on the farm. I want to feel settled, but something's holding me back. I think that *something* is the fear that I'll be forced to give it all up." More tears stream down my cheeks, and he hands me the red bandana he keeps in his back pocket.

"You're getting the cart before the horse, Stella. I'm sorry if I've pushed you too hard, asking you to marry me when we've only known each other a short time and buying the manor house without consulting you. We don't have to get married until you're ready, even if that means two years from now." He takes my hand. "If the worst happens and you lose the farm, I'll support you if you look elsewhere for a job."

"But Hope Springs is your home," I say, sniffling.

"My home is with you. I would prefer to stay here, but I'll follow you anywhere."

"You're too good to me, Jack. I don't deserve you." My heart swells with love for him. If I'm not careful, I'll lose him. I need to suck it up and stop whining about the what-ifs. "From now on, I'm going to stop worrying so much about the future and live in the here and now. We've both been working so hard lately. We've hardly had any time together. When this party's over, can we carve out some alone time?"

"You bet we can." He walks his fingers up my arm. "And I have some ideas of ways to spend that time."

19

EVERETT

Everett watches Presley sleeping peacefully beside him. She's classically beautiful with a creamy complexion, elegant features, and auburn hair splayed across her pillow. What does she see in a deadbeat like him? She deserves better. To have a chance at a future with her, he needs to give her his best self. And he can't do that on a bartender's salary. Especially not in a bar with no customers.

When she stirs, Everett takes her in his arms and makes love to her until she screams out in pleasure. Sex with Presley is different than anything he's experienced before. Even with his long-term girlfriend from his early twenties whom he was certain he would one day marry. His desire for Presley is consuming. She's under his skin, deep inside of him. This must be the real deal.

They lounge in bed for a long time afterward. When he finally tears himself away, he returns to his apartment to shower and dress before going to the library. He greets Rose, the librarian, with a peck on her cheek that brings a scarlet blush to her face. When he signs onto a computer, his heart jumps at the sight of an email from Wade Newman in his inbox. His excitement over hearing from Wade overpowers his concern that there are no emails from his mom.

Clicking open the email, he reads Wade's brief message.

Sorry about your old man. Hope he feels better soon. I am absolutely still interested in your work. When would be a good time for a phone conversation?

On impulse, Everett types out a response. *Because of hectic schedule, better for me to call you. Name a time, and I'll make it happen.*

He signs off the computer and leaves the library, winking at Rose on his way out. He's halfway back to the inn when he realizes his mistake. What if Wade returns his email right away and wants to speak with him today? Why didn't he accept Stella's offer of a computer for the bar?

The reservation office houses two desks with computers. One belongs to Naomi, but the other is free for any employee to use. When he arrives at the inn, the guest service agents are busy with patrons, and the office is empty. He quickly accesses his email, but there is no word from either Wade or his mom. When he returns to the office a second time around noon, the staff computer isn't working. He taps on the keyboard and jiggles the mouse, but the monitor remains black. Poking his head out of his office, he confirms the guest agents are still tied up and sits down at Naomi's computer, accessing his email. He has one message from Wade. None from his mom. Wade provides a contact number and asks that Everett call him at nine o'clock, Nashville time, on Friday morning. He scrawls Wade's number on Naomi's sticky note pad and exits his email account.

He doesn't hear her come in, and he's startled to look up and find Naomi looming over him.

"What do you think you're doing?" she asks, bug-eyed. "Why are you using my computer?"

Everett shoots up out of the chair. "My dad is sick and I'm waiting for an email from my mom."

Hand on hip, she says, "Your fake mom who lives in North Dakota, or your real mom in Georgia?" Naomi doesn't express any concern for Everett's father's health.

"Give me a break, Naomi. I'm not in the mood."

When he tries to brush past her, she takes hold of his shirt. "You didn't answer my question. Why are you using *my* computer? You know it's strictly off limits."

He nods at the staff computer. "Something's wrong with that one. I couldn't get it to turn on."

Naomi goes over to the computer and clicks a button on the back of the monitor. The computer comes to life. "It helps if you power it on."

Everett shrugs. "Sorry. I suck at electronics."

Naomi steps so close to him, he can smell garlic and onions on her breath. "I don't like you, Everett. Wanna know why? Because I don't trust you. I know for a fact you lied about your background. Wanna know how? Because I checked you out. I got your social security number off your employment application. You'll eventually screw up, Rhett, and when you fall, I'll make sure you go down hard."

Anger mixed with fear creates an adrenaline surge that pulses through his body. He grips her arm, squeezing tight. "Don't you dare threaten me. Here's a news flash for you, Naomi. I don't like you either. Then again, no one here does. If anyone's going down, it'll be you."

He storms out of the office and hurries back to the safety of his blue bar. How much does Naomi know about his past? She called him Rhett and mentioned Georgia. And at the meeting yesterday, she said his friend from Atlanta had booked two rooms for the weekend and was staying for the party on Sunday.

She was blowing hot air. Or was she? Who is that fisherman from Atlanta? Mack Lambert. Why is that name so familiar?"

Everett's adrenaline level tanks, and he begins to quiver all over. Naomi is scheming something. He's certain of it. Is she trying to get him fired? If so, why? What has he done to piss her off? Or is she just a vindictive bitch looking for trouble wherever she can find it? Regardless, Everett needs to tell Presley everything. He can't risk her finding out the truth about Carla and Louie from someone else. And he doesn't want their relationship to be based on lies. But he'll have to wait until after the party. Presley can't afford the distraction. For now, he should keep his distance.

He makes it through the rest of the day without seeing Naomi or Presley. Business is slow as usual. He spends the afternoon perfecting his signature cocktails for the party. Despite leaving work early, the library has already closed when he gets there. He's desperate for an email from his mom. A nagging feeling tells him something is wrong in her world. He hates to admit it, but not having a cell phone is becoming a problem.

Cecily, who also spent the afternoon experimenting, has sent him home with a to-go bag of sample finger foods for the party. But he's too worried about his mom to have any appetite. He removes his guitar from the closet and works on his new piece, a song about the challenges of being a recovering alcoholic. Everett can always count on music to calm his nerves and tonight is no different. When he hears his groupies calling for Music Man, he opens his window and performs his new song, "Just Say No." The crowd goes wild for it.

He performs for over an hour, the usual oldies that energize the crowd. It's Thursday night and they're ready to party. He's absorbed in his music, and when he hears clapping nearby, he's surprised to see Presley in her window.

He sets his guitar inside his apartment and makes his way over to her. "How long have you been sitting here?"

She smiles up at him. "About twenty minutes."

He rubs his one-day stubble. "I didn't see you."

"I noticed. You were totally into your music."

He squeezes in beside her on the windowsill. With their bodies close, he can smell the flowery scent of her perfume. He'd like nothing more than to take her inside and make love to her all night long. But he'd vowed to keep his distance until after the party. They sit in silence for a long while.

She nudges him with her elbow. "You're awfully quiet. Is something bothering you?"

He fakes a yawn. "I'm just tired."

"Why don't you ever talk about yourself, Everett? You know all about me, but I know virtually nothing about you. Except that you're from Georgia."

The hairs on the back of his neck stand straight up. "How do you know that?"

She gives him a playful shove. "The license plate on your truck, silly."

Damn. So, she noticed the plate after all.

She leans into him, resting her head on his shoulder. "I've been meaning to ask you if you're from Atlanta. I have a bunch of college friends from Atlanta. You might know some of them."

"I'm actually from North Dakota. Over the summer, I flew to Atlanta to see a buddy of mine. When I decided to stay on the East Coast, I bought that truck from one of his friends. I haven't gotten around to transferring the tags yet."

She pulls away from him, her gray eyes dark and full of suspicion. "What else are you hiding, Everett?"

He lets out a heavy sigh. "I'm sorting through some personal problems. I have some things I need to tell you, but I'd like to get through the party on Sunday first."

Irritation crosses her face. "I don't understand. Why wait until after the party?"

"Because you might not like what you hear. And I don't want you to be distracted from your job."

"We can work through anything, Everett, as long as you're truthful with me."

He pushes off the window to his feet. "The party ends at eight on Sunday. By the time we clean up, we'll get out of there by nine thirty or ten. We'll bring home some food, if there's anything left, and camp out on Big Blue. I'll tell you everything then."

"Promise?"

Leaning over to kiss her cheek, he whispers in her ear, "I promise."

Back in his apartment, he stretches out on his air mattress. He'd rather snuggle up to Presley in her comfortable bed. But he feels somewhat relieved now that she knows he's struggling with some issues. She won't be blindsided when he comes clean with her on Sunday night.

Promptly at nine on Friday morning, Everett places the call to Wade Newman from the landline in Billy's Bar. While he waits for him to pick up, Everett says a silent prayer Wade doesn't notice the Virginia area code.

On the third ring, he answers, "Wade Newman."

"Morning, Wade. It's Rhett Baldwin."

"Rhett, buddy, good to hear from you. How's your old man?"

"Hanging in there. He suffered a stroke." Everett repeats what his mom wrote in her email. "Fortunately, there was no permanent damage, but he's still not a hundred percent. Mentally, he's struggling. I've been helping my mom out. She really needs me right now." Everett cringes at how easily the lies depart his lips.

"You're a good son," Wade says, and Everett thinks, *I'm the lousiest son on the planet.*

"When do you think you'll be ready to launch your career?"

"Whenever you're ready, Wade. I can't put my life on hold forever." Everett hates the idea of leaving Presley. But she's from Nashville. His hope is she'll move back to Nashville with him, if she doesn't break up with him when he tells her about Carla.

"Well, look," Wade says. "Thanksgiving is only a few weeks away, and nothing ever gets done around here during the holidays. Why don't you plan to be in Nashville the first of January?"

Wade's proposed timing will give him a chance to sort out his mess of a life. "January sounds perfect."

"In the meantime, I'll be putting some things in place to launch your career."

Everett slumps against the counter as an enormous burden is lifted off his shoulders.

Wade goes on, "I've got your demo tape. I realize you've been busy with your old man, but have you been working on any new material?"

"I have a few songs I think you'll like. I'll polish them up and send them to you in a couple of weeks."

They talk logistics for a while longer, and when he hangs up with Wade, Everett goes straight to the library. He's disappointed to find his inbox empty. Something is wrong at home. He feels it in his gut. He considers calling his mom. But, if something is wrong, he'll be tempted to drop everything and drive home to Atlanta. And he can't leave Hope Springs until after the party. Until after he's talked to Presley.

20

PRESLEY

Presley works from her apartment on Friday morning, tying up loose ends for the party before meeting Lucy for lunch at noon. The island theme for Main Street's newest lunch spot seems all wrong for a small mountain town. Maybe the owner's goal is to offer patrons an escape from the dreary winters everyone complains about, which Presley has yet to experience. But when she enters Paradise Found, instead of feeling like she's in the islands, the riotous display of pink flamingos and fake palm trees makes her nauseous.

The tables, painted a high-gloss bubblegum pink, are all occupied by sophisticated middle-aged women with expensive hair highlights and trendy clothes on their well-toned bodies. The clientele who should be lunching at Jameson's.

Lucy manages to snag a table by the window. Sitting down opposite her, in a low voice intended for Lucy's ears only, Presley says, "I have my doubts about this place."

Lucy peers over her menu at Presley. "You think? *Vulgar* is the word that comes to my mind. Why aren't these refined ladies eating at Jameson's?"

"I just asked myself that very question. Maybe we need to do a better job of advertising our weekday specials."

One eyebrow cocked, Lucy says, "Maybe we need to do a better job of advertising period."

Presley opens the menu on the table in front of her. "They have twice the offerings we do." She pretends to read a text on her phone while she photographs the laminated pages.

"The owner is a young local woman in her mid-twenties who just graduated from culinary school in New York. From what I understand, her father bribed her into coming back to Hope Springs by setting her up in business." Lucy eyes the plates on a nearby table. "The food looks gross."

Presley follows her gaze. "I'll bet it tastes worse."

Lucy scrutinizes her. "What happened to your glow? Trouble in paradise already?"

Presley's face warms. "Maybe. I'm not sure."

"Wanna talk about it?"

Does she? She's not sure. Maybe it'll help to confide in someone. "Okay, so we were together on Wednesday night. And the sex was lovely, tender and meaningful. Being with him felt so right, like I could totally see myself waking up in his arms every morning for the rest of my life. But when I saw him last night, he was acting standoffish."

"Do you have any idea why?"

"Not a clue. I'm proceeding with caution until I know him better." She lifts the menu off the table and begins studying it, signaling to Lucy the discussion about her relationship with Everett is over. Presley doesn't want to tell her about the talk she and Everett have planned for after the party. If things don't go well, she won't have to explain.

The waitress, a thin woman with a beehive of inky hair, appears at their table. Cecily gave strict instructions on which menu items to try. When Lucy orders the crab cake sandwich,

Presley asks for the lesser of the two evils—the sesame-ginger chicken salad.

As soon as the waitress leaves, Presley says, "Now. Moving on to the purpose of this lunch. You promised to tell me why men can't be trusted. What happened in your marriage, Lucy?"

"It's a long story. Are you sure you want to hear it?"

Presley bobs her head. "Oh yeah! I totally wanna hear it."

Lucy settles back in her chair and crosses her legs. "Grant and I were childhood sweethearts, our families across-the-street neighbors. By the time we started high school, we were in a serious relationship. As you can imagine, living in such close proximity to each other drove our parents crazy. They watched us like hawks. But they worried needlessly, because Grant and I agreed to wait until we were married to have sex. Then, Grant's senior year in high school, his father accepted a job in Chicago."

"During your senior year? That must have been hard for both of you."

"I cried for months. But it was especially hard on Grant, because he loved—loves Hope Springs. There was never any doubt that he would one day make this town his permanent home. I committed early to Chapel Hill and was thrilled when Grant chose the University of Georgia for college over Notre Dame. A five-hour drive was easier and cheaper than a plane trip. Our freshman year, we managed to see each other once or twice a semester. I was disappointed when Grant spent that summer working in Nantucket, and by the time school started the following fall, we'd agreed to see other people. We still talked about one day getting married, but we both wanted time to ourselves, to enjoy the college experience."

The waitress delivers their lunch, plain white plates of blah-looking food. Lucy's crab cake is more ball than cake and is a third the size of her bun. And her side order of pasta salad is more mayo than pasta. Presley's grilled chicken breast is served over a bed of romaine lettuce, which would not have been her choice for a dish with an oriental flair.

Presley snaps several pics for Cecily. Lucy gives Presley half her sandwich, and Presley forks a portion of her salad onto Lucy's plate.

Lucy, with an expression of skepticism, watches Presley take a tentative bite of salad. "How is it?"

Presley gives her a so-so hand motion. "I don't understand the hype. What do you think of the sandwich?"

Lucy takes a bite. Her chewing slows down as a disgusted look crosses her face. "Agreed," she says, and sets it down on her plate.

"Back to your story," Presley says.

"Right. So, I had this huge crush on a guy at Chapel Hill. He was stud man on campus. Good-looking. Wealthy family. President of his fraternity."

Presley nods. "I know the type well."

"But he didn't know I was alive. At least that's what I thought. He shocked me by inviting me to his fraternity's formal in November of my sophomore year." Lucy toys with her pasta salad. "I've never been one to drink for the purpose of getting drunk. Even in college. But I remembered nothing that happened after dinner. It wasn't until March, when my pants started getting tight and I found out I was pregnant, that I realized he'd date-raped me."

Presley's mouth falls open, and she drops her fork to the plate with a loud clatter. Several customers glance in her direction, but she ignores them. "That's the worst thing I've ever heard. I'm so sorry, Lucy."

She stares down at her plate. "He stole my virginity. I never considered I might be pregnant. I had no morning sickness, and my period had always been irregular. In hindsight, my boobs were sore. By the time I took the test, it was too late to do anything about it. Not that I would have."

"Did you report the boy to the police?"

"What was the point? I had no proof. His word against mine. My parents were amazing about the situation. They made certain I received the care I needed both physically and mentally. The baby was born a week before classes started in August. I refused to even hold it. I don't even know if it was a boy or a girl. I gave it up for adoption. I just wanted to get on with my life."

Presley pushes her salad away. "I don't blame you." Lucy's story hits close to home. Did something similar happen to Rita? Is Presley the result of a rape? She gestures at Lucy's barely touched sandwich. "Are you gonna finish that?"

"No! Let's get out of here," Lucy says and signals the waitress for the check.

The day is warm for this time of year with temperatures in the low seventies. As they start out on foot toward the inn, Presley asks, "When did you and Grant get back together?"

"Ten years later. I'd finished sommelier school and was working in California. I ran into Grant at a party one Christmas when I was home for the holidays. He'd finished medical school and had begun his residency at the local hospital here. We stepped back into our relationship as though we'd never been apart. Within six months, he asked me to marry him and I moved back to Hope Springs."

"What kind of doctor is he?"

"An OB/GYN."

"Oh. Wow. How'd he react when he found out you put your baby up for adoption?"

Behind tortoiseshell sunglasses, Presley can see the lines around Lucy's eyes deepen. "I'll get to that part of the story in a minute."

Lucy pauses to look at an old-fashioned baby stroller in the window of an antique boutique. "Grant and I were eager to have children, but it took two years for us to get pregnant with Chris. Because it had taken so long the first time, we immediately started trying for another child. But I was never able to get pregnant again. Chris was eight years old when I was diagnosed with cervical cancer."

Presley squeezes her arm. "That's awful. I'm so sorry."

"Thank you." Lucy digs in her bag for a tissue to wipe her nose. "The truth is, I was fortunate. The doctor caught the cancer early. But, while I was spared from having to have chemo, the doctor recommended a full hysterectomy. Which meant no more children for me."

"You'd come full circle," Presley says. "You were on the opposite side of adoption."

"And I would have adopted a baby in a heartbeat, but Grant wouldn't consider it. He has nothing against adoption. He was simply content with our one child."

They begin walking again. "Depression set in, and when I started obsessing about finding the baby I'd given away, I told Grant about the rape and subsequent unwanted pregnancy. He was adamantly opposed to me trying to find my child. He was worried I'd disrupt his or her life."

Chill bumps break out on Presley's skin. With roles reversed, Lucy's story is so eerily familiar to her own. "How old would your child have been by then?"

"In college. An adult. Even so, Grant was right. I gave up my parental rights when I signed the adoption papers. I couldn't barge into this kid's life. And I eventually accepted that. But my depression worsened anyway. Some days I couldn't get out of bed. As Chris grew older, he developed his own interests and made his own friends. He needed me less and less, and I had nothing to occupy my time."

The sign for Hope Springs Farms comes into view ahead of us. "Did you consider going back to work?"

"There was no job to go back to. Things had begun to deteriorate at the inn by then, and none of the other restaurants in town were the caliber that employs a sommelier." With head lowered and shoulders stooped, Lucy stares at the pavement in front of her. "Everyone tried to help me. Grant and my family and friends. But the efforts were futile, because I wasn't willing to help myself. The six months after Grant left me were the darkest. I finally reached rock bottom when Chris, who was fourteen at the time, asked to go live with his father. I dragged myself to a therapist, and it's been uphill ever since."

Lucy removes her sunglasses and cleans them with the bottom of her beige cable-knit sweater. "Grant's generous alimony has allowed me to renew my certification and study to become a master sommelier. I'd planned to wait for Chris to graduate from high school before applying for jobs in other places. But then Stella came along and reopened the inn. Which has been a godsend, because I really don't want to move. My life is in Hope Springs."

They walk up the long driveway in silence. When they reach the portico, Lucy turns to Presley. "So, now you know the story of my pitiful life."

"Thank you for confiding in me." Presley gives her a quick hug. "I'm sorry for all you've been through. I wish you much happiness in the years ahead, because you deserve it."

Lucy's smile lights up her face. "I'm well on my way. I feel stronger every day. Working here and making new friends like you has given my life purpose."

Presley draws in a deep breath. "This homecoming party will either make or break both our careers."

21

PRESLEY

The team works long hours over the next few days preparing for the homecoming party. At three thirty on Sunday, Presley makes the final walk-through with Stella before the guests arrive at four.

Katherine has outdone herself with the flowers. Elaborate arrangements of elegant stems—hydrangeas, roses, lilies, peonies, ranunculus—in oranges and yellows and purples bedeck tabletops throughout the entryway and lounge.

Servers wearing black pants and white starched shirts position themselves near the front door to greet guests with drinks that Everett dubbed the Janis Jameson after Billy's mother, a woman known for her talents in the garden. The mixture of gin, elderflower cordial, and chilled Prosecco is served in coupe glasses and garnished with a tiny purple-and-white viola.

When a server offers Stella a drink, she takes two glasses, handing one to Presley. Clinking their glasses together, Stella says, "To a job well done, Presley."

Presley beams. She's proud of her accomplishment. "Let's hope the party has the desired outcome." She sips the tasty concoction. Regardless of what Everett is hiding about his past, he's a genius mixologist.

Glasses in hand, the two women walk down the hall to the solarium where a hyped-up Jazz is pirouetting around a colorful stage. Presley has hired a magician to perform hourly shows, and his assistant to tie balloons into animal figures for the children. The assistant, dressed as a clown, wears a pink wig and has hearts painted on her cheeks.

When Jazz sees them in the doorway, she toe-dances across the room and hugs Stella's waist.

Stella pats her half sister's head. "Are you excited for the party, Jazzy?"

Pushing away from Stella, Jazz bobs her head. "A lot of my friends are coming."

Presley bends over eye level with the child. "Do they know to meet you here for the magic show?"

Another head bob. "And later, after dinner, they're having s'mores and hot chocolate in the library."

"That's right, kiddo," Stella says.

Presley holds her hand out to Jazz for a high five. "And don't forget about the hayrides."

Her golden eyes grow wide. "Cool! I didn't know we're having hayrides."

Stella wags her finger at Jazz. "But you need to be careful. There will be a lot of people here tonight. Don't you dare go outside alone and be sure to check in with your mom and me periodically. Understand, Jasmine?"

"Understand, Stella," Jazz says, sassy-like, and leaps off.

Presley and Stella proceed to the library where a roaring fire in the stone fireplace warms the room. A server waits behind a wood-paneled bar to present guests with hot gin toddies—a mixture of gin, cinnamon-infused simple syrup, and lemon juice. The Panthers are playing the Falcons on the big screen television in the adjacent game room. With Mexican as the theme, harvest spiced margaritas are the specialty drink while the cocktail food includes mini tacos, shrimp tostado bites, and guacamole prepared on-site by one of Cecily's waiters.

Presley and Stella continue to the lounge where enlarged black-and-white photos depicting the inn's history throughout the decades are displayed on easels. In the center of the lounge, an enormous round table is set for a proper English tea featuring the inn's homemade blends accompanied by bite-size sweet and savory morsels.

They stop in at Billy's Bar to speak to Kristi, who is busy pouring a blue concoction of Sapphire gin, vermouth, and blue Curaçao into martini glasses and garnishing them with twists of lemon. A self-serve slider bar—offering burgers, barbecue, and pulled smoked chicken with all the fixings—stretches the wall beneath Billy Jameson's impressive display of memorabilia.

As they exit Billy's Bar, Presley smiles when she sees Cecily dressed in official chef's attire and standing in the doorway of her domain.

"Welcome to Jameson's," Cecily says, motioning them into the dining room.

Samples of Jameson's most popular menu items are presented on platters and in chafing dishes arranged on buffet tables. Open seating is available at long rows of tables draped in white linens. Adult diners will have their choice of red or white wines donated by a local winery.

On our way out, Stella gives Cecily a hug. "Everything is perfect."

Cecily holds up both hands, revealing crossed fingers. "Here's hoping the entire town shows up."

"The power of positive thinking." Stella glances at her watch. "Five minutes until showtime. We should get back to the front entrance." Downing the rest of her drink, she hands the empty coupe glass to a passing waiter. Presley follows suit with her nearly full one.

After many sleepless nights spent worrying no one will show up, Presley is relieved to see a long line of cars and hordes of people on foot making their way up the drive and sidewalks. Stella's grandmother and uncle are among the first group to enter the building. While Presley has heard much about Opal and Brian, she has yet to meet them.

Stella introduces Presley to her grandmother first. She takes the older woman's soft hand in hers. "I admire your work, particularly your mural in Jameson's," Presley says. Opal is a tiny woman with penetrating blue eyes and super short gray hair, growing back curly after chemotherapy. "I'm so sorry to hear you've been fighting leukemia."

"Past tense, my dear." Opal raises a balled fist. "I fought it and won. I kicked that leukemia into remission."

Presley laughs. "Good for you! You look wonderful. When you're feeling up to it, I'd love to talk to you more about your art. If you're interested, I have some ideas of ways we can utilize your talent."

Rosy spots appear on Opal's cheeks. "I'm definitely interested. You can get my number from Stella. Call me anytime."

"In that case, expect to hear from me this week." Presley turns to Brian, a refined man—upper fifties, maybe sixty—wearing gray flannel pants and a navy sport coat. "I'm Presley Ingram."

He smiles at her. "Brian Powers. I've heard a lot about you from my niece. She says you can work miracles."

"No pressure there," Presley says, rolling her eyes at Stella.

Stella smiles at her. "You've already performed one miracle in pulling this party together on such short notice."

Presley wonders why Brian never married. He's a successful

attorney, tall and handsome with white hair and his mother's blue eyes. He would make an ideal beau for Lucy.

"Be sure to visit the wine cellar," Presley says to him. "Lucy Jordan, our sommelier, has set up an elaborate tasting. Have you met Lucy?"

"Not yet," Brian says. "But I've heard wonderful things about her."

"Even if you're not a wine enthusiast, seeing the tasting room is worth the trip to the basement."

"Perhaps we should go there first. Mom." Brian offers Opal an arm and they start off toward the elevators. With a glance back at Stella and Presley, he says, "Good luck tonight, ladies."

Stella winks at him. "Thanks, Brian."

The entryway is now a logjam of people. Stella goes into action, meeting and greeting while directing them to other parts of the building and grounds.

Stella has assigned positions for the team members. Naomi, stationed at the reception counter, will answer questions and hand out brochures. Cecily is in charge of Jameson's, Billy's Bar, and the lounge. Everett will float between the various bars. Katherine will patrol the inflatables and oversee games on the back lawn. And Presley landed the job of organizing hayrides and overseeing the oyster roast at the barn. What's not to love about bluegrass music, a bonfire, and roasted oysters? The weather is ideal with brilliant blue skies and crisp, clean autumn air. She's dressed for the occasion in jeans, cowboy boots, and a cream-colored turtleneck sweater under a long puffy black vest.

For the next hour, Presley chats with locals as they wait in line for hayrides. She meets bankers and nurses, shop owners and schoolteachers. She quizzes them about their experiences at the inn. For some, this is their first visit. For others, they've been coming here since they were children.

"I didn't understand the extent of the renovations," one stay-at-home mom says. "A group of our friends gets together for birthday lunches at least once a month. We'll be trying out Jameson's for sure."

"Love the blue bar," says one dental hygienist. "Hope Springs is moving up in the world."

With a mischievous grin, an orthopedist specializing in sports medicine tells Presley, "I'm going to leave my kids with my parents and book a suite here next week for my wife's fortieth birthday."

"My in-laws are coming for Thanksgiving," an information technologist says with a pained expression. "Maybe I'll put them up here."

"You should!" Presley says. "We have plenty planned over the holidays to keep your in-laws busy and out of your hair while you cook your turkey dinner." She hands him a business card with all the pertinent contact information for the inn.

These conversations confirm Presley's suspicions. The inn's marketing efforts, or lack thereof, have failed.

Sometime later, she's standing beside the bonfire, listening to the band and eavesdropping on the surrounding conversations, when she meets Mark and Marcia Porter, a husband and wife marketing team in their thirties dressed from head to toe in black.

Marcia's eyes go wide behind heavy black eyeglass frames when she reads Presley's name badge. "*You're* the event planner? We've been trying to get in touch with you."

"Or whoever's in charge of your marketing plan," Mark adds.

Marcia vigorously nods. "We've called and come by numerous times. We've left messages with your guest services manager. But no one ever contacted us."

Because Naomi never relayed the messages, Presley thinks.

Mark says, "Your direct dial numbers should be front and center on your website."

Aren't they? Presley doesn't know. Maintaining the website doesn't fall under her job description.

Marcia continues, "I mean . . . I hate to say it, but y'all need to get your act together."

"We're working through some issues," Presley says.

"Seriously, your marketing materials are blah." Marcia sticks out her tongue. "Your agency is better suited for banks and hospitals. And you really should be using a local firm, not one in Roanoke."

"Calm down, honey." Mark casts his wife a warning look before shifting his gaze to Presley. "As you can see, my wife is passionate about her work. We both are. We'd love a chance to sit down with you and . . . Stella, is it?"

Presley nods. "That's correct. Stella Boor is the new general manager."

"She did a brilliant job with the renovations," Marcia says. "The place is gorgeous."

"With the right marketing campaign, we can have this inn booked to capacity and your restaurant teeming with customers like that," Mark says, snapping his fingers.

Marcia thrusts a business card at Presley. "Please have Stella call us."

Presley pockets the card. "I absolutely will. Enjoy the party. I hope to speak with you soon."

Mark and Marcia may be pushy, but they're right. First thing in the morning, Presley will have a serious discussion with Stella about marketing.

As she's turning away from the Porters, Presley runs smack into Rita and Emma Reed. "Well . . . hello there," she says. "Welcome to Homecoming."

Surprise registers on Rita's face. "You're that girl, the one who . . ."

"Fell on her face in front of your house? That's me. I'm Presley Ingram."

"Presley Ingram?" Rita gives her a closer look. "What a pretty name. Where are you from, Presley?"

"Nashville, originally. But I moved to Hope Springs three weeks ago. I'm the new event planner."

Emma says, "Cool! I've been considering a career as a wedding planner. I'd love to talk to you more about it. Can you come to dinner one night this week?" She elbows Rita. "Is that okay, Mom? If Presley comes to dinner?" Emma doesn't wait for Rita to respond. "Wednesday or Thursday would be best for me. Does either work for you? Do you have any food allergies or dietary restrictions?"

Presley laughs out loud. This girl who was so rude to her when she tripped on their sidewalk is suddenly her best friend. "Your outgoing personality will serve you well in planning events and dealing with diva brides."

Rita smiles. "Emma's wanted to be a wedding planner since Santa brought her Barbie Bride. I attended at least a thousand Barbie and Ken weddings."

Emma covers her face with her hands. "Mom! Stop!"

"I had a Barbie Bride," Presley admits. "And I'd love to come to dinner. Wednesday night would be best."

"Perfect." Someone in the distance distracts Emma, giving Presley the opportunity to study her. Despite her casual attire—Barbour coat over jeans and cowboy boots—she's strikingly pretty with dimples, a tiny turned-up nose, and prominent cheekbones.

Emma tugs on her mother's coat jacket. "I see Chad. I'm going to talk to him."

"Okay, sweetheart." Rita waits until Emma is out of earshot.

"Chad is her boyfriend. They've been dating forever. We'll see if their relationship can stand the test of college."

Presley looks around for Abigail. "Did your other daughter come with you?"

"Abigail? No, she's at home studying for a calculus test tomorrow. Crowds aren't her thing."

A server approaches with a tray of spiked oyster shooters. Rita accepts one and swallows it in one gulp, handing the empty shot glass back to the server. "Delicious. Oysters are one of my favorites. You all did a wonderful job with the party. Lucy Jordan, the sommelier here, is my sister."

"Lucy and I are friends," Presley says, and then it dawns on her. Rita's sister's name is Anna, not Lucy. Is it possible there are three Townsend sisters? It's not only possible, it's entirely probable since Presley's knowledge of the family is based on information gathered from random websites. Lucy has mentioned sisters, but never by name. Her story of putting her baby up for adoption comes rushing back to Presley. Is Presley that baby? She feels a crushing weight against her chest, and she struggles to catch her breath.

Rita braces Presley's arm. "Do you feel okay? You're very pale."

She shakes her head to clear it. "I'm fine. I felt lightheaded for a minute. We've been working so hard these past few days, I haven't taken the time to eat a decent meal."

Presley has been waiting for the right moment to talk to this woman, who she is certain . . . was certain is her mother. But now, all she can think about is getting away from her. "Have you been down to the cellar yet? Lucy has organized an impressive wine tasting."

"No, I came outside first to help Emma find Chad." Rita glances over at her daughter. "Now that she's occupied, I'll sneak down to the wine tasting. Thanks for agreeing to talk to Emma about your career. Does seven o'clock work on Wednesday?"

"That'd be lovely."

As Presley watches Rita stroll back toward the main building, a second wave crashes down on her. If Lucy Jordan is her mother, based on the story she told Presley at lunch, her father is a rapist.

22

EVERETT

P resley nailed the theme. The party feels like a homecoming with the citizens of Hope Springs talking loudly and laughing, hugging and backslapping, as though they haven't seen one another in years. And some of them probably haven't. Even though the town is small, everyone has such busy lives these days.

As Everett moves through the crowd from bar to bar, he overhears bits of conversation. Overall, the guests are impressed with the renovations. Men speak of bringing clients for drinks at Billy's Bar, and women make plans for girls' nights out and celebratory dinners at Jameson's. One young woman suggests to her fiancé they have their wedding reception here next fall while another wants to rent out the game room for a football party in honor of her boyfriend's birthday.

Everett deems the party a success. He anticipates a drastic increase in business soon. At least for the restaurant and bars. The room bookings may take a little longer.

A thickening in his throat surprises him. While he's worked at the inn only a short time, he's grown to love the vast rooms and mountain views. Except for Naomi, the other members of the team have become his friends. He enjoys the mixology aspect of bartending, and meeting new people, but he finds the work unfulfilling. During the past two months, he hasn't been working toward anything. He's been biding time. While he's ready for the next stage of life, leaving the inn come January will be bittersweet. He can't even bring himself to consider a life without Presley. He'll have to convince her to come to Nashville with him.

He's leaving the library when Jazz sneaks up behind him, tugging on his shirttail. When he turns around, she leaps into his arms, and he twirls her around a few times before setting her back down. When she wobbles, he holds onto her until the dizziness passes. He will definitely miss Jazz. How can a kid with such a pure spirit come from a rotten soul like Naomi?

"Are you having a good time, kiddo?" he asks.

"Yes! Come see the magician!" Taking him by the hand, she tries to drag him down the hall.

"I'm working right now, Jazzy. You'll have to tell me all about it tomorrow."

She sticks out her lower lip. "Okay."

He offers a fist bump, and she reluctantly touches her tiny balled fist to his. Tossing a wave over her shoulder, she stalks off in the solarium's direction.

The kid needs a dad. It makes Everett sad to think she might never get one. Naomi's already run off one husband. No matter how beautiful she is, no man in his right mind would marry her.

As he hustles from bar to bar, Everett rehearses his speech in his head. In a few short hours, he will tell Presley everything. The burden of his lies has weighed him down since he arrived in Hope Springs, but even more so in recent weeks as his feelings for Presley have deepened. He hopes she'll be understanding. If not, while he may lose his chance at happiness with her, he'll at least be able to live with himself again.

Everett is so engrossed in his own thoughts, he doesn't believe his eyes when he sees Presley talking to Carla and Louie out by the bonfire. He blinks hard and rubs his eyes. What on earth are Carla and Louie doing here? Wait a minute. Is it possible? Memories flash back and he finally connects the dots. He met the fisherman from Atlanta, Turkey Neck, at Blue By You one night. Carla introduced them. "Meet my uncle, Mack Lambert." Only he isn't Carla's uncle. He's her neighbor, her father's best friend.

Everett imagines the conversation between Mack and Carla at a neighborhood barbecue. "I ran into your buddy, Rhett. He's working as a bartender up in the mountains of Virginia. He's going by the name of Everett. Claims he's from North Dakota. But I swear he's the guy I met with you at Blue By You. What's his deal? Why's he in hiding? Is he wanted by the police or something?"

Presley's conversation with Carla and Louie appears to be cordial. They haven't stirred up any trouble yet. Maybe they don't know about his relationship with Presley. His gaze shifts slightly to the right, to Naomi, who is staring straight at him with a grin so smug he wants to smack it right off her face.

She tried to warn him. *I just got off the phone with your friend from Atlanta. He booked two rooms for this weekend. I convinced him to stay through Sunday to attend the party.* Everett had assumed that by *friend*, she meant the fisherman from Atlanta.

Everett pushes his way through the dwindling crowd to Presley's side. "What're the two of you doing here?" he says to Carla and Louie.

Carla loops her arm through his, leaning possessively against him. "We came to see you, silly."

"Correction! *Carla* came to see you. *I* came to give you this." Drawing back his hand, Louie punches Everett in the eye. Everett stumbles backward, and Louie tackles him to the ground. "You stole my money, your rotten a-hole, and I want it back."

Carla squeals, "Stop!" as she kicks at them with her pointy-toed boot.

They roll around on the ground until Everett wrestles his way on top and begins pummeling Louie with his fists. He manages several hard blows to Louie's face before Martin, the head of security, jerks Everett to his feet and sets him down in front of Stella.

Stella's face is beet red, and her nostrils are flaring. Her arm shoots out, finger pointed at her cottage. "Come with me! All of you! Now!"

Martin takes Louie and Everett by their collars and marches them down the narrow road to the caretaker's cottage. Everett feels as though he's on his way to the guillotine with Queen Stella leading the procession and her attendants—Naomi, Carla, and Presley—bringing up the rear.

Their party of seven packs into the tiny living room. Presley remains by the door, with one hand on the knob as though preparing to bolt. Carla uses her brother's body as a shield, as though she needs protecting from the man who impregnated her. Everett's eyes travel to her swollen belly. *Damn, she's still pregnant.*

Louie, who is bleeding from his nose and a cut above his eye, catches Everett staring. He takes another swing at him, but Martin holds Louie off.

Stella stares Louie down. "If you go after him again, I'll have you arrested." She turns to Everett. "What is wrong with you? This is beyond embarrassing for me to have one of my employees cause such a scene at a party we're hosting. Start talking, Everett. What's this about?"

"Everett?" Louie snorts. "Where'd you come up with a fancy name like that?"

Stella's jaw drops. "Your name isn't Everett?"

Louie answers for Everett. "I've known him all my life. Ain't never called him nothing but Rhett."

Stella's eyes still on Everett, she says, "So these people are friends of yours from North Dakota."

Louie barks out a *ha*. "North Dakota? The three of us are from Georgia. Born and raised in Atlanta." Louie takes Carla by the arm and jerks her forward. "This here's my sister, Carla. Rhett knocked her up and split town with three thousand dollars in cash that belongs to me."

"I knew it!" Naomi says. "You *are* a thief. I thought there was something sketchy about you when I caught you using my computer the other day? How much did you steal from the inn, Rhett?"

"I didn't still a dime from the inn," Everett says to Naomi, and to Louie, he adds, "And I have touched none of your money."

Everett risks a glance toward the door. Presley is gone. When did she leave? How much did she hear?

Stella massages her temples. "This sounds like a personal matter to me. Everett . . . Rhett . . .whatever your name is, go home. Take the rest of the night off. We'll talk in the morning."

Everett is crossing the room on his way out when he hears Stella say, "Martin, politely escort our guests back to their rooms."

Everett, to avoid the lingering partiers, follows the road around the main building to the front. His vision blurred by tears, he stares at the sidewalk as he walks home. He craves a drink. Town Tavern is closed. He'll go to the market for beer or wine. A memory from two years ago comes flashing back. He's lying drunk and bloody from a bar fight at his parents' front door. The door opens and his mom is standing over him. She's shaking her head, her expression twisted in a grimace. *You're better than this, Rhett.*

Everett hurries inside to the safety of his apartment. He throws open his window and straddles the sill. Town Tavern is open for brunch on Sundays but closed on Sunday nights. Downtown is quiet with few cars on the road and only a scattering of people walking home from the party.

So, Carla has decided to go through with the pregnancy. He's going to be a daddy. Shouldn't he have experienced something when he saw her baby bump? A tug at his heartstrings or butterflies in his gut? But he feels nothing for this child. No tenderness or pride or concern for its wellbeing. Is that because he feels nothing for the baby's mother? Or is it because he's a vile human being like his old man?

An honest and hard-working woman, a friend he's known most of his life, is having his child out of wedlock, and all he can think about is another woman. Presley is lost to him now. He's almost certain of it. He could try to explain. But what's the point. A relationship between them would never work. He and Presley are nothing alike. Everett comes from redneck trash, and Presley from wealth and privilege.

The sound of his guitar echoes throughout the silence as he fine-tunes his latest masterpiece, his best work yet, a song he calls "Raven" about a red-headed beauty who has stolen his heart. He sees Presley's shadow on the sidewalk below long before her body comes into view. With head bowed and shoulders slumped, she doesn't look up at him, even though he's certain she can hear him. A moment later, her apartment door closes with a thud, and light spills through the window.

He continues to play his guitar and sing into the wee hours, not for Presley but for himself. He's lost his way, and he's counting on his music to guide him back.

Everett, unshowered and unshaven and wearing sunglasses to hide his black eye, goes to the bank when it opens at nine the following morning. He never transferred any of Louie's money to his mother. His conscience wouldn't let him, not until he knew for certain Louie owed him the money. Withdrawing the full three thousand dollars in cash from his account, he continues down the street to the library.

He checked his email sporadically over the weekend whenever he could sneak away from the inn. On his last visit to the library yesterday before the party and still having heard nothing from his mom, he sent her an urgent message asking her to please let him know she's okay. Today, thankfully, he has an email from her waiting in his inbox. The message is brief: *Call ASAP.*

Panic sets in and he hurries to the checkout counter.

"Can I use your phone?" he asks Rose. "I have an emergency and I need to call my mom."

Rose's eyes narrow as she scrutinizes his black eye.

"Please, Rose! I wouldn't ask if it weren't important."

She lowers her gaze to the desk phone. "Is it local?"

Everett shakes his head.

She removes her cell phone from the pocket of her pink cardigan and slides it across the counter to him. "Go outside to make your call, and don't forget to bring me back my phone."

"I won't. I promise." He gives her his most genuine smile. "Thank you. And my mom thanks you."

Outside, he paces the sidewalk in front of the library while waiting for his mom to answer. He calls three times before she finally picks up. In a suspicious tone, she asks, "Who's this?"

"It's me, Mom."

She begins to cry. "Oh, Rhett."

"What's going on, Mom? Are you okay?"

"No, son, I'm not okay."

The bottom falls out of his stomach. "Where are you?"

"In the hospital. Your father went off the deep end. After beating me into a coma, he suffered a massive stroke."

Everett grips Rose's phone tighter. "Is he—"

"Yes!" she sobs into the phone. "He's gone."

Everett stops pacing. Is she seriously sad the bastard is out of their lives? "I hate to speak ill of the dead, but you're better off without him. You know that, don't you, Mom?"

Her voice is meek. "Yes. I know that. He nearly killed me. I'm just so emotional right now. The doctor has me on a lot of painkillers. I really need you, Rhett. I hate to ask you, but can you please come home?"

Everett hates that she has to ask. "Of course, Mom. I'll be there tonight. Tell me the extent of your injuries."

A rustling sound comes over the line, and his mom says, "The doctor just walked in. He can tell you better than me."

Lowering himself to the library steps, Everett rakes his fingers through his hair as Dr. Mullins speaks of broken ribs, a punctured lung, a severe concussion, and an arm broken in two places. "Those are the worst of her injuries. She has other minor cuts and bruises. I've been a doctor for thirty years, but I've never seen an assault of this magnitude."

If his father wasn't already dead, Everett would kill him with his bare hands. "When did this happen, Doctor?"

"An ambulance brought her in last Wednesday. She came out of the coma yesterday. We've been trying to reach you, but our calls keep going to your voicemail."

Guilt expands in Everett's chest, making it difficult for him to breathe. "I've been having trouble with my phone. I'm out of town now, but I'll be home tonight, by midnight at the latest."

"Good! Your mom needs you. I'll expect to see you during my morning rounds tomorrow."

After returning Rose's phone, Everett takes off running. He doesn't stop until he reaches the inn. Covered in sweat, he charges through the front doors. He ignores Naomi when she calls after him as he hurries around the corner to Stella's office. Her door is open and she's talking on the phone.

When she sees Everett, she tells the person on the other end she'll call them back and hangs up.

Everett expects Stella to be angry, but she smiles at him when she waves him into her office and her tone is sincere when she says, "Come in, Everett. Or should I call you Rhett?"

"Either is fine. Everett is my given name." When his butt lands in the chair opposite her desk, his legs begin to bounce up and down. He can't be here right now. He came here to explain about last night, but his thoughts are too jumbled to make any sense. He doesn't care about this job. Stella will probably fire him, anyway. He has a career waiting for him in Nashville. He needs to be on the highway to Atlanta. The only thing that matters is getting to his mom.

He jumps to his feet. "I'm sorry, Stella. I just got off the phone with my mom. I have a family emergency. I need to get home as soon as possible."

Stella's brows become one. "Oh. I'm sorry. Is everything okay?"

"Honestly, no. But it will be. Despite what Naomi says, I didn't take any money from the inn."

"I want to believe you, Everett. I truly do. But I can't ignore the fact that you lied on your employment application."

He hangs his head. "I don't blame you."

Coming from behind her desk, Stella, with one hand cupping his elbow, walks him to the door. "Your family is the most important thing right now. Be careful on the drive."

Stella is a remarkable person, honest with strong morals. She's worked hard, she's persistent, and she should have success. When they reach the door, he leans down and gives her a hug. "I mean this as a friend, Stella. Beware of Naomi. I'm not sure what's driving her agenda, but she doesn't have the inn's best interests at heart."

Everett doesn't wait for Stella's response. He rushes back toward the reception desk. Relieved to find Naomi gone, he asks Valerie, the guest service agent, to ring Louie Daniels' room. "Tell him he has a guest in the lobby who needs to speak with him."

Valerie's searching her computer for the room number when Louie and Carla emerge from the elevator. Louie's battle scars are way worse than Everett's. Both his eyes are black, and blood oozes from a gash above his right eyebrow.

Everett walks toward them. "Here's your money." He shoves the bank envelope at Louie. "It's all there, if you wanna count it."

"I believe you." Louie takes the envelope from him and shoves it in his pocket.

"I didn't steal your money, Louie. I forgot I had it in my truck. Then, after I left town, I had no way to get it back to you. Be honest, man. What is the money for? Was Waylon paying you on the side for our gig?"

His bloodshot eyes bulge. "Dude! No! I would never cheat you. You're like a brother to me. Waylon bought an old dirt bike of mine."

Everett's cheeks burn. He's reached a new level of low. "I'm sorry for doubting you."

"And I'm sorry about the way I acted yesterday. We can work this out, Rhett. The band needs you."

Everett lets out a sigh. "You will find out soon enough, so I might as well tell you now. I've been talking to Wade Newman. He wants me, Louie, not the rest of the band. It's a tough break, I know. But that's how it goes sometimes. Sorry, bro." Everett turns and heads toward the door.

Carla calls after him, "Wait! Rhett! What about the baby? This is your kid."

Everett returns to where they're standing. "I'm not the father, Carla. I'm the sperm donor. You made the decision to get pregnant on your own. You can raise it on your own."

This time, when he turns his back on them, he keeps on going.

23

PRESLEY

P resley works from home on Monday morning. Still dressed in exercise clothes from her yoga workout, she answers emails and prepares notes for her wrap-up meeting with Stella at noon.

Around ten thirty, she's still at her desk when she notices Everett . . . Rhett . . . whatever his real name is . . . hoofing it down Main Street toward their building. He's wearing a red baseball cap, flannel shirt, and torn jeans. Why the sunglasses when it's cloudy out? Is he trying to hide a black eye? He crosses Marshall Street with barely a glance in either direction, and seconds later, she hears the downstairs door slam followed by footfalls on the hardwood stairs. Leaving her desk, she goes to her entryway and presses her ear against the door. He makes three trips—down, up, and back down again—before finally leaving for good. She moves to the window, and seconds later, his truck appears on the street below. As he waits at the stop sign for a line of traffic to pass, she peers into the passenger side windows of his truck. In the front seat is his guitar, and loaded in the back are an air mattress, duffel bag, and hanging clothes.

When the traffic clears, he makes a right-hand turn and disappears out of sight.

Presley is angry with him for so many reasons. He told so many lies, she questions whether anything he said to her is true. She expected him to come over last night after the party. Not that she would have let him in. But he didn't even try to see her. He was home. She heard him playing his guitar. Does he not realize he owes her an explanation? Or does he not care? With his cover blown, he has little choice but to move back to Atlanta to be with his girlfriend while they await the arrival of their baby.

Presley thinks back to their conversation a few weeks ago when she spilled her guts to him about being adopted. He spoke of unwanted pregnancies and abortion. His unwanted pregnancy is the *thing* he's been hiding, the problem he's been trying to sort out. The situation seems relatively simple to Presley. The girl is pregnant. He's the father. Based on the size of her baby bump, abortion is no longer an option. Their choices are adoption, raising the kid on the fly as single parents, or marriage. But hiding out in the mountains isn't one of them. Only a coward would do that.

"You are way better off without him, Pres," she says to her reflection in the mirror as she applies makeup for work. Her brain understands this. But her heart is struggling to accept it. She thought they had something special, a rare and pure love. "Boy, did you get this one wrong. Don't ever trust your people reader again."

After blow-drying her hair, she puts on a winter-white long-sleeved sheath with black suede tall boots and a gray cashmere cape. She's not dressing to impress anyone. She's dressing to make herself feel better. And it works. She feels good about herself as she walks to work. She's grateful to have her career and her birth mother to focus on. She was up half the night thinking about Lucy and the boy from Chapel Hill who raped her. The thought of having a rapist's blood running through her veins makes her skin crawl. She wipes the thought from her mind. Why go down that rabbit hole until she knows for certain she's Lucy's daughter?

Her mood improves tenfold when she sees the inn bustling with activity. In addition to the many people moseying about the lounge, small groups of men and women are having drinks in Billy's Bar, and all the tables in Jameson's are occupied.

Stella, who is waiting for her at a table by the window, stands and greets her with a hug. "Look at this crowd," Presley says.

"I know! Isn't it wonderful?" Stella gives Presley a squeeze before turning her loose. "Don't you look lovely. Is there a new man in your life?"

"Nope, there's a new *me* in my life." Draping her cape over the back of her chair, Presley sits down opposite Stella. "I didn't expect to see results so soon."

"Me either," Stella says, her face aglow. "I almost feel guilty taking up a table."

Presley cranes her neck to look back at the hostess stand. "We're good. There's no one waiting in line."

"After last night, we deserve to celebrate." Stella gestures at the ice bucket bearing an uncorked bottle of sparkling rosé beside her. "Compliments of Lucy. She specifically requested that you have a taste." Stella uses air quotes to emphasize *taste.* "The vineyard is local. Lucy feels with rosé being so popular, this one will be an excellent and affordable choice for brides on a budget."

"In that case, I'll have a sip." Today of all days, Presley may make an exception and drink a whole glass. Maybe she'll even have seconds.

Their waiter, Ron, arrives. "Ladies." He gives a slight bow. "May I pour you some wine?"

"Please!" Stella and Presley say in unison.

With his hand cupped over his mouth as though sharing a secret, Ron says, "Everyone's raving about Cecily's salmon salad special."

Presley doesn't bother looking at the menu. She already knows it by heart. "Then that's what I'll have."

"Make that two." Stella hands Ron their menus, and when he leaves, she holds her glass out to Presley. "To the future of Hope Springs Inn."

Presley clinks her glass. "To the future." The wine is delicious, crisp and dry despite the bubbles that tickle her nose. She takes several more sips before removing her iPad from her work tote. "I made some notes about the party. The most urgent thing we should discuss is our marketing plan. I met a young couple last night, Mark and Marcia Porter, who own their own marketing firm here in Hope Springs." She slides the Porters' business card across the table to Stella. "According to Mark and Marcia, and I have to agree with them, our advertising materials are blah." She taps a fingernail on the business card. "This couple is convinced they can quickly turn things around for us."

"I'm one step ahead of you on finding a new marketing agency." Stella picks up the business card and studies it. "I've been talking to several large nationwide firms, but their fees are so high, and none of them seems to understand my vision."

Presley opens her iPad, accesses the internet, and flips it around so Stella can see. "I spent some time studying the Porters' website this morning. I have to admit, I'm impressed. They represent some large national companies, although most of their business is local."

While Stella explores the website, Presley guzzles the rest of her wine. What has gotten into her today? Is she celebrating the success of the party? Or is she drowning her sorrows about Everett?

"Interesting. They handle the marketing for Paradise Found."

"I saw that," Presley says. "Lucy and I ate lunch there last week. The food was horrible, but there wasn't an empty table in the place. Women love the pink and green theme. Mark and Marcia have done an excellent job promoting them."

Stella hands Presley the iPad and drops the business card into her purse. "I'll schedule a meeting with them as soon as possible."

Something across the restaurant catches Stella's attention. Presley risks a glance and sees Naomi standing in the doorway. When Naomi locks eyes with Stella, raw hatred passes between them. Naomi hurries away, and Stella drains the rest of her sparkling wine and refills both their glasses.

"There's something else you should know, Stella. Mark and Marcia have been trying to reach you. They've called and come by in person. And they've left messages with our guest services manager. Did Naomi ever give them to you?"

"She did not." Stella doesn't elaborate, but her face is set in stone.

"Do you believe what Naomi said last night, about Everett stealing from the inn?" Presley realizes she's overstepping her boundaries, but the wine has suppressed her inhibitions and loosened her lips. And, if she's honest with herself, she's desperate for information about Everett.

"I'm not sure I *believe* her allegation," Stella says. "But I can't ignore it either. Not after everything else we heard last night about Everett . . . Rhett." She chuckles. "What *are* we supposed to call him?"

Presley shrugs. "I've been wondering the same thing. Since we know him as Everett, I guess we should call him that."

Stella stares into her wine. "Sadly, we may never see him again to call him anything."

Presley's gray eyes are wide. "Did you fire him?"

"I didn't have to fire him," she says. "He had a family emergency. He took off for Atlanta this morning."

Presley's stomach clinches, and she fears she might throw up. "Is he coming back?"

"Honestly, I don't know. He was in such a hurry to leave, I didn't ask too many questions."

Presley doesn't say it, but she's thinking, *He lied about everything else. Maybe he lied about the family emergency as well.*

Ron delivers their lunch, and they dig into their salads. The salmon is grilled to perfection and the mixed lettuces are crisp and tossed in a delicious lemon basil vinaigrette. Cecily is rapidly becoming famous for her savory cheese biscuits, her grandmother's recipe that she refuses to share. Presley scarfs down two and refrains from asking Ron for more.

While they eat, their conversation shifts to the holidays. "People are booking online and calling for room reservations for Thanksgiving," Stella says. "At this rate, we'll sell out by the end of the day. I get the impression a lot of them are locals with family coming in from out of town."

"That's great news!" Presley says. "I think we've turned the corner."

For the rest of lunch, Presley shares some of her many ideas for holiday events with Stella. Afterward, to work off their wine buzzes, they take a long stroll around the grounds. When they encounter Opal painting down by the lake, Presley makes a date with her to have coffee on the veranda the following morning at nine. At the construction site, while Stella has a word with the architect, Jack gives Presley a tour of the spa building. In addition to a high-end gift shop, a rental office for water sports and a lunch cafe occupy the main level. Spa facilities take up the third floor, and the second floor is all about fitness with an indoor lap pool, dance studios for classes, and a workout room with state-of-the-art equipment.

They rejoin Stella in front of the building where excavators dig for the outdoor pool. "The Summer House Wellness Center will be our crowning jewel," Presley says to Stella excitedly. "My brain is spinning with ideas."

Stella laughs. "Then take your brain back to your office, or your apartment, wherever you work best, and make lots of notes while these ideas are still fresh."

"I'll do that! See you in the morning." Phone in hand, typing ideas into her Notes app as she walks, Presley heads back up the hill toward the inn. She's approaching her apartment building when the first sprinkles of rain from an incoming storm system ping her face.

24

PRESLEY

Presley's head is splitting from the wine she consumed at lunch. She pops two Advil and changes into yoga pants, an Alabama sweatshirt that once belonged to an old boyfriend, and her fuzzy socks. Curled up with a blanket on Big Blue, she works on her laptop for hours, creating Pinterest boards and brainstorming ideas for events. The distraction keeps her from obsessing about Everett and Lucy, but when she finally closes her laptop at almost eight o'clock, reality hits hard. When the walls of her lonely apartment close in on her, she slips on her rain boots and coat, grabs her purse, and darts across the street to Town Tavern.

Inside the restaurant, she's greeted with flashbacks of her dinners here with Everett. The point in coming here was to get her mind off him. But the tavern's decor, neon lit signs on the walls and wooden booths, makes for a cozy spot to hang out on a rainy night. She spots a familiar face at the bar.

She taps Katherine on the shoulder. "Hey there."

Katherine looks back at Presley with red-rimmed hazel eyes. "Oh. Hey. What're you doing out on such a nasty night?"

"I live in the building across the street," Presley says with thumb over shoulder. "I could ask you the same thing."

"My husband and I had a fight." She dabs at her eyes with a paper cocktail napkin.

"I'm sorry. Do you want some company, or would you rather be alone?"

Katherine smiles at Presley. "I could definitely use the company right now. Are you eating or drinking or both?"

"Eating." Presley climbs onto the barstool beside Katherine. "I still have a hangover from the two glasses of sparkling rosé I drank at lunch with Stella. I'm a lightweight. I rarely drink much." Presley eyes the clear beverage in Katherine's glass. "What about you?"

She clinks her ice cubes. "Club soda." She slides a menu across the bar to Presley. "Wanna share some appetizers?"

"As long as we can get the ones with the most carbs."

When she laughs out loud, Katherine's face is transformed into a striking figure who reminds Presley of Meredith Grey, America's most beloved fictional doctor on *Grey's Anatomy*.

The bartender, Pete, a young guy just out of college, arrives to take their orders. Accustomed to seeing Presley with Everett, Pete asks, "Where's your insignificant other tonight?"

"He had to go out of town unexpectedly," she says in a deadpan tone.

Pete takes the hint and doesn't press for specifics. "What can I get you ladies?"

Presley orders for them. "We're going to split a few appetizers. We'll have the nachos, buffalo chicken wings, and a quesadilla. And a club soda for me."

Katherine pushes her glass toward him. "I'd like a refill, please." He takes her glass and walks away. "I'd rather be drowning my sorrows, Presley. But since I can't drink, stuffing my face with comfort food will have to do."

"Why can't you drink?" Presley bites her tongue. "I'm sorry. I'm being nosy."

"Not at all. I'd like to get it off my chest, if you can stand listening to my sad story."

Presley grins. "I'll tell you mine, if you tell me yours."

"Deal." Katherine shifts in her seat to face Presley, with a smile not reaching her hazel eyes. "My husband and I are trying to start a family, but so far, I've been unable to conceive. I want to schedule an appointment with a fertility specialist, but Dean, my husband, says we haven't been trying long enough."

Pete returns with their drinks, and Presley takes a sip of club soda. "How long have you been trying?"

"A year, give or take a month or two. I admit things have been stressful with Dean starting a new job in the college's admissions office and me getting my business up and running. We probably should wait a little longer. I'm just impatient. I'm not getting any younger, and I'd like to have more than one child."

Me too, Presley thinks. A vision of Everett holding a newborn baby comes to mind. Carla's baby. Will Presley ever find the right guy to settle down with? "How old are you, Katherine?"

"Thirty-five next month. And you?"

"I turned thirty in June," Presley says.

Pete brings their food, and they load up their plates with helpings from each of the appetizers.

Presley's eyes roll back in her head as she savors a bite of quesadilla. "This is so good."

Katherine dips a buffalo wing in blue cheese dressing and gnaws it to the bone. "This will give me heartburn for sure."

Presley points a nacho at Katherine. "You know, Katherine, sometimes you have to wait a couple of months to see the doctor of your choice. Why not schedule an appointment with the fertility specialist for January? You can decide later if you want to keep it."

Katherine sits straight up in her chair. "I never thought of that. That's exactly what I'll do. Dean will surely be on board with seeing a specialist by January."

Presley stuffs the nacho in her mouth. "Who knows? Maybe you'll get pregnant before then."

"Maybe," Katherine says, but she doesn't sound very hopeful. "Start talking. I want to hear your sad tale. Does it have anything to do with your *insignificant* other?"

While they finish gorging themselves, Presley tells Katherine about both Everett and Lucy. By the time she's finished talking, she feels nauseous from eating too much and depleted from unburdening herself of her problems.

Katherine gives her hand a squeeze. "Oh, honey. You're handling the stress so well. I'd never have guessed you were going through so much. What're you gonna do?"

"About Everett? There's not much I can do. Our relationship is over. He made that clear when he left town without telling me. Even if I wanted to get in touch with him, I can't call him, since he doesn't have a cell phone. As for Lucy, I figure I'll let that situation play itself out. I'll know when to make my move." Presley places her hands on the bar, fingers splayed. "In the meantime, I'm going to stay busy."

"I'm sure you have plenty to occupy your time, but I would love some help decorating the inn for the holidays."

Presley comes out of her chair a little. "I would absolutely love that. A fun project is just what I need."

Katherine smiles. "Honestly, that's a load off my mind. I'm not sure what Stella was thinking when she put me in charge. I'm great at poinsettias and greeneries, trees and wreaths. But I'm over my head when it comes to ornaments and trimmings."

"Come on, Katherine. I don't believe that."

"It's true." Katherine wipes her mouth and tosses her napkin on her plate. "I've been talking to the people at a Christmas tree farm about an hour away. They'll give us a discount if we buy more than one tree. I'm going to check out their offerings this weekend. Would you like to come with me?"

Presley grins. "Yes! Count me in! What're you thinking in terms of how many trees you want to put up in the inn?"

"We need a Rockefeller Plaza-worthy tree for the center of the lounge with a combination of live and fake trees in other key rooms. I'm wondering if we can get away with having a white, musically themed tree in Billy's Bar?"

"Themed trees are the bomb," Presley says. "We could have a nature tree in the library and one with sports-related ornaments in the game room."

"And a tree that glimmers and shimmers in the solarium. We can brainstorm on the way to the tree farm this weekend."

When Katherine covers her mouth to stifle a yawn, Presley signals Pete for the check and they plunk down their credit cards. "I'm so glad I ran into you tonight, Katherine. Having the holidays to focus on will keep our minds off our problems."

Presley feels pounds lighter as she traipses back across the street in her rain boots. She doesn't realize she's humming Everett's tune until she's unlocking her apartment door. She hasn't been able to get the song out of her head since she first heard him sing it. She doesn't know the title. It's not the one about his mama but the one about a man who's lost his way. She sits down at her desktop computer and googles Rhett Baldwin. What she learns transports her back fifteen months.

She's just arrived home from being out at dinner with friends. Loud music greets her at the back door. Wanting to avoid a scene with her mother, she tiptoes down the hall toward the stairs. But her mother hears her.

"Presley!" Renee calls out. "Is that you? Come here a minute."

She can tell from her slurred speech that her mother's been

drinking. Sure enough, when she enters the study, her mother is sprawled on the sofa, stemless glass in hand with a red wine stain down the front of her white blouse.

"What is it, Mother?"

"Listen! This young man sounds like Johnny Cash. He wrote this song himself. It went viral on its own. I'm gonna sign him and make him a star."

Presley had ignored her at the time. Renee's alcoholism was at its worst, a month before a bout with pancreatitis marked the beginning of her downward spiral toward death.

She has no trouble finding a video of the song on YouTube. The man singing into the microphone and strumming his guitar like a professional is Rhett Baldwin, aka Everett. She replays the video over and over, listening carefully to the lyrics. In the song, this man, who Presley assumes is Rhett, turns to his mama for help when his excessive drinking and fighting gets out of control.

The first night they met, Everett told Presley he doesn't like the person he is when he drinks. He posted "Show Me the Way" to YouTube eighteen months ago. Presumably, he's been sober for at least that long. But that means nothing. Renee quit drinking too many times to count. The ease in which Presley downed those two glasses of wine at lunch today serve as a reminder of how fast one can fall off the wagon. She spent her young adulthood taking care of one alcoholic. She has no interest of traveling down that path again. Presley let her infatuation with Everett overpower her common sense. As much as she's missing Everett right now, she knows their breakup is for the best.

25

EVERETT

Because of heavy traffic around the Charlotte area, the drive to Atlanta takes Everett longer than expected. His mom is asleep when he arrives at the hospital at nearly eleven o'clock on Monday night. The sight of her face, bruised and swollen beyond recognition, is like a knife in his heart. Her broken left arm is in a cast past her elbow, and a rectangular gauze bandage that presumably covers a laceration is taped to the side of her neck. Tubes provide oxygen and deliver fluids to her lifeless body. Her lips are slightly parted, and he can see the gaping hole in her upper jaw where her left canine tooth is missing. That bastard. How could any man do this to any woman, particularly one as sweet and honest as his mother? She took care of his mean ass for thirty-four years. And this is the thanks she gets?

Everett lowers himself to the recliner beside her bed, but he's too wired from his trip to sleep. He watches his mom sleep instead, vowing to let nothing bad happen to her ever again. He finally drifts off around two, and when he wakes, his mom is staring at him with roadmap eyes through slit eyelids.

Everett sees how much it pains her when she tries to smile through cracked lips. In a weak and raspy voice, she says, "If you're trying to outdo me with the black eye, you've lost the contest."

"No doubt about that." Everett doesn't explain his black eye, and his mom doesn't hound him with questions. She knows he'll tell her the truth when he's ready. He doesn't hold back his tears. "I'll never forgive myself for leaving you here with him."

She reaches for his hand with her unbroken arm. "Hush now, sweet boy. You have your own life to live. The last thing I want is to be a burden to you."

"You've never been a burden. It's you and me against the world. Remember, our words for when times are rough?"

She nods. "You and me against the world. Did you sort through your problems?"

He shakes his head. "Things are more complicated than ever."

"Since we're both in a bad place how about we support one another while we figure out our lives?"

"I'd like that very much. I definitely need my mama right now."

"And I need my son." She squeezes his hand before letting go.

Doctor Mullins enters the room wearing a white jacket over blue scrubs as though he's been in the operating room. He's a distinguished-looking rich dude with hair graying around the temples. The doctor gives Everett's eye a hard stare, but doesn't say a word about it.

"How're you feeling today, Mary?" the doctor asks in a gentle voice that makes Everett soften toward him.

"A little better." His mom looks at her doctor with pleading eyes. "Can I go home today, Doctor? My son is here to take care of me now."

"Hmm." He listens to her chest with his stethoscope. "I'm

pleased with your progress, but I'd feel better if we give it one more day."

Mary presses, "Tomorrow morning, then?"

The doctor smiles at her. "As long as you don't have any setbacks between now and then." He spends several minutes typing on his iPad before leaving the room.

For the rest of the morning and into the afternoon, Mary's room is a constant beehive of activity. Around three o'clock, his mom says, "Go home, Rhett. You need a shower. When's the last time you ate anything?"

Food is the last thing on his mind. How can he think of eating with his mom in so much pain? But he hasn't showered since Sunday morning, and he can barely stand the smell of himself. "Maybe I will." Everett gets up from the chair and stands beside the bed. "I want to stock up on groceries and get the house ready for your homecoming, anyway."

Mary grabs a fistful of blanket. "I have no idea what condition you'll find the house in. I remember little about that night. But don't worry about cleaning anything up. We can do all that later. Just get some rest. You look like you could use it."

Everett kisses her forehead. He's not going to argue with her. "I'll check in with you later, Mom. Maybe I'll come back later. I can bring you your favorite salad from Panera Bread."

She cups his cheek. "Please, baby, don't go to the trouble. All the medications I'm taking have zapped my appetite. Just be here in the morning to take me home."

He pats her thigh beneath the blanket. "Don't worry. I'll be here first thing."

They only live five miles from the hospital, but Everett drives it slowly, dreading what he'll find at home. A rancid smell assaults his nose when he pushes open the front door. They took his father away, right? Everett takes tentative steps through the small entryway to the living room where the furniture is overturned, lampshades are askew, and picture frames are smashed on the floor. The beige rug sports a large rust-colored stain that he assumes is his mother's blood. He sniffs his way to the kitchen and stops short in the doorway. The trash can is knocked over with trash strewn across the floor. Everett identifies an empty package of raw chicken breasts as the source of the godawful smell. Grabbing the broom from the pantry, he sweeps up the trash, bags it, and takes it outside to the supercan.

After unloading his truck, he removes his cell phone from under his mattress and plugs it into the charger. He cleans the kitchen and straightens the living room, rearranging the furniture to hide the blood stain. Stripping off his clothes, he leaves them in a heap on the bathroom floor and takes a long hot shower. He's dressing in sweatpants and a long-sleeved T-shirt when the doorbell rings. Stuffing his feet into his bedroom slippers, he hurries down the hall to the door.

A kid of about twenty—wearing jeans, a red jacket, and a backward baseball cap—thrusts a brass urn at him. "Delivery from Pearly Gates Funeral Home."

Everett stares down at the urn, afraid to touch it. The kid is holding his father's remains. He's tempted to pay the guy his last hundred bucks to dispose of the ashes at the city dump, but he needs the money to buy groceries.

"Thank you," Everett says finally, taking the urn from him.

"Here." The kid removes an envelope from his back pocket and gives it to Everett.

Everett watches him walk down the sidewalk. Tripping on an uneven paver, he stumbles forward several feet, but he doesn't fall. He jogs the rest of the way to the funeral home van and speeds off.

Closing the door, Everett takes the urn to the living room and places it on the mantel. Stepping back, he stares at the vessel that houses his father's remains. He feels no sadness or remorse, only reassurance that his father can no longer hurt them.

Everett tears open the envelope and reads the invoice. They owe Pearly Gates Funeral Home five thousand dollars for burning his father's body, something Everett would gladly have done for free.

He takes the invoice to his room and hides it in his backpack. He has no clue where he will get five thousand dollars, but he doesn't want his mom to know about it, when she's already so stressed out about the hospital bills.

He unplugs his fully charged phone and spends a few minutes installing updates. Since August twenty-nine, the night he split town, he's received over two thousand unread text messages and over a hundred missed calls from friends. He deletes them all.

Checking his email, he discovers a message from Wade Newman with a contract and bank deposit request form attached. He's stunned. Wade never mentioned an advance, but a windfall is just what he needs right now.

He goes down the hall to the spare bedroom Mary uses as her sewing room. Seated at her dinosaur desktop computer, he signs into his account and prints out the contract and bank forms. His eyes pop out of his head at the dollar amount printed in the advance section of the contract. Fifty thousand dollars. If he's careful, he can pay his mom's bills and make this money last a good long time. When a wave of relief rushes over him, he gets up and does a little victory dance around the sewing room. His problems are far from over, but his life just got a heck of a lot easier.

26

PRESLEY

Promptly at seven o'clock on Wednesday night, with a bouquet of Katherine's garden-grown flowers in hand, Presley rings the doorbell at 237 Hillside Drive. She neglected to exchange contact information with Emma or Rita at the party, and since she has no way of confirming their plans, she hopes they haven't forgotten about dinner.

Emma, her hair still wet from the shower, swings the door open. "Come in!" The teenager wraps her fingers around Presley's wrist and jerks her inside. "I hope you like lasagna. I wanted to make something super special for you, but I've been studying for a physics test tomorrow."

"I love lasagna," Presley says. "But I don't want to keep you from studying. I can come back another time if tonight doesn't work for you."

"Don't be silly. I have to eat dinner, and you're already here. Besides, everything's almost ready." She gestures for Presley to follow her. "Come on back. Mom and Abby are in the kitchen."

Presley has imagined this house a thousand times. She expected 1950s *Happy Days*. While the layout is traditional— central hallway with living room on the left and dining room on the right, the decor follows current-day trends of neutral palettes with pops of color. They round a corner into an updated kitchen with stainless steel appliances and stone countertops, white with gray veining. Rita stands at the island tossing a salad while Abigail sets four places at a farm table in the adjoining family room.

When she sees Presley, Rita puts down her salad tongs and gives her a hug.

"I love your home," Presley says.

Rita smiles. "Thank you. The girls and I took over the house after my parents moved into a retirement home last year. They lived here nearly sixty years. The place needed a face-lift. We hired a contractor to remodel the kitchen and baths, but the girls and I did most of the painting and wallpapering throughout the rest of the house."

Abigail finishes setting the table and comes to stand beside her mother, smiling shyly at Presley.

Rita places an arm around her younger daughter's waist, pulling her close. "Emma is the one with style. She was in charge. Abigail and I took orders from her." Rita gives Abigail a squeeze. "Didn't we, sweetheart?" Warmth spreads throughout Presley's body at the abundant love in this kitchen.

Emma cracks the oven door and peeks inside. "The lasagna's ready. I hope you don't mind if we eat," she says to Presley. "I really need to get back to studying."

"Anything's fine with me," Presley says. "What can I do to help?"

Rita removes a vase from a cabinet. "You can put those lovely flowers in this."

Presley takes the vase from her. "Katherine, the groundskeeper at the farm, cut these especially for you."

"That's very thoughtful of you both," Rita says. "Thank you."

Rita and the girls put the finishing touches on dinner while

Presley arranges the flowers in the vase. "Where are you girls thinking about going to college?"

"Cornell is on the top of my list," Emma says. "As I'm sure you know, they have one of the best hospitality management degrees in the country. Chad and I want to go to the same school, but I'm not sure he can get in with his grades."

"Cornell?" Presley says. "Smart girl."

Emma hooks her arm around her sister's neck. "Abigail's the smart one. She's going to be a doctor. And she's athletic. She's already committed to play lacrosse at UVA."

This surprises Presley. Not the UVA part. At the hockey game, she heard UVA was recruiting Abigail. "You're going to play lacrosse? Not field hockey?"

Emma cuts her eyes at Presley. "How do you know she plays field hockey?"

Presley loves it that Emma is so protective of her family. "I've seen you with your hockey sticks, when I walk by in the mornings and you're on your way to school."

"Oh. Right. Duh." Emma hip-bumps her sister. "UVA wanted Abby for hockey, too. But lacrosse is her passion."

"Congratulations. DI Lacrosse is a huge deal." Presley smiles at Abigail who looks uncomfortable being the center of attention.

When Emma announces dinner is ready, they fill their plates with lasagna, salad, and crusty bread. At the table, the three Reed women take their places—Rita at the head with Emma on her right and Abigail on her left—and Presley sits down in the vacant chair beside Emma. After Rita offers a simple blessing, they commence eating.

"So, Presley," Emma says, forking off a chunk of lasagna. "When did you decide to become an event planner?"

"When I was about six," Presley says with a little laugh. "My mom was always throwing parties to entertain her clients. I learned a lot from hanging out with the florists and caterers."

"What does your mother do?" Rita asks.

"She was a producer for a major country music record label."

Emma drops her fork. "Shut up! That's badass. Does she represent any big names?"

Presley lists the names of some of Renee's top stars.

Emma says, "Cool! I wanna meet her. Is she coming to see you soon?"

"Unfortunately, my mom died a few months ago."

Emma gasps, her hand flying to her mouth. "I'm so sorry."

Rita dabs at her mouth with her napkin. "That must have been difficult for you."

Presley presses her lips into a thin smile. "It's been a tough year."

Jabbing a forkful of lettuce, Emma says, "So, tell me about your career, Presley."

Presley pinches off a bite of crusty bread. "Well, let's see. After graduating from Alabama, I worked for a few years at a country club in Nashville before accepting a job with a firm in New York that plans elaborate affairs for movie stars and politicians. I was getting ready to move to New York when my mom became ill. Her disease was debilitating but not crippling. With my help, she was able to work until a month before she died. I pretty much ran her life."

"That's what I wanna do! Plan parties for the rich and famous."

They talk for a while about the pros and cons of a career in event planning. Abigail is noticeably quiet, and Presley attempts to draw her in, to no avail.

When they finish eating, Emma says, "Thank you for sharing your experience, Presley. I don't mean to be rude, but I really need to study. I'm trying to keep my grades up."

"I totally understand. And thank you for having me." Presley wipes her mouth and sets her linen napkin on the table. "You have the right personality for event planning, Emma. You're creative and resourceful and outgoing. You will do great."

Emma's face lights up. "Do you think so, really?"

"I do," Presley says. "Would you be interested in working with me over the holidays? I'd have to clear it with Stella first, but I could use your help. As an intern. I'm not sure we'd be able to pay you."

Emma's blue eyes are enormous. "Are you kidding? *I'll* pay *you* for an opportunity like that." She whips out her phone. "What's your number?"

Presley recites her cell number and seconds later her phone pings with the text from Emma. "I'll call you as soon as I confirm it with Stella."

"That will look so great on my résumé." Emma shoots out of her chair and gathers all their dinner plates.

"Leave those in the sink, honey," Rita says. "I'll get them later."

Abigail stands to leave. "It was nice to see you again, Presley."

"And you as well, Abigail."

Rita waits until they're gone. "Would you like a cup of tea? I took some of Emma's specialty, lemon blueberry cheesecake bars, out of the freezer."

"She bakes, too?" Presley says, shaking her head in amazement. "What doesn't that kid do?"

"Emma's pretty remarkable. Both my girls are special in different ways. You would think Abigail would have self-confidence issues from having an overbearing sister like Emma, but she's sure of herself. She's just quiet by nature." Rita snickers. "I'd be willing to bet she was working calculus problems in her head during dinner." She pushes back from the table. "How about that dessert?"

"I'd love some, as long as you let me help you clean up first."

"If you insist," Rita says. "I'll get an apron for you."

While the tea brews, they clear the table and load dishes in the dishwasher. Rita tells Presley about her job at the high school. "Before my divorce, I was a stay-at-home mom. When I moved back to town from Charlotte, I had to find a job to help pay the bills. Russell Freeman, the high school's principal, is an old childhood friend. He offered me an administrative job in his office. It's fine for now. I like being around the kids. I'm still trying to figure out what I want to do for the rest of my life."

Presley laughs. "I'm sure you will in time."

Working side-by-side with Rita feels natural to Presley, like they've known each other longer than a few days. Rita is her aunt, and Abigail and Emma are her cousins. Will they accept her into their family when she tells them Lucy is her birth mother? Is this even what she wants? She answers her own question with no hesitation. She's never wanted anything more in her life.

"Let's go to the living room. It's my favorite room, but we hardly ever spend any time in there." Rita places the teacups and dessert plates on a small acrylic tray and leads Presley down the hall to the living room.

Presley pauses in the doorway to admire the room, which is decorated in shades of gray on the walls and upholstery with accent colors in pinks and yellows. "I see why you like this room. It's so feminine and happy." She scrutinizes the family photographs in silver frames that clutter the baby grand piano. Emma and Abigail are pictured at various ages. There are several of Rita and Lucy from childhood with a third girl who must be their sister, Anna. She leans over to look at an image of a handsome young couple, not much older than Presley, in formal evening attire. The man is dashing, a James Dean looka-like. There's something vaguely familiar about his wife, a beautiful redhead with pale gray eyes. Studying the photograph closer is like looking in a sepia-toned mirror. The woman can only be her grandmother.

"Are these your parents?" Presley asks.

Peering over her shoulder, Rita says, "Yes, Sam and Carolyn Townsend in their much-younger days. I would kill for my mother's hair. Out of all her offspring, children and grandchildren, only Lucy's son, Chris, got her auburn hair. Seems like such a waste on a man, but he carries it well. Did you meet Chris at the party?"

"No, I'm sorry I didn't. But I've heard a lot about him from Lucy."

"He was only there briefly with his father. He's a good boy. And his father is a good man. I was sorry when he and Lucy ended their marriage." Rita takes the photograph from Presley. "You look enough like my mother to be her twin. Presley, are you . . .? You are, aren't you? You're the child Lucy put up for adoption."

Presley's shoulders cave. "I'm not sure, but I think there's a good chance I might be."

Rita returns the photograph to the piano. "How did you find us? On 23andMe?"

"After my mom died, when I was going through her desk, I found your address on a torn envelope in my adoption file." Suddenly light-headed, Presley says, "Can we sit down?"

"Yes, of course."

Seated side-by-side on the sofa, Presley tells Rita about finding the envelope and making the split-second decision to come to Hope Springs. "I thought *you* were my birth mother at first. Lucy told me what happened to her in college and about giving her baby up for adoption. When I found out at the party that you and Lucy are sisters, I put two and two together and realized Lucy must be my birth mother."

"What a small world," Rita says, but she doesn't seem all that surprised by the coincidence.

Another piece suddenly falls into place for Presley. "Or is it, Rita? You mentioned 23andMe. Lucy claims she never searched any ancestry websites. Is someone in your family on 23andMe?" Presley turns to Rita. "Are you on 23andMe?"

Rita looks away while she sips her tea. "My sister was in such a dark place. I would have done anything to help her find the child she put up for adoption." She gets up and walks aimlessly around the room, fluffing pillows and straightening lampshades. "When my online search proved futile, I begged our parents to tell me everything they knew about the adoption. Back then, Lucy wanted nothing to do with the baby. She thought the less she knew, the easier it would be for her to forget about it. Fortunately, my parents were wise enough to realize Lucy would one day need to know more.

"They helped choose the adoptive parents. After much harassment, they gave me your parents' names. I researched your parents, and when I learned your father had passed away, I sent a letter to your mother." Rita returns to the sofa. "That's my handwriting on the envelope you found in your mother's file."

Presley takes a minute for this information to sink in. "So, you knew who I was when we met at the party and I told you my name?"

Rita gives a solemn nod. "I figured it best to let the situation play itself out. Emma, with her bubbly personality, was instrumental in making that happen."

Presley feels both betrayed and manipulated. "So, you wrote to my . . . to Renee? What did you say?"

"I explained about my sister's depression and asked her to

please call me to discuss your adoption. I never heard from her. Honestly, I didn't really expect to."

"What *did* you expect?"

"I hoped that one day you would find your way back to us. And you have."

A moment of awkward silence passes between them. "So, you're okay with me being here?" Presley asks.

"I'm thrilled with you being here, honey. You're my niece, my sister's child." Rita fingers a lock of Presley's hair. "And Lucy will be overjoyed. When are you planning to tell her?"

"I have no clue. I wanted to get to know you better first. I figure I'll know when the time is right."

"I'll support you in any way," Rita says. "If you'd like, you and I can tell Lucy together."

Presley ponders this idea. "Maybe. Let's wait a few days to see if an opportunity presents itself first."

27

EVERETT

After being released from the hospital, aside from visits to the toilet, Everett's mom sleeps for thirty-one hours straight. When he wakes her to take her meds, she gulps them down with water and falls right back asleep. The meals he brings to her room on trays go untouched. This is about more than Mary needing rest. She's slipping into depression. Finally, on Thursday evening, he makes her get out of bed for dinner.

"Rise and shine." Bursting into her room, he turns on the overhead light and bedside table lamp. "You've slept long enough. I made your favorite teriyaki chicken for dinner." When he jerks back the covers, he gets a whiff of her sour smelling body.

"Go away, Everett." She pulls the blanket back over her.

"Sorry. No can do. You can't hide out in your bed forever. Time to face the rest of your life. And I will help you, just like you helped me when I was at my lowest. We'll take it one day at a time. First off, you need to shower. You stink to high heaven."

She cries out when he eases her into a sitting position, but he doesn't let that deter him. "You're stiff from lying in this bed.

You'll feel better once you get up and move around. Besides, I have some exciting news I want to share with you over dinner."

He wraps her cast in a plastic bag, securing it with duct tape, and turns on the water in the shower. "I'll be right outside if you need me." He steps out of the bathroom and waits beside the door, listening in case she calls out for him.

She emerges twenty minutes later wearing a clean nightgown and bathrobe that smells like scented drier sheets. Her curly blonde hair is combed straight and hangs like wet noodles to her shoulders. Her face appears slightly less swollen and the bruises are transitioning from inky purple to green.

Everett settles her on the sofa before going to the kitchen to prepare their plates. When he returns to the living room with their trays, Mary is staring at the urn on the mantel. She doesn't ask where it came from or what it is.

After bowing their heads and reciting the simple "God Is Great" blessing, Everett devours his teriyaki chicken, while his mom merely picks at hers. "You need to eat, Mom, to get your strength back."

"These meds make me feel so yucky." She sets down her fork, abandoning her dinner. "You mentioned you have news. I hope it's good news."

"It's great news." He smiles at her over a forkful of salad. "I signed a contract yesterday with a major country music label."

Her mouth drops open. "You did not."

He nods. "Yes, I did."

"Oh, Rhett! That's the most wonderful news ever. I'm so proud of you. If I weren't so darn sore, I'd hug your neck." She kisses the tips of her fingers and touches them to his cheek. "You've worked so hard. You deserve success."

"Success isn't guaranteed, but Wade, my producer, seems confident I'll do well. I'm going to Nashville, Mom." He angles his body toward her. "*We're* going to Nashville. I want you to come with me."

Mary's smile fades. "You're sweet to think of me, but I can't leave Atlanta. My life is here."

"What life, Mom? Dad is gone. I'm moving away."

She moves her tray from her lap to the cushion beside her. "My friends are here, and my business."

"When's the last time you went to lunch or out for drinks with friends."

"My customers are my friends," she says, her jaw set.

"Your customers aren't your friends. They're rich ladies who tell you about their fancy parties and dysfunctional families while you're pinning up their clothes." When her chin quivers, he experiences a stab of guilt for making her cry. "I'm sorry, Mom. I didn't mean to hurt your feelings."

She wipes at her eyes with her napkin. "I guess there's some truth to that. But it took me a long time to establish my business. I can't just start over in Nashville."

"Why not? If you get in with the right crowd, word will travel fast. Who says you have to continue with alterations? Maybe you should try something new. I'm sure there are plenty of opportunities in Nashville for a gifted seamstress. Maybe Carrie Underwood needs a wardrobe assistant."

She bites on her lower lip, as though the idea appeals to her. "I'll think about it."

When Everett tells her about his deal with Wade, Mary appears more interested in the urn than what he has to say. She waits patiently for him to finish eating before excusing herself for bed.

Mary wakes before Everett the following morning. He finds her sipping coffee at the small round table in the kitchen. "Morning," he says, kissing the top of her head. "Feeling any better today?"

"No. But I will soon. I've decided to back off on the pain pills. They're making me depressed." She nods at the coffee maker. "Get some coffee and sit down. I want to ask you something."

Everett smiles at the authoritative tone of her voice. "Yes, ma'am." His mom is on the mend.

He pops a pod into the Keurig machine he gave her for her birthday in April. She loves the coffee maker as much as she loves her new sewing machine, his gift to her last Christmas. When the coffee finishes brewing, he joins her at the table. "What's up?"

"I want to know what happened that made you leave Atlanta in such a hurry. Are you in trouble with the law?"

"No, it's nothing like that." Everett walks her through the events of August twenty-nine. He tells her about Wade coming to his show and Carla's pregnancy and Louie's money.

Mary's face remains expressionless, and when he finishes talking, they sit in silence for a long while. "Regardless of how Carla got pregnant, that child is your flesh and blood, Rhett. Your responsibility."

The disappointment in her tone deflates him. He hasn't let her down since that morning two years ago when she discovered him on her doorstep. That was rock bottom for him. He never wants to go there again.

"Carla tricked me, Mom. She went off the pill without telling me and used my semen to get pregnant. I feel violated."

"Puh-lease," Mary says, rolling her eyes. "I agree that what she did was underhanded, but Carla is a lovely girl with a genuine heart. I don't blame her for wanting to start a family. Would marrying her be such a bad thing?"

"I'm not marrying someone I don't love. You, of all people, should understand that." A vision of Presley lying beside him in bed, with her auburn hair fanned out on the pillow, enters his mind. Tears fill his eyes, blurring his vision as he stares down at the table. When he looks up again, his mom is studying him intently.

"You're the bravest man I know, Rhett. You've always been my rock. How many times did you take beatings that were meant for me? What are you so afraid of now?"

"I'm not afraid of anything?"

"Really? Then why did you run away like a coward?"

Ouch. He slouches down in his chair. "Maybe I'm not ready to be a parent."

"You have to grow up sometime. Don't you want to have children?"

He shrugs. "Until Carla got pregnant, I'd never thought much about having children. It was just one of those things in the far-off future that I would worry about when the time comes. Maybe I'd be fine with not having children."

She strokes his hand. "You're nothing like your father, Rhett. You're a better man than he ever was. And you'll be a better father."

Everett jerks his hand away and sits up straight in his chair. "Is that what you think? That I'm worried I'll beat my wife and kids?"

"Isn't it?"

Everett jumps to his feet, kicking his chair out of the way. "I need some air."

Changing into running clothes, he heads out into the brisk morning. He takes off down the road at a sprint, running as fast as he can until he struggles to breathe. Until he realizes he's running from the truth. He knows he has the alcoholic gene. What if he has the abusive gene? His father never hit his mother, never even raised his voice to her, until after Everett was born. His father hated him. Of that much he's certain. What if something goes so wrong in his life and Everett lets it get the best of him? He's lost control of his anger many times before. But only with guys. Never with a woman. Not until that day he was tempted to slap Naomi.

Even if a miracle happened and things worked out with Presley, would he want to have children with her? He can't honestly answer that. Just as he's not sure he can be a part of Carla's baby's life. It's in the best interest of the child to keep it away from him.

When he finally returns home two hours later, Mary, dressed in jeans and a sweater, is standing in front of the fireplace looking at the urn. She doesn't acknowledge Everett, and wanders from room to room for the rest of the day, lost in her thoughts.

They eat dinner in a companionable silence. He's thrilled to see his mom devour two slices of the store-bought supreme pizza.

"How're you feeling without the meds?" he asks.

"More pain but less nausea is the trade-off for giving up the narcotics. But I feel less depressed and more like myself."

On Saturday, Mary surprises him by making his favorite Mexican dinner—beef enchiladas, homemade guacamole, and virgin margaritas. She's not much of a drinker either. It's hard to enjoy a cocktail when you live with an abusive alcoholic.

She still winces in pain sometime, but mostly, she's moving around a lot better.

"What's all this?" he asks when he sees the kitchen table set with placemats, linen napkins, and a small purple mum in the center.

"We're celebrating your success."

"That's awfully sweet of you, Mom." Everett kisses Mary's cheek as he holds her chair out for her.

"I've been thinking about moving to Nashville with you," Mary says, draping her napkin across her lap. "But I have some questions."

"Fire away." He forks off a bite of enchilada and stuffs it in his mouth.

"The timing is ideal. Our lease here is up at the end of December. But what would I do with all our stuff?"

"Haul it off to the dump." Everett stops chewing and flashes her a mischievous grin. "Seriously, Mom, aside from the family photo albums, what do we own that's worth keeping? We have a hodgepodge of furniture and knickknacks that you've picked up at yard sales and second-hand stores over the years. Other people's junk."

She smiles, covering her mouth to hide her missing tooth.

He points his fork at her. "The first thing we'll do when we get to Nashville is take care of that tooth."

"What about this?" She waves her cast at him. "Who will take this off when the time comes? My doctor is here."

"That's no big deal. We'll find an orthopedist in Nashville."

We eat for a minute in silence. "I would at least like to take my sewing machine and clothes."

His mom has a closet full of classic, never-go-out-of-style clothes she's created out of fine fabrics she saved her money to buy. Sadly, Everett has never seen her wear a single one of those outfits.

Everett's face grows serious. "You can take whatever you want, Mom. If we need to hire movers, we will. However, I had in mind for the two of us to go on an adventure. We'll sell your minivan. It's probably worth about ten grand. And we'll load whatever will fit in the back seat of my truck. We'll donate everything else to Goodwill."

"Have you spoken to Carla yet? You can't leave Atlanta with that business unfinished."

"I'm aware. I'm still trying to decide how to handle it."

With a look of reproach, Mary says, "There should be no decision, son."

Her reprimand stings, and they eat in silence for a few minutes.

Finally, he says, "We're in no hurry to get to Nashville. If you want to make a detour to Charleston or New Orleans or Disney World in Orlando, we can."

"Or to Hope Springs so you can see your girl," she says with a wide smile, this time not bothering to hide the gaping hole in her mouth.

He loads up a chip with guacamole. "What girl?"

"The one who has stolen your heart," she says. "Don't bother denying it. I'm your mama. You can't lie to me. You hide it well, but I've noticed a faraway look in your eyes."

Everett takes a long drink of margarita, wishing it had tequila in it. His food goes cold while he tells his mom about Presley. About how her gray eyes twinkle when she laughs, and her hair is the color of sugar maple leaves in the fall. How she's funny and smart and how he wants to be around her all the time.

"She sounds lovely," Mary says in a soft voice. "What happened between you two?"

He explains about Carla showing up at the homecoming party and Naomi accusing him of stealing money from the inn.

"Son." His mom reaches for his hand. "You've never known true happiness, and I want that for you. I'm the wrong person to offer advice on romance, but if you think she may be the one, don't let Presley get away. As for Stella, you must clear your name with her as soon as possible. The last thing you want is an allegation hanging over your head as you start your new career. Such a thing could come back and bite you in the rear end."

"Don't worry, Mom. I have every intention of clearing my name. I just haven't figured out how to do it yet."

Everett takes his plate to the microwave and waits for it to reheat. When he returns to the table, he asks, "Have you ever known true happiness, Mom?"

"Every single minute I spend with you."

This chokes him up, and he pauses a minute to steady his voice. "I mean with Dad. Did he ever make you happy?"

"For about a day when we first met." She drags a chip through the guacamole, but she doesn't eat it. "The truth is, we were happy for a long time. And I loved him with all my heart. That's why I stayed with him all these years. I took my vows seriously when we married, for better or worse, in sickness and in health. And he was sick, Rhett. Not just the diabetes, but the alcoholism."

"If you move with me to Nashville, I vow to help you find that happiness again." He chucks her chin. "I want that for *you*."

28

PRESLEY

Presley spends most of her time at work with Lucy on Thursday and Friday. They compose the wine list for the official Thanksgiving feast Cecily is planning at Jameson's and brainstorm ideas for the art show/wine dinner auction Presley has scheduled for the first weekend in December. Presley has plenty of opportunities to break the news to Lucy. But she doesn't share Rita's optimism that Lucy will be overjoyed to learn Presley is her biological daughter. And the now-familiar fear of rejection holds her back.

Her days are meaningful, packed with planning sessions for the upcoming holidays, but unbearable sorrow fills her nights. She misses Everett like crazy. She cries herself to sleep and wakes feeling drained. While she's furious at him for lying to her, she's also devastated by the hole he left in her life. Her apartment that had begun to feel like home now feels desolate. She envisions Everett everywhere. In her bed with his arm propped behind his head. Leaning against the kitchen counter, sipping on coffee. Sitting next to her in the open window. Eating pizza on Big Blue. Reminding herself that she doesn't need his kind of problems does little to comfort her aching heart.

She works from home less than before and spends more time at the inn, which is now buzzing with activity. Jameson's is booked every night and room reservations are on the rise. When Presley tells Stella about Emma, Stella says, "By all means, hire her! An intern is just what we need. We'll pay her something, although it probably won't be much. If things continue to go well, we'll go on a hiring spree after the holidays. One of those positions will be a full-time assistant for you."

Presley relishes the idea of having an assistant to help with the job's more monotonous tasks.

When Stella meets with Mark and Marcia Porter on Wednesday, their fresh ideas, endless enthusiasm, and comprehension of the tourism industry win her over. She hires them on the spot, and on Friday, the Porters present an advertising campaign that blows their team away.

"If we work all weekend, we can begin rolling it out on Monday," Mark says.

Marcia explains, "We're planning a major overhaul of your website, but for now, a few carefully placed high-resolution images of the grounds and newly remodeled rooms will at least be an improvement over what you already have."

Lucy, sitting next to Presley, whispers, "Do you think those two ever sleep?"

Cupping her hand over her mouth, Presley whispers back, "There's no way they came up with that campaign in two days. I'll bet they've been secretly working on it for weeks, hoping to win our account."

Lucy laughs. "You know it."

Early Saturday morning, Katherine and Presley leave in Katherine's pickup truck for the Christmas tree farm. They have no shortage of things to talk about during the sixty-minute drive.

They've no sooner exited the city limits of Hope Springs when Katherine says, "I took your suggestion and scheduled an appointment with the fertility specialist. You were right. I can't get in to see her until mid-January. But I feel so much more relaxed, just having the appointment on my calendar."

Presley smiles over at Katherine. "Good for you! Now, cook your husband his favorite meal and put on some sexy lingerie. Stop worrying about conceiving and have a little fun."

Katherine inhales a deep breath, letting it out slowly. "You know, I can't remember the last time we had sex for enjoyment. I will do that very thing tonight."

Presley chuckles. "I'm sure Dean will appreciate the attention."

They drive on for a while in silence. When Presley thinks about how much she'd love to show Everett a night of romance, she reminds herself that he betrayed her.

Drew Terry, the owner of the Christmas tree farm, is waiting for them when they arrive. He's a mountain of a man, about Presley's age, tall and broad-shouldered with thick sandy hair. His wife, Susan, runs the gift shop that sells seasonal indoor plants like poinsettias, Christmas cactuses, and amaryllis, in addition to nature-themed fake trimmings.

Katherine and Presley spend hours picking out three trees for key spots at the inn. An enormous Fraser fir, tall and full, for the lounge. A beautifully shaped cedar for the solarium. And a short, fat spruce to accommodate the lower ceilings in the entry hall. Katherine negotiates a reasonable price for the fifty-plus wreaths Stella wants for the exterior windows on the first floor.

On the way back to Hope Springs, Katherine says, "I found a source for old-fashioned outdoor ribbon. The red velvet and gold metallic kind. I ordered miles of it. You don't, by any chance, know how to make a bow?"

When Presley shakes her head, they say in unison, "YouTube."

Katherine stomps on the gas pedal as she passes a tractor

trailer. "Stella mentioned that there were boxes of Christmas decorations in one of the basement storage rooms, but I've been too busy to check them out."

"I'll do that," Presley volunteers. "How soon can we decorate?"

"I'm sending my crew for the trees and wreaths next Friday. But Stella won't let us decorate until after Thanksgiving. She says Thanksgiving deserves its moment in the limelight."

Presley laughs. "I don't disagree with that. If you need any help with Thanksgiving flowers, I'm your girl. I have plenty of extra time at the moment."

"No word from Everett?"

"None. Stella hasn't heard from him either." Presley presses her palms against her temples. "Despite all the bad stuff I know about him, I can't get this guy out of my head."

"Only time cures the breakup blues, I'm sorry to say. But food definitely helps. Let's get some lunch." Without waiting for Presley's response, Katherine pulls off the highway into a roadside diner parking lot. "This place comes highly recommended."

Presley casts her a skeptical glance. "Seriously? What truck driver do you know who's eaten here?"

"Not a truck driver. A Christmas tree farmer."

Based on Drew's suggestion, they order cheeseburger platters, which are phenomenal, and Presley eats every morsel on her plate.

They arrive at the inn around two. Not ready to face her lonely apartment, Presley retreats to the basement in search of Christmas decorations. She passes through the tasting room, careful not to disturb Lucy's wine tasting and continues on to the sizeable storage room at the end of the dark hallway.

The storage room is filled with rolling coatracks and castoff furniture. Boxes marked Christmas Ornaments are stacked in the back corner amongst a forest of fake Christmas trees. She randomly selects one of the larger boxes and rips the packing tape off the top. Inside, nestled in layers of yellowed tissue paper, are Christopher Radko tree ornaments. She carefully unwraps several, lining them up on the concrete basement floor. The ornaments are old, but they've aged well. Presley envisions them grouped together on the fat tree in the entryway, making an impressive display to welcome guests. In the other boxes, Presley discovers an extensive collection of Byers' figurines, an entire Boehm nativity set, and a Swarovski star tree topper.

"Wow. Look at all this," Lucy says when she enters the storage closet an hour later. She drops to her knees on the floor beside Presley. "These must be worth a fortune." She picks up a nutcracker ornament and studies it. "This takes me back years. My mother had a collection of Radko ornaments. I wonder if they're still in the attic at the house, or if Mom and Dad took them to Shady Grove with them."

Here's my opportunity. Presley sucks in a deep breath. *Now or never.* "I had dinner with your sister and nieces in that house on Wednesday night."

"You did?" Lucy furrows her brow. "I didn't realize you knew Rita."

Presley never mentioned meeting Rita for fear Lucy would ask questions she wasn't prepared to answer.

"We met briefly at the homecoming party. Emma invited me to dinner to interrogate me about a career in event planning."

Lucy laughs. "That sounds like Emma. She's a resourceful one."

"That's exactly the word I used to describe Emma when I asked Stella to hire her as an intern."

"What did Stella say?"

"She was thrilled. Emma is all set to work with me over her Christmas break."

"Emma is hardworking and creative," Lucy says. "She'll make an excellent intern."

Presley stares down at the angel ornament in her hands. She's afraid to see Lucy's reaction when she drops the bomb. "I need to tell you something, Lucy. I have reason to believe I'm your biological daughter, the child you gave up for adoption."

The ornament Lucy is holding slips from her hands and crashes to the floor in a million pieces. "Why would you say something like that? I told you my story in confidence, and now you're making up lies." She scrambles to her feet and flees the storage room.

Presley runs after her. "Lucy, please! At least give me a chance to explain." When they reach the wine shop, Presley corners Lucy behind the checkout counter. "I was adopted as a baby. I came to Hope Springs in search of my birth mother. I had reason to believe she—"

Lucy screams. "What do you want from me? If it's money, I don't have any."

"I don't know what I want, honestly, but it's not money. I inherited plenty from my . . . from Renee. I guess maybe I'm looking for a certain kind of closure."

"Well, I can't give it to you." Lucy comes from behind the counter, and with surprising force, she shoves Presley out of the way. By the time Presley catches her balance and exits the shop, Lucy is on the elevator and the doors are closing.

Presley considers taking the stairs to the main floor, but she decides not to go after her. This is not at all what she'd expected. Not what she'd hoped for. Lucy completely shut her down without even hearing her side of the story.

With tears blurring her vision, she returns to the storage closet and repacks the ornaments in the boxes. She's stopped crying and has somewhat pulled herself together by the time she finishes the task an hour later. She's finally ready to go home and is waiting for the elevator by the wine shop when she hears the muffled sound of crying. Looking around, she spots Jazz crouched down in the far corner of the cellar.

Hurrying over, she kneels down beside the child. "What's wrong, sweetheart?"

Jazz sobs, "I ran away from home. Stella's not in her cottage. Can you find her for me?"

"Of course." Presley sits down on the floor, pulling Jazz onto her lap as she removes her phone from her purse. The Wi-Fi reception can sometimes be spotty in the cellar, but the call goes through on the first try.

Stella answers on the third ring, sounding groggy as though just waking from a nap. "What's up, Presley?"

"I'm in the wine cellar at the inn. Jazz is here looking for you. She says she ran away from home."

"Damn it, Naomi," Stella says to herself and then to Presley, "I'm at Jack's. I can be there in ten minutes. Can you stay with her until I get there?"

"Of course. Jazz and I will wait right here."

Presley drops her phone back into her bag and hugs Jazz tight. "I had a bad day too. Wanna talk about it?"

"No!" Jazz buries her head in Presley's chest. "I just want Stella."

Presley kisses her hair. "I know, sweet girl. She'll be here in a few minutes."

Rocking the child gently, she hums the tune that is never far from her mind these days. Presley is not the only one in need of someone to show her the way.

Stella arrives looking disheveled, sweatshirt on inside out, and short curls springing out from her head. It appears as though Presley interrupted Stella's Saturday afternoon alone time with Jack. *Good for her!*

Stella takes Jazz from Presley. "Thank you, Presley. How did you find her?"

"I was in the storage closet going through boxes of Christmas decorations. I was getting ready to leave when I heard crying."

"Wanna go to my cottage?" Stella asks Jazz who nods, her face planted in Stella's neck.

The threesome rides together in the elevator to the first floor. Stella thanks Presley again when they part in reception. She retrieves her belongings from her office and leaves the inn.

Her heart breaks for Jazz as she walks back to her apartment. No telling what Naomi did to that sweet child to make her run away. Presley got mad at Renee . . . at her mother plenty of times, but her mother never made her angry enough to run away. Renee was a good mother, critical at times but supportive in Presley's many endeavors. While Renee was not an affectionate person, Presley never doubted her mother's love for her. Presley never felt unsafe in their home.

Stop feeling sorry for yourself, Presley. You have a good thing going in Hope Springs. Your job is challenging and rewarding. Your teammates are your family—Cecily and Stella and Katherine. You don't need a new mother, and you don't need a boyfriend. You only need you.

When she reaches Main Street, Presley places a call to Rita. "I told Lucy. She was definitely not overjoyed."

Rita sighs into the phone. "Uh-oh. Tell me what happened."

Presley gives her a blow-by-blow account of Lucy's reaction.

"I'm not surprised. Lucy can be a wild card."

Presley's mouth falls open. "Now you tell me."

"Don't worry about it, Presley. This is typical behavior for Lucy. She flies off the handle but usually calms down quickly. Give her some time. Do you want me to talk to her?"

"Only if she comes to you first," Presley says, and ends the call.

She usually calms down quickly. Except when a woman claims to be her biological daughter. Presley should never have listened to Rita. She blindsided Lucy. She doesn't blame Lucy for reacting the way she did. Lucy confided in Presley about the child she put up for adoption. And now Presley is claiming to be that child. Of course, Lucy is suspicious. And Presley doesn't blame her. Lucy undoubtedly thinks Presley is a delusional girl looking to replace the mother she lost.

29

STELLA

Jazz skips alongside me on the way to the cottage, her reason for running away seemingly forgotten. Are all kids this resilient? Or has all the trauma she's experienced in her short life made her an expert at shrugging things off? "Have you eaten dinner yet?" I ask.

Jazz stops suddenly in the middle of the road. "I haven't eaten since lunch and I'm starving."

Alarm bells go off inside my head. This active little girl eats at least two healthy snacks in between meals when she's with me. "Shall we have Cecily make us a pizza?"

"Yes!" Jazz bounces on her toes. "I love pizza."

I smile down at her. Jazz and I had our first fight over pizza on the night before she came down with bacterial meningitis. She insisted she hated pizza, and I was adamant that all kids love pizza. She went to bed without dinner that night. The next day, she landed in the hospital for a week. The poor kid was getting sick, and I never realized it. Was that only five months ago? It feels like a lifetime.

Grabbing her hand, we run the rest of the way to the cottage. Jazz jumps up and down on the sofa like a trampoline while I turn on the gas logs. "Can I spend the night, Stella?" After one last jump, she lands on her bottom. Pressing her hands together, she begs, "Puh-lease!"

"We'll see." I need to know why she ran away before I decide how to handle the situation.

Remaining by the fire, I call Cecily to place our order. "One Margherita pizza coming up," Cecily says. "I'll have one of my waitstaff run it over to the cottage when it's ready."

"You sound chipper. Pre-wedding bliss?"

"I'm on top of the world," Cecily says. "I'm getting married in six weeks and business is booming. We're booked solid tonight with a waiting list."

"That's awesome! I'd offer to come get the pizza, but I have Jazz with me."

"I didn't know you had Jazz tonight. In that case, I'll bring the pizza myself, so I can give her a hug."

I hang up with Cecily and turn to Jazz, my expression now serious. "We need to talk, kiddo. I have to call your mommy and tell her where you are. I'm sure she's worried about you. You're only six years old. Do you understand how dangerous it was for you to run away from home?" I cringe when I think of what could've happened to her. Naomi's rental house is only a few blocks from the inn, but Jazz could've been hit by a car or kidnapped.

Jazz folds her arms over her chest in a huff. "I'm six and a half."

I laugh. "I stand corrected. But still, you must promise me never to run away again." Moving to the sofa, I sit down beside her. "What's this about, anyway?"

"I got in a fight with Mommy. My dance school is performing *The Nutcracker* for our Christmas program this year. My teacher asked me to dance the role of Clara in the first act, but Mommy says I can't do it. She says ballet is stupid, and I have to quit."

My heart pounds in my ears. This has been a point of contention between Naomi and me since the beginning. At my insistence, Naomi had agreed to let Jazz continue to take ballet lessons. "Does your mommy know you left the house?"

Jazz shakes her head. "She sent me to my room. She thinks I'm still there. Her *boyfriend* is over. I snuck out when they were kissing on the sofa." Jazz pretends to stick her finger down her throat as though gagging herself.

My face remains impassive, even though my insides are stewing. "Okay, doodlebug. I'm going to turn on *Frozen* and go outside to call your mom."

I tickle Jazz for a minute before leaving the couch. After starting the movie, I put my coat back on and slip outside. My first call to Naomi goes to voicemail. Instead of leaving a message, I try again. Naomi answers on the fourth ring. "What do you want, Stella?"

"Jazz is with me at the cottage. She ran away from home. You don't even know she's gone, do you?"

"What're you talking about? She's in her room." I hear footsteps on hardwood floors followed by the sound of a door creaking open. "That little brat. She was here when I checked on her fifteen minutes ago."

Brat? Who calls their child a brat? "You're lying, Naomi. You didn't check on her fifteen minutes ago. Jazz has been at the cottage with me for at least that long. Before that, she was hiding in the wine cellar at the main building."

When I see Cecily cutting across the lawn with our pizza, I point at my phone and motion her inside.

For once, Naomi doesn't argue. She knows she's at fault. "I'll come and get her."

"You can come get her after church tomorrow. Jazz is spending the night with me. Enjoy your date."

I end the call as Cecily emerges from inside the cottage. "What's going on?

I drop the phone into my coat pocket. "Naomi's giving me a hard time."

Cecily rolls her eyes. "Naomi gives everyone a hard time, Stella. I have the upmost respect for you, except when it comes to Naomi. You really need to do something about her. Soon. Before something really bad happens," she says and heads back toward the main building.

Her warning sends a shiver down my spine. She's right. Enough is enough. I need to find a way to take Naomi down. To get Jazz away from her and get Naomi out of their lives for good.

Sucking in a breath of frigid air, I go back inside, locking the door behind me.

Despite the circumstances, I enjoy my evening with my baby sister. When she begs to watch *Frozen 2*, I grant my permission as long as she promises not to give me any lip when I wake her early for church tomorrow.

"You mean this?" She fingers her lip, trying to be funny. "Why would I do that, anyway? I like going to church with you. Can we walk?"

"If it's not too cold," I say, hugging her tiny body close to mine.

Jazz keeps an extra set of everything at my cottage. I love seeing her small clothes hanging next to mine in the closet. After helping her brush her teeth and put on her nightgown, I read to her from the stack of children's books beside the bed. I wait until I'm certain she's asleep before turning out the light and leaving the room.

I brew a cup of lavender tea, and wrapped in a blanket on the sofa, I call Jack. When I tell him why Jazz ran away, he reiterates what Cecily said earlier. "You've given Naomi ample opportunity to prove herself. She won't change, Stella. She's rotten to the core. When are you going to do something about her?"

"As soon as I figure out a plan."

"I know you're worried, baby. Do you want me to come over?"

"Thanks, but no. I already feel guilty enough for being in your bed when I should have been here for Jazz."

"Don't you dare go there, Stella. Our time together this afternoon was the first in weeks."

He's right. I'd promised we'd spend more time together after the party, and today was the first opportunity I found. "I enjoyed our time together, by the way." I nestle under the blanket, thinking back on our few brief hours of bliss.

"Me too. Are you feeling better about us, about our future together?"

Torn is what I feel. Being alone with Jack today reminded me of how good we are together. But Jazz running away is evidence of my unsettled life.

"Can I do it again to be sure?" I ask in a teasing tone.

"Yeah, baby! Are you free tomorrow afternoon?"

"I will make time for you."

"Is Jazz spending the night?"

"Yes. I told Naomi to pick her up after church. Do you think I should buy Jazz a cell phone?"

"Is she old enough to know how to charge it?"

"Kids these days are smarter than we are about electronics. I've been thinking about getting her a basic phone, like a flip phone without all the bells and whistles, to use in case of emergencies."

"After what happened tonight, I think that's an excellent idea."

I haven't officially joined a church in Hope Springs. Most Sundays I attend chapel at Jefferson College, but when Jazz accompanies me, we go to Hope Springs Episcopal, a small stone church on Main Street. Although she's disappointed when I insist on driving to church, Jazz talks through breakfast and in the car about which of her friends will be at Sunday school today.

Grabbing a coffee from the fellowship hall, I sit in on a Bible study with a group of my peers. An hour later, I'm waiting outside of the classroom when Jazz emerges from Sunday school. When I lead her toward the parking lot, she says, "Aren't we going to church?"

"Not today, kiddo." I feel guilty for making her miss. To the best of my knowledge, Naomi never takes her to church. "We need to run an errand before your mommy picks you up."

We drive out to the cell phone store on the outskirts of town. When I tell her why we're here, she drags me over to the display of iPhones. "Can I have a smart phone? Pretty please."

"Not hardly, kiddo. This phone is only for you to use in an emergency. I hope it never happens again, but if you ever feel like running away, call me and I'll come get you. You're not allowed to leave your house alone until you're twenty years old. Understood?"

Jazz gives me an exaggerated eye roll. "Twenty? Give me a break."

I rub my knuckles on top of her head. "You give *me* a break."

The salesclerk shows us our options, and I choose the simplest of the two. She's patient in explaining to Jazz not only how to charge the phone but the importance of keeping it charged.

Thirty minutes later, we're on our way back to the inn. "Let's keep this between us, okay, kiddo? I'm not sure how your mommy will feel about you having a phone."

"I won't tell her. Promise." Jazz stuffs the phone in her coat pocket.

"I don't like doing anything behind your mom's back, but I want you to be able to reach me if you need me."

"K. I get it. Can we go for brunch, now?

"Sure! Why not?" I haven't heard from Naomi. Why race back to the inn on her account? "Where do you want to go?"

Jazz has several favorite restaurants on Main Street, but she surprises me when she says, "Jameson's."

"Jameson's is fine with me, but are you sure you don't want to eat at Lucky's or Town Tavern?"

"Nope. I wanna go to Jameson's. Cecily's making me chocolate chip Mickey Mouse pancakes."

"Oh, I see. You and Cecily schemed this brunch."

Jazz gives me a sheepish grin. "Maybe."

I park my car at the cottage, and we walk over to the veranda. Betsy, the hostess, greets us with a smile and seats us at my favorite table alongside the railing. She hands me a menu and places several sheets of plain paper and a basket of crayons in front of Jazz.

Bruce, one of my favorite waiters, arrives with a carafe of coffee, filling my cup to the brim. He bows to Jazz, and in a formal voice says, "And what can I get for you, miss?"

Jazz giggles. "Orange juice, please."

The sky is clear and the sun bright. The air is chilly, but the space heaters provide plenty of warmth. We beat the church crowd, but within a few minutes, the veranda and the dining room buzz with activity. While Jazz colors, I stare out across the grounds to the mountains, thinking about how much my life has changed in the past six months.

Cecily appears table side with order pad in hand. She winks at Jazz. "Are you still going with the Mickey Mouse pancakes, kid?"

Jazz smiles and gives her a thumbs-up.

Cecily turns her attention to me. "What about you, boss?"

I study the menu. Even though I know the offerings by heart, I have trouble deciding between my favorites. "I'll have the arugula and goat cheese egg-white omelet, please."

She jots down our order. "Anything else?"

"That's all. Looks like a full house for brunch."

"As I told you last night, business is booming. We sold out for both seatings for Thanksgiving Day. I've been working on the menu."

Stella nods at the empty chair beside Jazz. "Can you sit for a minute? I have an idea I want to run by you."

"Sure!" Cecily slides into the seat. "What's up?"

"What do you think about having a mock Thanksgiving dinner sometime before the big day? I'd like to invite the other team members plus some family and a few friends as a way of showing my appreciation for all the hard work and support these past few months."

"In other words, you want to have a Friendsgiving!" Cecily's face is bright. "I love the idea. It would give me a chance to have a trial run on a few new dishes. When were you thinking of having it?"

"What about next Sunday? Since the restaurant is closed on Sunday nights."

"Perfect," Cecily says. "Can we get together one morning this week to go over the menu?"

"Text me some times, and let's get it on the calendar."

"Will do." Cecily rises from the table. "I'm off to fix chocolate chip pancakes."

Jazz looks up from coloring and smiles. As she watches Cecily walk away, she asks, "Am I invited to the Friendsgiving?"

"Of course. Do you want to design the invitation?"

Jazz's golden eyes grow big. "Really?"

"Sure! You've got paper and crayons right here."

While we wait for our food, I show Jazz how to draw a turkey by outlining her hand. She colors the palm area brown and fills in the finger feathers in red, yellow, green, and orange.

"Here." She slides the paper over to me. "Is this good?"

Lifting the paper, I study the turkey. "It's excellent. I'll type in the wording at the top, scan it, and email it out to all our invitees."

Our food arrives, and we discuss the upcoming holidays while we eat. Her face lights up when she talks about dancing the role of Clara in the Christmas performance. "Will you talk to Mommy about letting me be in the performance?"

"I'll do my best, kiddo." Although I have a sneaking suspicion this situation is more about Naomi trying to undermine me than her not wanting Jazz to dance ballet.

After brunch, when we find Naomi waiting for us in front of the cottage, I say to Jazz, "Run inside for a minute while I talk to your mom."

When Jazz starts up the steps to the porch, Naomi grabs onto her coat hood. "Get in the car, Jasmine. I have to be somewhere."

As she stomps off toward the silver sedan, Jazz sticks her tongue out at her mother's back.

I press my lips thin to stifle a smile. I wait for the car door to slam before I say to Naomi, "She has her heart set on dancing in the Christmas performance."

"So that's what this is all about."

"Yes, Naomi. You're well aware of how much ballet means to her. Continuing with her lessons is a condition of our agreement."

Naomi's glare pins me against the side of my cottage. "You can shove our agreement where the sun don't shine, Stella. I haven't had a drink since early July, and I'm attending AA meetings regularly. As of today, my period of probation is officially over. If I don't want my daughter to take ballet, she's not going to take ballet."

Several threats come to mind, but I bite my tongue until it bleeds. I have no evidence to back any of them up. Yet.

With head held high, Naomi rounds the corner of her car to the driver's side. I'll let her think she's won for now. But she will get what's coming to her if it's the last thing I do.

As they drive off, I stare at the ground, kicking at the gravel in the road. I can't bear to see Jazz's disappointed face in the backseat window.

When I turn toward the cottage, I spot Brian and Opal coming up the sidewalk from the lake.

"What was that about?" Brian asks.

I explain about the ballet lessons and Jazz running away and Naomi's new boyfriend. "I did what you asked of me. I've given Naomi the benefit of the doubt one too many times. My staff is losing respect for me because of it. But no more. I will get my sister away from that monster."

Opal pulls me in for a half hug. "We're behind you all the way, Stella."

When I look over at Brian, he nods his head in agreement. "We'll figure it out. Billy put certain measures in place for this very reason."

I watch mother and son walk slowly across the road and climb the steps to the terrace. Inside the cottage, I locate the flash drive my father left me. When I insert the memory stick into my laptop, my father's face fills the screen. I've watched this video countless times since Brian gave it to me back in July. While I never had the pleasure of meeting my father, for six months, I've been living his life, seeing the inn emerge from a state of near ruin through his eyes.

He talks about his relationship with my mother, the love of his life, and his regret in not having the chance to know me. "I've used private investigators to keep tabs on you all these years, Stella. You're the best of Hannah and me. You're intelligent and independent. Your gusto for life and enthusiasm for the hospitality industry makes you the ideal person to run the inn."

And he speaks of his affair with Naomi, and how she tried to trap him into marriage by getting pregnant. When I get to the part where he talks about Jazz, I listen carefully, as though I haven't already committed his words to memory. "As for Jazz, I trust you've fallen in love with her by now. It's easy to do. I have faith that you'll take care of your baby sister in the event something happens to Naomi. Or in case Jazz needs you."

The words I'm looking to hear come straight from his lips. *In case Jazz needs you.* She totally needs me right now. To protect her from her mother.

30

PRESLEY

Presley wakes in a funk on Sunday morning. With the day stretching long ahead of her, she lounges in bed, scrolling through Instagram until she can no longer stand looking at pics of her friends enjoying their weekends with their significant others. She pads in bare feet to the kitchen for coffee and takes her steaming mug to the window. The sun is high in the sky, bright and happy and clashing with her dark mood. Why couldn't it be stormy today?

She turns away from the window to face her empty living room and Big Blue. It's not yet ten o'clock. She'll go insane before lunchtime if she doesn't find a way to occupy her time. She's not in the mood for work or exercise, and while her stomach growls in hunger, she has no appetite for food. Retail therapy has worked for her in the past. Why not go out and buy something pretty, like a painting from a local artist, for her apartment?

She dresses in jeans and a fleece and brushes her hair back into a ponytail. Slipping on her running shoes, she heads down to Main Street, only to discover the art galleries are all closed. Retail therapy comes in all shapes and sizes. She'll go to Target to tackle the long list of household items she's been meaning to buy. But when she sees the crowded parking lot, she keeps on going. She rolls down her window, the brisk air clearing her head, and cranks the volume on Pandora's Southern Rock Radio. With no destination in mind, she drives in a trance with her eyes on the road and her mind on Everett and Lucy. Twenty minutes later, she finds herself in the mountains. She parks at the next overlook and gets out of her car. Standing on a boulder, she stares out at the seemingly endless landscape of mountains surrounding her. The beauty of the scene takes her breath. This is God's creation, and she's merely a small part of his universe. Spreading her arms wide, she tilts her head back. "I'm here, God, waiting for you to show me the way."

She lowers herself to a sitting position, and for the next two hours, she contemplates her life, where she's been and where she's headed. She's on her journey. From now on, she'll take life one day at a time, no matter what happens with Lucy and Everett.

Presley returns to town feeling revived, as though someone pushed her reset button.

She begins the new week by diving into her work, the one thing she can count on to satisfy and fulfill her. But Lucy is determined to make things difficult for her. Lucy leaves when Presley enters a room, ignores her calls, and responds to her texts and emails with curt messages. Presley understands if Lucy no longer wants to be friends, but her hostility toward Presley makes for an unhealthy work environment for the other team members. She needs to clear the air with Lucy before Stella senses the tension between them.

Midafternoon on Wednesday, Presley makes the trip to the wine cellar to confront Lucy. When the elevator doors open, Lucy is standing before her, waiting to get on. As Presley exits the elevator cart, Lucy backs herself into the cellar. Lucy, who is normally meticulously groomed, is not wearing any makeup, which underscores the inky shadows under her eyes on her pale face.

Glancing around, Presley is relieved to see they're alone. "We need to talk."

Lucy turns her back on Presley and enters the wine shop, going behind the checkout counter to the iPad point of sale terminal.

Presley approaches the counter. "Have you spoken to Rita yet?"

"I've spoken to her. Regardless of what Rita says, the situation is too coincidental for me to believe."

"Coincidental?" Presley scoffs. "Rita confronted your parents about your adoption. Your parents gave her my parents' contact information. Rita wrote to my mother. And my mother left the return address from the envelope in my adoption file for me to decide whether to pursue a relationship with you. The situation is anything but coincidental."

"What about the part where you and I became friends? Are you saying that wasn't planned?"

Presley raises a finger. "*That* was coincidental. I befriended you because I enjoy your company. I had no idea of your connection to Rita."

"At lunch that day, when I was confiding in you about being date-raped and the subsequent pregnancy and adoption, did it ever occur to you that you might be my child?"

"Never. I admit the similarities in our situations hit home, but the idea that you might be my birth mother never crossed my mind. Rita is the one who lives at the return address on the envelope. I thought she was my birth mother. Since I didn't know the two of you were sisters, I had no reason to suspect I was your child." Presley's throat swells, and she chokes out,

"Having a rapist for a father isn't something a girl dreams of when searching for her biological father."

Lucy's eyes cloud over, and she braces herself against the counter. She's apparently never considered how any of this might affect Presley. Presley has seen a different side of Lucy these past few days. A side she doesn't particularly care for.

Presley backs away from the counter. "I understand if you no longer want to be friends, but we have to work together. We both love our jobs. There's no reason one of us should have to quit because of this."

Lucy stares at Presley, her eyes glazed and expression blank.

"Just think about it, Lucy. We'll talk more later."

When Presley turns to leave, Lucy says to her back, "You look like them, you know?"

"Them who?" Presley asks still facing the door.

"My mother and son. I realize there's a very good chance you're my child. But I'm afraid. I've wanted this for so long. It seems too good to be true."

Presley doesn't know what to say, and she's afraid she'll burst into tears if she tries to speak. She nods, her eyes glued to the basement floor as she moves from the shop to the elevator. She has no idea where they go from here. But at least this is a start.

When she emerges onto the main floor, Stella calls her into her office. "You're just the person I want to see. Close the door. Have a seat."

As Presley takes a seat in the chair in front of the mahogany desk, she notices Stella's grave expression. "What's up? Have I done something wrong?"

Stella's lips curve into a soft smile. "Not at all. I'm beyond thrilled with your performance. I have a delicate matter I need to discuss with you that concerns Naomi. I need your word that none of this will leave this office." She taps her desk.

Presley sits up straighter. "You can trust me, Stella."

"I know that. But thanks for saying it, anyway." Stella folds her hands on her desk. "How much do you know about my relationship with Naomi?"

"That Jazz is your half sister, and that your shared father's family were the original owners of the inn. Does this have something to do with Jazz running away on Saturday night?"

"That was the icing on the cake. Billy, my father, brought me to Hope Springs not only to run the inn but also to be near Jazz. He was worried about his youngest daughter's safety. And he had good reason. Naomi is emotionally unstable. I need to know if Naomi has done anything to cause you concern or interfere in your job in any way."

Presley nods. "During my first week here. She claims I misquoted the room discount rate to one of my brides. I contacted the bride to confirm that I'd given her correct discount rate, which I had. There's no way to prove Naomi was lying. In the grand scheme of things, it was not that big of a deal."

Stella looks up from the legal pad where she's been frantically taking notes. "Except that a lot of small deals are adding up to a very big deal. Every staff member I've spoken to has a similar story. Unfortunately, this big deal still isn't enough to fire her. I'm gathering evidence in the event I need it down the road."

"I'll be honest with you, Stella. When I first came here, before I understood your relationship with Jazz, I couldn't figure out why you'd hired such an unpleasant woman to be your guest services manager. Imagine what our guests must think of her."

"To Naomi's credit, she's usually polite and accommodating to the guests," Stella says. "I would never have kept her on this long otherwise."

"Have you spoken to Everett about Naomi? Her allegations against him were the most serious."

"I would, if I knew how to get in touch with him." Stella positions her ink pen over paper, prepared to write. "By any chance, do you have his number?"

"Sorry. No. But if I hear from him, I'll have him get in touch with you."

"Please do." Stella tosses the pen on the desk and relaxes back in her chair. "On a more cheerful note, Cecily and I are organizing a Friendsgiving for Sunday night. I plan to email the invitation this afternoon. I'm counting on you to come. Bring a date if you like."

Presley's ego deflates. She's the event planner. Why didn't she know about this Friendsgiving? "That sounds like fun," she says in a flat tone. "What can I do to help?"

Stella shakes her head. "Not a thing. I want you to relax and enjoy yourself. The party is a way to show my appreciation to the team members for their hard work these past few months. And to say thank you in advance for the extra long hours you'll be putting in over the holidays."

"Speaking of which." Presley removes her iPad from her bag. "If you have a minute, I'd like to go over my proposed calendar of events for the holidays."

"A diversion is just what I need." Stella checks her watch for the time. "I don't have to be anywhere for another hour."

For the next thirty minutes, they discuss tree lightings and Santa brunches and a dinner dance for the locals in mid-December. When Presley leave Stella's office at almost four o'clock, she decides to finish out her workday from her apartment.

She's sitting at her desk twenty minutes later when her phone rings with a call from an Atlanta area code. Expecting one of her brides, she answers in a cheerful tone.

"Presley, it's Everett." The sound of his voice warms her body, but her blood quickly runs cold.

"What do you want?"

"To explain. I have a lot of explaining to do, actually. Starting with why I left town so suddenly. My father gave my mother the beating of her life, right before he had a massive stroke and died."

She knows so little about his background, and he's told so many lies she's expecting another one, but you can't make up this kind of family dysfunction. "I'm sorry. How's your mother?"

He lets out a sigh. "Recovering, but slowly. I'm an only child. She really needs me right now."

Presley's sympathy for him is short-lived. His mother is the one she feels sorry for. Not Everett. "Maybe it wouldn't have happened if you'd been *there* instead of hiding out *here* from your pregnant girlfriend."

"Carla isn't my girlfriend, Presley. I was upfront with her from the beginning. She knew I wasn't interested in a long-term relationship, yet she quit taking her birth control without telling me. She intentionally got pregnant to trap me into marriage. When Carla told me about the baby, I freaked out and left town. I've been so confused these past months. I'm not the type to shy away from my responsibilities. My mom helped me see why I was running scared. I'm afraid of being a father, scared to death I'll turn out to be an abusive alcoholic like my old man."

"I would be, too, in your shoes." Presley means it as a dig, and he apparently takes it that way, as evidenced by the silence filling the line. She doesn't need his kind of problems. Been there. Done that.

She leaves her desk and moves to the sofa. "Why did you call, Everett? What do you want?"

"To clear my name. I'm not a thief. I never spent a dime of Louie's three thousand dollars. And Naomi's lying about me stealing from the inn. I was checking my emails the day she caught me using her computer."

Presley believes him. Her people reader wasn't wrong about

him. Deep down, he's a good guy who got caught in a difficult situation.

"Stella's the one who needs to hear this. You should call her. But I'll warn you, she's got a lot going on right now with Jazz."

"Is Jazz okay?" His genuine tone is proof of how much he truly cares about the kid. *And he's worried he won't make a good father.*

"Jazz ran away from home on Saturday night. I found her hiding in the wine cellar at the inn. Stella hinted that her running away had something to do with Naomi."

"Poor Jazz. She's an exceptional kid. She deserves better than Naomi."

"She deserves a father. Do you think maybe the reason you're so worried about being a father is not because you're afraid you'll be a bad father but because you so desperately want to be a good one?"

Once again, silence fills the line, but Presley knows he's still there by the sound of his heavy breathing.

"Are you going to marry her, Everett?"

"Who? Carla? Heck no! My relationship with Carla is over. You're the one I want, Presley. I miss you."

And I miss you so much, she thinks. There's a chance they can work it out, but she's not sure she wants to. So much has happened and she has so many doubts. "Why did you call, Everett?"

"I wanted to hear your voice."

Gripping the phone, she asks in a soft voice, "Are you coming back to Hope Springs?"

"I'm moving to Nashville, Presley. I signed a contract with Wade Newman at Big Country Records."

Pressure builds in Presley's chest, and she finds it difficult to breathe. She knows Wade Newman. Wade was her mother's biggest adversary, but he was also Renee's friend. Wade only signs the very best. Presley is not surprised, because Everett has the potential to be one of the best. This is just one more thing Everett kept from her. One more secret. She's not interested in having a long-distance relationship with a rising country music star she can't trust.

"Have a nice life, *Rhett*," she says before hanging up on him.

31

EVERETT

E verett lies in bed for hours, staring at the ceiling and thinking about Presley. While there were awkward moments during their conversation, he was making progress with her until he made the mistake of telling her about Nashville. Why did that make her so angry? She knows music is his passion. Is it because he never told her about Wade? Does she perceive that as another lie?

She asked him twice why he called. Once, he told her to clear his name. The second time, because he wanted to hear her voice. Both true. What *was* his ulterior motive in calling her? What exactly does he want from Presley? A long-distance relationship? The closest airport to Hope Springs is Roanoke, and none of the airlines offer nonstop flights from Roanoke to Nashville. The seven-hour drive from Nashville to Hope Springs is faster than flying but not something anyone wants to do every weekend.

His mom's words ring out in his head. *If you think she may be the one, don't let Presley get away. You've never known real happiness, and I want that for you.* How does one choose between an amazing woman like Presley and a career as a country music star?

Presley was spot-on about one thing. The reason he's so worried about being a father is not because he's afraid he'll be a bad father but because he so desperately wants to be a good one. He rolls over to a sitting position. After all these months of uncertainty, he understands exactly what he needs to do. Grabbing his phone off the bedside table, he sends Carla a text asking if he can see her.

She responds right away. *Meet me at my apartment in thirty minutes.*

He gives her text a thumbs-up. In rush-hour traffic, he has just enough time to get there.

When he emerges from his room, he hears his mom's sewing machine, but he doesn't tell her he's leaving or where he's going.

When he arrives, Carla, still dressed in blue scrubs from work, is leaning against the hood of her Subaru Outback. She earns good money working in the neonatal intensive care unit at Emory Hospital. She'll be able to offer the baby a modest living, even without his support. When she sees him, she lowers her head and stares at the ground.

He parks in the space beside her and turns off the engine. He allows his gaze to linger over her swollen belly. His baby is growing in there. His son or daughter. Will he have a passion for music like Everett? Will she have her mother's brains and independent determination? Will he love his mother as much as Everett loves his?

Getting out from behind the wheel, he goes around to the passenger side and stands in front of Carla. He opens his mouth to speak, but before he can say anything, she holds up a finger to silence him.

"Me first. I owe you an apology, Rhett. What I did was wrong on so many levels. I let my desperation to have a baby cloud my judgment. You don't owe me or the baby anything."

"And I'm sorry for going MIA. You took me by surprise. And I needed some time to think. But, regardless of how it came about, that's my kid in there." He dips his head at her baby bump. "I don't know what the future holds for me. I may have a successful music career, or I may fall on my face. Financially, I'll do what I can. But I want to be a part of his or her life. You and I were friends long before we started sleeping together. Based on that friendship, we can offer our child a stable life."

"Seriously? Do you mean it?" Tears spill over her lids and slide down her cheeks.

"Yes, I mean it. I'm sorry it took me so long. I had some growing up to do." When he pulls her in for a hug, she breaks down in sobs.

"Shush!" he says into her hair. "Everything's gonna work out."

"I've been so scared. I don't regret getting pregnant. I'm thrilled about the baby. But I feel so alone."

"You're not alone anymore."

When she finally stops crying, she invites him inside for a cup of tea. They talk about the amazing care she's getting at Emory, her due date of March twenty-seven, and her recent ultrasound, which revealed a healthy fetus.

Carla blushes. "Call me old-fashioned, but I decided not to find out the sex."

"Good! I prefer to be surprised." When she cocks an eyebrow at him, he adds, "I'll do everything in my power to be here for the birth."

They talk for another hour, and when he leaves her apartment, even though he's scared out of his mind that he'll let his kid down, he's comforted in knowing he's doing the honorable thing. At home, he finds his mom standing in the middle of the kitchen staring into an open cupboard.

"What're you doing?" he asks, leaning over a pot on the stove to sample her marinara sauce.

"Trying to decide what to take with me to Nashville," she says with mischief in her smile.

He places the lid back on the pot. "Does that mean . . ."

"Yes! I'm moving to Tennessee with you! If you'll still have me."

"You bet I'll still have you." He wraps his arms around her in a hug. When he squeezes too tight, she grimaces, but she doesn't complain.

"I have one condition," Mary says when he sets her loose. "I insist on making a detour through Hope Springs. I won't be able to sleep until you've cleared your name."

He was planning to call Stella in the morning but speaking to her face-to-face is even better. And he needs to see Presley. He's not yet ready to give up on their relationship.

"Fine by me." Everett turns his attention to the collection of chipped and broken dishes in the cupboard. "Why would you take any of this junk?"

She slams the cabinet doors. "What about these?" she asks, opening the cupboard beside it that houses her cookware.

"Jeez, Mom. Those pots were cheap when you got them as a wedding gift. I'd be embarrassed to give them to Goodwill."

"But what will we cook with when we get to Nashville?"

"It'll cost less to buy new stuff than to pay for a truck to move all this." He gestures at the pots and pans. "Besides, part of the adventure is starting anew, with no baggage from our past."

This from the man who just committed to a lifetime of supporting a child he never planned on having.

Mary closes the cupboard doors. "In that case, I'll take my

Keurig, my sewing machine, and my wardrobe. When are we leaving?"

Everett's been ready to leave Atlanta since he got here ten days ago. "I see no reason to hang around. My old high school buddy, Marty, does odd jobs for a living. I can pay him to haul everything off, either to Goodwill or to the dump. We can box everything up tomorrow and leave first thing on Friday morning. We'll spend the weekend in Hope Springs. I'll book a room for you at the inn."

"That'll cost a fortune," Mary says. "Can't I stay with you at your apartment?"

Everett laughs. "Not unless you want to share my air mattress with me. We can afford to live a little, Mom."

"As long as you promise not to go overboard." Her hands on his shoulders, she walks him over to the table. "Now, sit down and I'll get our dinner."

They make plans while they eat. Everett hasn't seen his mom this excited and animated since . . . since never. While she's doing the dishes, he accesses the inn's website on his phone and reserves one of the smaller, less expensive rooms. For a woman who's never stayed at a luxury resort, she'll feel like a queen in a royal palace.

They stay up late, making plans for the future, and first thing on Thursday morning, he goes to a nearby grocery store to collect empty boxes. They work tirelessly throughout the day, and by dinnertime, their meager belongings are packed into boxes. The few they'll take with them are stacked by the front door. The rest are neatly organized in the living room for Marty to distribute to the dump and Goodwill next week.

On their last night in the only house Everett has ever thought of as home, they order pizza and eat on trays in the living room. Mary has been quiet most of the day, and he senses she's reminiscing about the past.

"What're we gonna do about that?" she asks, her eyes on her husband's urn.

"Let Marty take it to the dump?" Everett suggests, only half joking.

"You don't mean that, Rhett." Based on her serious tone, his mother will not be satisfied until they properly dispose of his dad's ashes.

"Did you have something in mind to do with his remains?" he asks, peeling a pepperoni off his slice of pizza and popping it in his mouth.

She shakes her head. "Not really. He didn't really have a special place."

Everett can think of one—the Hotlanta Lounge, a seedy neighborhood bar where his dad hung out before his health failed. "Why don't we take the urn with us? There are many beautiful spots in the mountains."

"That would be perfect," she says without hesitation.

"That's what you had in mind all along, isn't it? Your real reason for wanting to detour through Hope Springs."

His mom gets up and takes her plate to the kitchen. When she returns, she says, "Is it so wrong of me to want to give my husband of thirty-four years a proper burial?"

"Not at all, Mom." Everett knows his mom hasn't loved his father in years. The good Christian woman in her wants to make certain his dad's spirit is free from the alcoholic life that imprisoned him on Earth.

Mary, who hasn't been outside the city limits of Atlanta in years, insists they make multiple detours and pit stops on their way to Hope Springs. In addition to numerous stops at quaint-looking gift shops, they have lunch at the Biltmore in Asheville and play the slot machines in the casino at the Greenbrier in West Virginia.

His mom grows quiet after leaving the Greenbrier, and they're almost at Hope Springs when she speaks again. "I've been thinking a lot about my family since I came out of the coma. I follow my brothers on social media, and I know my parents are still alive. After I start back to work and save enough money, I'm thinking of making a trip to Texas to see them. Would you be willing to go with me?"

Everett hesitates before answering. "As much as I want to meet your family, I think you should go alone this first time."

She sighs. "You're probably right. We have a lot to talk about that doesn't concern you. Maybe I'll test the waters with my brothers, to see if my parents would be receptive to a reunion."

"That's a good idea. But do it now, before you start back to work. I'll pay for your plane ticket."

Mary shakes her head. "I can't ask you to do that. You've already done so much for me."

"You're not asking. I'm telling you, I'm buying you a plane ticket."

She covers her mouth with her hand, her eyes wide and shining. "I love you, son."

"And I love you, Mom."

Even though they left Atlanta early this morning, they don't arrive in Hope Springs until dinnertime. They stop at Town Tavern for dinner before going to the inn. The place is hopping with the usual Friday night crowd. Girls stare at Everett as he and Mary make their way through the crowd waiting for tables on the sidewalk. Is it possible they recognize him from the balcony? He smiles to himself. Is this what his future as a country music star holds?

Bar seating is first come, first served, and two stools open up as they enter the restaurant. Everett introduce his mom to Pete, and they order hamburgers without looking at the menu. They're both exhausted, and even though she doesn't admit it, he can tell Mary is overwhelmed by the noisy tavern.

As they're leaving the restaurant, he pauses to look up at Presley's darkened apartment. Is she working a party at the inn? Or is she out on a date with a new guy?

At the inn, Everett doesn't recognize the guest services agent who checks them in, and he's grateful not to run into any of the staff on the way up to his Mom's second-floor room.

Mary gasps at the decor. "This is so pretty, honey. Are you sure we can afford this?"

He smiles at her. "Yes, Mom. We can afford it. Are you sure you'll be okay here alone? I can have them bring up a rollaway."

She eyes the fluffy bed longingly, and Everett knows she's looking forward to spending the night here alone. "I'll be fine, sweetheart."

"Okay then," he says, kissing her goodbye. He has his own agenda and sleep is not part of it. But his heart sinks at the sight of Presley's still-darkened windows when he approaches his apartment building. Just as well. He should rest up before talking to her.

At nine the next morning, he joins his mom on the veranda for breakfast. Their mission for the day is to find a final resting place for his dad. But first, he needs to speak with Stella. And he's glad to run into her as they're leaving Jameson's after breakfast.

"Everett, this is a surprise. I didn't know you were back in town."

"Just passing through, actually." Stella gives him a quizzical look that he ignores. "Stella, this is my mom, Mary Baldwin."

Stella extends her hand and smiles softly at Mary. "Very nice to meet you."

"Do you have a few minutes?" he asks Stella. "I really need to talk to you."

"Of course. I'm heading to my office now."

"Let me get Mom settled in the lounge, and I'll be there in a second."

"Take your time," Stella says to him, and to Mary, "I hope I see you again during your stay."

Everett leads his mom to an empty chair by the window. "Are you sure you don't mind waiting here for me?"

"Not at all, son. Clearing your name is the reason we came. I'll have a good time watching the people," she says, making herself comfortable.

He kisses the top of her head. "I shouldn't be long."

But he ends up talking to Stella for over an hour. She's understanding about Carla, sympathetic about his family situation, and seemingly thrilled about his music career. He can tell she believes him about Louie's money, and when he assures her he didn't steal from the inn, she says, "I never really thought you did."

"I hope you nailed Naomi for the missing money."

Her expression darkens, as though the situation is weighing heavily on her. "Not yet, but I'm working on it." She opens her top drawer and slides an envelope across her desk. "This is your last paycheck. I didn't know where to send it."

"Thank you." Taking the envelope, he stands to leave.

Stella walks him to the door. "I'm hosting a Friendsgiving on Sunday night. I'd love for you and Mary to come. We can give you a proper send-off."

"We hadn't planned to stay. But I'll talk to Mom and let you know."

Truth be told, he wants to talk to Presley first. Whether he stays for the party or leaves for Nashville on Sunday morning as planned is up to her.

32

STELLA

I'd interpreted Naomi's accusation against Everett as yet another one of her empty threats. Is it possible she stole money from the inn? Is there any money even missing? Our accounting department hasn't notified me of any discrepancies in our accounts. Why would Naomi need to steal when my father provided for her in his will? Maybe it's not about the money. Maybe it's about the thrill. Maybe she's trying to satisfy some sick and twisted deep-seated yearning. Or maybe she wants me to crash and burn so she can take over the inn.

Lifting the phone receiver, I punch in Brian's number. After exchanging pleasantries, I tell him why I'm calling. "I have a hunch Naomi is embezzling funds from the reservations department. But I don't understand why she would need money when she has her salary plus whatever allowance she receives from Billy's estate."

"That money is intended primarily for Jazz's benefit," Brian explains. "Naomi gets a modest monthly stipend, and she's required by the terms of the trust to submit an account of her expenditures."

"So, if she wants to buy a designer handbag, she must use her own money?"

"Exactly. I haven't been shopping for women's accessories lately, but I imagine some designer bags are costly."

I fall back in my chair. "In that case, she may very well be robbing the till."

"If your hunch proves correct, you have grounds to fire her. Then what?"

Twirling in my chair, I look out the window across the front lawn. "Then I risk her leaving town with my baby sister. You've told me before that Naomi has no other family. Are you certain about that?"

"Positive. I investigated her thoroughly. Naomi is an only child, and her parents and grandparents are all deceased."

"She has no one to turn to, and unless she's been accumulating stolen cash under her mattress, she has limited funds to get far if she decides to run."

In a warning tone, Brian says, "Tread carefully, Stella. You never know what trick Naomi might have up her sleeve. I'm here for you if you need me."

"Thanks, Brian." Feeling the onset of a headache, I massage my temples. "I hope you got the invitation for the Friendsgiving tomorrow night."

"I did," he says. "And I responded to Cecily. Opal and I will both be there. We're looking forward to it."

"Me too. I'll see you then."

I press the button to disconnect the call, and looking up Diana's cell number on my Rolodex, I quickly tap it out on the phone's keypad. She answers on the first ring. "Good morning, Diana. I'm sorry to bother you on a Saturday, but I have an urgent matter to discuss with you."

"Sure! I'm actually in my office, catching up on some work. What's up?"

I tell my accountant about my suspicions.

"I haven't noticed any inconsistencies in the accounts," she says. "But I may have missed something. Can I do a little digging and get back to you?"

"Please. Call me on my cell. I'll be around the farm, although I might not be in my office."

I drop the phone in its cradle. If Diana unearths proof that Naomi's been stealing from the inn, I will not hesitate to fire her. I've been working my butt off to turn this place around, and she's been undermining me at every turn. Naomi might have something up her sleeve, but I'm fairly confident it doesn't involve leaving Hope Springs.

The wall's closing in on me, I jump to my feet, and stuffing my cell phone in my back pocket, I leave my office. The lounge is crawling with people. I recognize some locals but most, I presume, are guests. There's a long line outside Jameson's, waiting for a table for lunch, and a crowd in Billy's Bar watching college football.

I take the elevator to the basement and sit in on a wine tasting Presley has organized for a group of guests. Lucy does a commendable job of explaining how to taste and what to look for in terms of flavors and aromas in the sampled wines. Do I detect tension between Lucy and Presley? They're usually an entertaining pair for these groups. Both are uncharacteristically quiet, although I catch them sneaking glances at each other. What is up with them? I thought they were friends.

When the tasting ends, after mingling with the guests for a minute, I leave the main building and wander down to the maintenance shed where Katherine is unloading wreaths and trees from the back of our landscape trailer.

"I love that smell," I say, inhaling a deep breath of Christmas. "Do you need some help?"

Katherine hauls a large tree out of the trailer and holds it upright. She's strong for a slight woman. "I won't say no to an extra pair of hands."

We spend the next hour setting the trees in buckets of water and giving the wreaths a good soaking. When we finish, we stand back to admire the trees leaning against the building.

"You did a great job, Katherine. The trees are so fat and full and healthy. They should last through New Year's."

She gives me a playful nudge with her elbow. "If we work hard, Presley and I could have the inn decorated in time for Thanksgiving."

"No way!" I say with a laugh. "I've told you, Thanksgiving deserves its day of glory. Besides, we have a lot of locals booked at Jameson's for Thanksgiving dinner. If we spoil it for them, they won't come back the following week for our big lighting ceremony."

Katherine considers this. "You're right. I didn't think of that." She gives a little shrug. "Just as well. I've ordered the most amazing autumn flowers, and I have some interesting concepts for the Thanksgiving arrangements."

"I'm sure they'll be beautiful."

Katherine opens the door to her truck. "I guess my work here is done for the day."

"Enjoy the rest of your weekend. I'll see you tomorrow at the Friendsgiving. I hope you're bringing Dean with you."

She snickers. "Dean is thrilled. He could eat Thanksgiving food every day of the year."

After Katherine leaves, I consider going back to the inn but decide to walk through the spa building instead. Having no workmen or architects around gives me a chance to scrutinize the progress, and I make long lists on the Notes app on my cell phone. Although I've managed to kill the better part of the afternoon, I've yet to receive word from Diana. At almost five o'clock,

I'm walking back up the hill toward the inn when she finally calls.

"I'm sorry, Stella. I don't know how I missed it. The discrepancies are there, plain as day. Naomi was crafty about her thievery. She stole small amounts that add up to a whopping sum. Over the past six weeks she's pillaged over ten thousand dollars from the reservations department. This is all on me. I totally understand if you fire me."

Diana is not the one I aim to fire. I sit down on a nearby park bench. "Don't be so hard on yourself, Diana. This is a lesson learned for both of us. Going forward, we need to be more careful. Is there a way to get documentation of the theft?"

"The pages are coming off the printer now. It will take some time, though. I can have the file ready for you by tomorrow morning."

"That would be great," I say. "I wouldn't ask you to put in such long hours on the weekend if it wasn't important."

"I'm happy to help in anyway."

After ending the call, instead of continuing up to the main building, I go to the cottage, get in my Jeep, and speed down the front driveway. My phone rings with a local number I don't recognize, and I ignore it. Naomi's car isn't in her driveway, but I pound on her front door anyway. No one answers. Walking around to the garage door, I'm surprised to find it unlocked. I tiptoe into the house, passing through the kitchen to the living room where I find the television on, tuned into Nickelodeon, and a half-eaten bowl of popcorn and empty juice box on the coffee table. *Strange.* Even Naomi is responsible enough to turn the TV off.

I leave the door unlocked and get back in the Jeep. I want to talk to Jack before I make my next move, and I'm almost at his house when my phone rings again from the same unknown number. I answer with a tentative hello, and a female voice asks to speak with Stella Boor. In the background, I hear what sounds like a wild animal howling.

"Speaking. Who's calling, please?"

"Detective Kathy Sinclair with the Hope Springs Police Department. I have your sister with me at the station."

My heart skips a beat. My sister is only six. She can't be in trouble. Is that Jazz I hear crying in the background? "What's wrong, Detective? Is Jazz okay?"

"She's fine, although quite upset as you can probably hear. I was on my way home from the station a while ago when I found her wandering around on a street about five blocks from her house. She claims she got lost on her way to find you at Hope Springs Farm. She's adamant we call you instead of her mother. I got your cell number from the operator at the inn. Can you come to the station?"

"I'm on Main Street now. I'll be there in five minutes." When we hang up, I place another call to Brian, explaining what little I know about the situation. He promises to meet me at the station. Before we hang up, I ask him to call Jack for me.

At the police station, a rookie officer shows me to a small room with a table and chairs and no windows. When Jazz sees me, she stands abruptly, kicking her chair out of the way, and rushes into my outstretched arms. "Mommy found my phone and took it from me. I wasn't running away, Stella. I promise. You told me not to. I was trying to get to you. But I got lost."

"Shh! It's okay, Jazzy. I'm here now, and I'm not going anywhere." Over the top of Jazz's head, I study the woman more closely. She's gorgeous with golden brown skin and high cheekbones, and her warm smile speaks to how much she cares about her job. "Do we know where her mother is, Detective?"

"Jazz claims her mother went out with her new boyfriend. As best I can tell, she's been gone for some time."

"Are you saying Naomi left Jazz home alone?"

The detective gives me a solemn nod. "It appears so."

"I've just come from their house. That explains why the door was unlocked and the television left on." My blood reaches the boiling point, and I pace in circles around the room as I jiggle Jazz to calm her. "This is the final straw, Detective. Naomi is not a fit mother. I'm ready to take whatever measures necessary to have this child removed from that home. I assume that means getting social services involved. Will you make that call?"

"I'm one step ahead of you. The agent is already on the way. She should be here momentarily."

The door bangs open and in files Jack, Brian, and a stern-looking older woman I assume is with the Virginia Department of Social Services. Jack hurries to my side, giving me a half hug and rubbing Jazz's back. I'm relieved when Brian takes charge in discussing the situation with Cynthia Greene, the social services agent.

I'm shocked at how easy the process goes. Cynthia, who is outraged to hear that Naomi left Jazz at home alone, immediately grants me temporary custody of my sister. "The case will go to juvenile court early next week," she explains. "We'll be in touch with you regarding those details. Sometime tomorrow, we'll arrange for you to get the child's clothes and whatever other belongings she might need from the home."

"Who will notify Naomi of this development?" I ask. "And what if she tries to take her away from me?"

Detective Sinclair says, "I will personally wait at Naomi's house until she returns tonight. Quite frankly, I'm curious what time that will be. I'll let you know as soon as we've spoken. If she tries to take Jazz from you, you should call the police immediately."

"I'll be honest with you, Miss Boor," Cynthia says. "These situations can sometimes get ugly. Down the line, you may need to request a protection order."

I bring myself to my full height, shifting Jazz to my opposite hip. "I understand. And I'm . . ."—I glance up at Jack who winks at me—"*we're* prepared to do whatever it takes to get permanent custody."

At that instant, every remaining concern I have about marrying Jack dissipates. My doubts were never about him. I love Jack with my whole heart. He loves me, and he loves Jazz. We are a family. We will grow old together raising our children in the manor house. I will do everything in my power to make a success of the inn. But if the worst happens, with Jack's support, I'll figure out a new path for my career.

After the paperwork is completed, I thank the detective again and say goodnight to the social services agent. Brian walks us to the parking lot. "Billy knew this day would come. No regrets, Stella. You're doing the right thing."

"I should've done it a long time ago." I strap Jazz into her car seat and close the back door. "Diana has documented evidence that Naomi's been embezzling money from the reservations department. To the tune of ten thousand dollars. Needless to say, she's no longer employed at the inn."

Brian rakes his fingers through salt-and-pepper hair. "Naomi won't take any of this lying down. We need to prepare ourselves for a fight."

"Bring it on. She's not getting Jazz back no matter what." I thank Brian for his help and kiss his cheek in parting.

Jack follows me to the cottage, and we settle Jazz on the sofa between us. She refuses to eat dinner or talk about anything that happened today. She even rejects my offer to turn on Sponge-Bob. She only wants to be held, and we are happy to oblige. It's not long before her eyelids flutter, and she drifts off to sleep.

I smile up at my fiancé. "I'm sorry, Jack. This will put a crimp in our sex life."

"That's the least of my concerns at the moment. Not that I won't miss seeing your beautiful naked body in my bed." When he leans over to kiss my lips, he squishes Jazz, making her squirm. She stretches out, pushing us farther apart.

I offer him an apologetic smile.

"Welcome to our new normal," he says. "I'm worried about the two of you living in this tiny cottage and having to share a bed. Don't you want to move into my house? I have enough bedrooms for the three of us to each have our own."

"Thanks for the offer, but Jazz feels safe here, and we're used to sharing a bed. Although we could fit a cot in the bedroom. Maybe I'll have housekeeping bring one over tomorrow."

"I'm hoping to have the new house finished by Christmas. Maybe by then, she'll be ready."

"Christmas is weeks away. A lot can happen between now and then. Let's take things one step at a time. First, we need to get through the hearing on Monday." I kiss my fingertips and touch them to his cheek. "I love you. Please be patient a bit longer. I promise we'll have our happily ever after."

"I'll wait as long as it takes."

We stare at each other across the sleeping child. We don't speak. Words aren't necessary to express the love we feel for each other and for Jazz.

Finally, he breaks the silence, "Wanna watch a movie?"

"Sure! I won't be able to sleep until I hear from Detective Sinclair anyway."

"You pick the movie while I put this kiddo in the bed." Jack lifts Jazz off the sofa and carries her in his arms to the adjacent bedroom.

I find a station playing reruns of Meg Ryan movies. We watch *When Harry Met Sally* followed by *You've Got Mail*. We're halfway through *Sleepless in Seattle* when we hear from Detective Sinclair.

"Naomi just arrived home, if you can believe that. I found Jazz at four fifteen this afternoon. To my best estimate, she'd been alone since around two o'clock. It is now nearly eleven. Which means that child would've been alone for nearly nine hours."

Tears prick my eyelids. "Do you know if Naomi has been drinking?"

"I assume so. She arrived home in an Uber. Why?"

"With all the confusion at the station, I failed to mention she's a recovering alcoholic." While I hate that Naomi's drinking again, it makes my case stronger.

"I'm adding that to my report now. I'll make certain social services has my report first thing in the morning. I don't think you'll have any trouble from Naomi tonight. But call nine-one-one immediately if you do."

"You've gone above and beyond on this case, Detective. Thank you."

Within minutes of me hanging up with Sinclair, I receive a text from Naomi: *You won't get away with this, Stella.*

I already have. And BTW, I have documented proof that you stole over ten thousand dollars from the inn. You're fired.

33

PRESLEY

Presley is stretched out on Big Blue, reading a romance novel and pretending she's not alone on a Saturday night, when the sound of Everett's distinct voice wafts through the closed window from the balcony. He sings "Show Me the Way" followed by "Go Home, Mary." It breaks Presley's heart to think about how much his family has suffered. Alcoholism and abuse.

Presley thinks back to earlier in the day when she spotted Everett and his mother in the lobby at the inn. She spied on mother and son from inside Billy's Bar. The abuse was evident in Mary's broken arm, missing tooth, and yellowing bruises around her eyes. How devastating to have the man you promised to love, honor, and cherish cause you such pain. Why did Mary stay with Everett's father? Because she loved him? Or were they so poor she couldn't afford to leave him?

Presley had softened toward Everett when she saw the way he doted on his mother. He helped Mary into a chair by the window and knelt down beside her when he spoke to her. His lips lingered in her hair when he kissed the top of her head in parting. *A man will treat his woman the way he treats his mother.* Everett may have trouble telling the truth, but he's a gentle soul.

He would never intentionally hurt someone he cares about. If he keeps his drinking under control. But that is a big *if*, a chance Presley's not willing to risk. She does not want to end up like Mary.

His next song is one Presley has never heard before about a red-headed woman named after the King of Rock and Roll. She leaves the sofa for the window. Sliding the bottom sash upward, she sits on the sill with her slippered feet on the balcony. The lyrics in his song speak of his love for Presley and how her presence in his life brightens his world.

Everett's music is showing *her* the way. Right back to him.

When the song ends, the crowd on the sidewalk at Town Tavern goes wild. Presley waits for the applause to die down. "You wrote a song about me."

"I did. Do you like it? I've been working on it for a while."

"I love it. Does it have a title?"

"I'm not sure yet. I'm thinking of calling it something simple —like "Presley."

"I'm flattered, Everett. I hope you don't mind if I continue to call you Everett. That's who you are to me."

"You can call me whatever you like. Everett is my given name. So, are you flattered enough to forgive me?"

She smiles, but he can't see her in the dark. "No way I'm making it that easy for you."

Everett's groupies on the street chant for more.

Presley laughs. "Get used to it. This is your future. You can't disappoint your fans."

"Wanna come sit with me while I sing?"

"I'm fine where I am."

He performs for over an hour until the crowd on the street diminishes.

Everett places his guitar inside his apartment, but he doesn't leave his window. "So, you're not going to forgive me?"

Her people reader was right about him all along. He lost his way for a while. His circumstances led him to make some bad decisions. But his core beliefs are rock solid. "I'm not one to hold a grudge, Everett. I forgive you for the lies, although it hurts that you didn't have enough faith in me to tell me the truth."

"I know, and I'm sorry. I'd like to make it up to you if you'll give me another chance. Will you give *us* another chance, Presley?"

"What's the point? You're moving to Nashville to become a country movie star."

He lets out an audible sigh. "Can I at least come over to your window, so we can talk face-to-face?"

"I don't think so, Everett. There's nothing left to say. I can forgive the lies, but I'm not yet ready to forget about your addiction. I just buried one alcoholic. I can't go through that again."

"Whoa. Wait a minute. I haven't had a drink in over two years." She hears anger in his voice.

"But you write about it in the song."

"And the song went viral because my fans could hear my raw emotions. I'm not gonna lie to you, Presley, I fight the temptation to drink nearly every single day. But I've stayed sober for two years. I've told you before. I don't like the person I am when I drink. And I never wanna hurt the ones I love like that again.

"There are no guarantees in life, Presley. I'm in love with you. All I'm asking for is a chance. I want a future with you. We'll take it one day at a time. If we're both committed, we can make a long-distance relationship work."

"You're about to embark on a lifestyle that revolves around partying. The temptation will be great, and I'm warning you in advance, I won't be forgiving if you fall off the wagon. I can't go through that again."

"Understood. Having you in my life is all the more reason for me to stay sober."

"I need some time to think, Everett. Are you staying for Friendsgiving tomorrow night?"

"We hadn't planned on it, but I will if it means spending more time with you."

"I'd like to meet your mom." Perhaps meeting Mary will help her decide whether to give him another chance.

"In that case, we'll stay. Mom wants to meet you as well."

Presley stays in bed uncharacteristically late on Sunday morning. She stares at the ceiling as she struggles with her decision whether to give Everett another chance. One thing he said last night keeps repeating itself in her mind. *There are no guarantees in life.* Presley knows that as well as anyone. What's the worst thing that can happen? If it doesn't work out between them, their relationship wasn't meant to be. At least, she won't go through the rest of her life wondering what might have been.

Thanksgiving was like every other holiday at Presley's house when she was growing up—a catered affair with a merry mix of guests who had nowhere else to be. Even Christmas was an endless stream of parties. After attending several gatherings on Christmas Eve, Renee and Presley stayed up late opening all their presents and then slept in on Christmas Day, only to start the round of open houses that lasted all afternoon and well into the evening. What will she do on the real Thanksgiving this year? Everett will be gone and she has no family. She won't hold her breath waiting for an invitation from Lucy. She's grateful to have work at least to focus on.

The smell of roasting turkeys in the kitchen makes her mouth water when she enters the kitchen at the inn early that afternoon. Cecily puts her in charge of setting the community table. After helping Katherine fashion a cornucopia centerpiece, she returns to the basement storage closet where she found the Christmas ornaments and remembers seeing boxes labeled Holiday China. Opening a few, she discovers a gorgeous set of plates with colorful turkeys in the center surrounded by a decorative brown-and-white border.

On her cell phone, she searches the internet for turkey china patterns and identifies this one as Johnson Brothers' Woodland Wild Turkeys. She loads the three boxes of china onto a luggage cart and rolls it up to the kitchen. After gingerly hand-washing each piece, she sets the table and stands back to admire the effect. Everything looks splendid and is ready for the guests who will be arriving soon.

"Now, that's a perfect Thanksgiving table if ever I saw one."

Presley places a hand over her racing heart, startled to find Stella and Jazz standing next to her. "Thank you. I'm pleased with the way it turned out. Katherine deserves the credit for the centerpiece."

"I'll be sure to compliment her." Stella's wide smile doesn't quite reach her eyes. Something is troubling her.

Jazz tugs Presley's hand. "Guess what, Presley. I'm going to be living with Stella from now on."

"You are?" Presley looks to Stella for confirmation. "Really?"

Stella nods. "If all goes well in juvenile court tomorrow." She cuts her eyes at Jazz. "It's a long story. I'll tell you another time."

"Is Naomi . . ."

"No longer employed here," Stella says in a curt tone.

Presley does a mental victory dance around the restaurant. She's sorry Jazz has to suffer, but the child will be much better off living with Stella. She offers the kid a high five. "I hope that means I'll be seeing a lot more of you."

Jazz grins at her in return.

The sound of voices draw their attention as guests begin to file into the restaurant. Brian and Opal. Katherine and Dean.

Lucy. Jack and Cecily's fiancé, Lyle. When Everett and Mary arrive, Presley goes over to greet them. Despite being shy, Everett's mother is delightful as she peppers Presley with questions about Nashville.

"Mom's a seamstress," Everett explains. "She made the dress she's wearing."

"It's stunning," Presley says of the simple but elegant burnt-orange wrap dress. "I'm impressed."

Pink dots appear on Mary's cheeks. "In Atlanta, I had my own alterations business. I'll be starting over in Nashville."

Everett rests a hand on his mother's shoulder. "Maybe Presley can pass along your contact information to some of her friends who might need alterations."

Presley nods. "And my mom's friends as well. Although, if you're looking for a change, you might shop around before you jump back into alterations. Nashville has an incredible number of live shows. I'm sorry. I'm overstepping—"

"Not at all." Everett winks at his mother. "That's exactly what I've been telling Mom."

When Cecily announces dinner, Stella makes a brief speech, thanking everyone for their dedication these past months, and follows it with a sweet blessing. They load up their plates from a smorgasbord of Thanksgiving dishes concocted with Cecily's unique flair. Brian heads up the table at one end and Stella the other. Presley is seated in the middle, sandwiched between Everett and Mary, and Lucy is to Brian's right. Lucy totally has a crush on him, and Brian appears eager to return her flirtation.

Presley hasn't spoken to Lucy since she confronted her on Wednesday. Yesterday, at the wine tasting, they proved they can work together despite their differences. But it's not the same as it was. They were only friends a short time, but Presley misses that friendship already.

A festive mood falls over the table while they eat. They talk about the upcoming holidays and the steady rise in business.

"Last I checked, room reservations for the New Year's weekend are nearing capacity and Christmas isn't far behind." Stella's gaze shifts to Everett. "If you have any interest in working over the holidays, we could really use your help in managing the bars. I will comp you a suite in the carriage house. I would love to have you and Mary as my guests."

Everett looks questionably at Presley. "Should I?"

Presley doesn't hesitate. "I'd like that." Decision made. She wants nothing more than to give him another chance.

Everett looks around Presley at Mary. "What do you think, Mom? Should we come back for Christmas?"

Mary casts a tentative glance at her son. "If I don't go to Texas to visit my family, I would love to come."

Everett smiles at Stella. "Count me in. And I'll be in touch about Mom's plans."

"Be sure to bring your guitar. You can entertain our guests in Billy's Bar. We'll even advertise, our very own up-and-coming country music star."

"I'm gonna be a big star, too," Jazz says, grinning from ear to ear. "I'm dancing one of the leading roles in our Christmas program."

All eyes shift to the sweet little girl as she tells us about her part as Clara in *The Nutcracker*. If she's upset by the recent drama in her life, she doesn't show it.

The table lingers over coffee and caramel pumpkin cheese-cake. When they finally disperse, Presley is walking toward the front entrance with Everett and Mary when Lucy pulls her aside.

"I wanted to talk to you about your biological father. Despite what he did, he wasn't such a bad guy. I was crazy about him, actually. He had a winning personality, and he was a true leader amongst his peers. He was a star athlete in high school. He was handsome and intelligent. He planned to follow in his father's footsteps to become a lawyer. He—"

"Stop!" Presley quiets her with her hand. "You don't have to sell me on him, Lucy. My adoptive father was a wonderful, loving man. I only regret that he died too young. But his memory lives on in my heart. I'm sorry for what this other man did to you, for what you went through because of it, but if it hadn't happened, I wouldn't be here."

"That's very true." Lucy loops her arm through Presley's, and they drift through the lounge to the entryway. "We can't change the past, but we can do something about the future. I don't know how to be a mother to a thirty-year-old woman."

Presley places a hand on her arm. "Then don't try to be. How about we go back to being friends and see where that leads us."

Presley waits by the front door while Everett walks Mary to her room. When he returns, Everett asks, "Can we go to your apartment?"

Looking up at him, she says, "Don't hurt me, Everett."

Taking her by the shoulders, Everett presses his lips gently against hers. "I won't, babe. I promise."

Hand in hand, they walk as fast down Main Street as Presley's heeled boots will allow. At her apartment, they make crazy love, first on Big Blue before moving to her queen-size bed. Their passion is tender one minute and bestial, like on their first night together, the next.

Around midnight, with Everett wearing his boxer shorts and Presley his blue button-down shirt, they go to the kitchen for a snack. Seated at her island, a pint of cookie dough ice cream between them, they talk about everything that has happened in their lives since he left for Atlanta. She tells him about Lucy and

Rita, and he tells her about his decision to be a father to Carla's baby.

"You made the right decision. You'll be an excellent father." Presley stabs at the ice cream with her spoon. "I hope you don't mind me asking, but why did your mother stay with your father?"

He drags his tongue up the back of his spoon. "I don't mind you asking, but I don't know the answer. She loved him once. I think she felt sorry for him. And I guess she was scared of being on her own."

"What about her family in Texas? You wrote about them in the song, and at dinner, she mentioned she may visit them for Christmas."

"Mom grew up in a modest but respectable Catholic family. Her parents had their hearts set on her marrying a close friend of the family's son. When she fell in love with poor white trash, they disowned her."

"That's a shame. I don't understand why some parents feel the need to control their children like that."

"Sadly, in her case, they were right."

"Why aren't you going with her to Texas? Don't get me wrong, I'm thrilled you'll be here with me."

"I've never met her family. It will be less awkward if she makes this first trip alone."

"Right. I guess that makes sense."

Presley sets her spoon on the counter and wipes her lips. "I've been thinking, why don't you and Mary live in my mother's house? We're not closing until mid-January, which will give you plenty of time to find your own place."

"I couldn't," he says, although Presley can tell her offer intrigues him.

"Why not? You'd be doing me a favor. I worry about the house being empty. You know, because of busted pipes and break-ins and stuff like that."

Spoon in mouth, he stares up at the ceiling as he considers the idea. "I'd rather not waste money on a hotel room, and it would only be for a couple of weeks . . . if you're sure."

"I'm positive." Presley puts the lid on the ice cream and returns the carton to the freezer. "If your mom ends up going to Texas, you're welcome to stay with me when you come for Christmas."

He stands to face her. "I would like that very much."

"Understand that I'll expect sexual favors in lieu of rent."

In a deep husky voice, he says, "That's the least I can do."

Throwing her arms around his neck, she pulls him down and makes love to him on the kitchen floor. Being with Everett feels right. She will live in the moment and see where their relationship takes them. They will work together to show each other the way.

Did you enjoy this title? Please consider leaving an honest review on my Amazon Page.

ALSO BY ASHLEY FARLEY

ACKNOWLEDGMENTS

I'm grateful to many people for helping make this novel possible. Foremost, to my editor, Patricia Peters, for her patience and advice and for making my work stronger without changing my voice. A great big heartfelt thank-you to my trusted beta readers —Alison Fauls, Kathy Sinclair, Anne Wolters, and Laura Glenn. And to my behind-the-scenes team, Kate Rock and Geneva Agnos, for all the many things you do to manage my social media so effectively.

I am blessed to have many supportive people in my life who offer the encouragement I need to continue the pursuit of my writing career. I owe an enormous debt of gratitude to my advanced review team, the lovely ladies of Georgia's Porch, for their enthusiasm for and commitment to my work. To Leslie Rising at Levy's for being my local bookshop. Love and thanks to my family—my mother, Joanne; my husband, Ted; and the best children in the world, Cameron and Ned.

Most of all, I'm grateful to my wonderful readers for their love of women's fiction. I love hearing from you. Feel free to shoot me an email at ashleyhfarley@gmail.com or stop by my website at ashleyfarley.com for more information about my characters and upcoming releases. Don't forget to sign up for my newsletter. Your subscription will grant you exclusive content, sneak previews, and special giveaways.

ABOUT THE AUTHOR

Ashley Farley writes books about women for women. Her characters are mothers, daughters, sisters, and wives facing real-life issues. Her bestselling Sweeney Sisters series has touched the lives of many.

Ashley is a wife and mother of two young adult children. While she's lived in Richmond, Virginia for the past 21 years, a piece of her heart remains in the salty marshes of the South Carolina Lowcountry, where she still calls home. Through the eyes of her characters, she captures the moss-draped trees, delectable cuisine, and kindhearted folk with lazy drawls that make the area so unique.

Ashley loves to hear from her readers. Visit Ashley's Website @ashleyfarley.com

Get free exclusive content by signing up for her newsletter @ ashleyfarley.com/newsletter-signup/